HOUSE OF LIES

*previous novels
by the same author*

The Song of the Forest
The Sound of the Sea

House of Lies

A Novel

Colin Mackay

BLACK ACE BOOKS

First published in 1995 by
Black Ace Books, Ellemford, Duns
Berwickshire, TD11 3SG, Scotland

© Colin Mackay 1995

Typeset in Scotland by Black Ace Editorial

Printed in Great Britain by Antony Rowe Ltd
Bumper's Farm, Chippenham, SN14 6QA

All rights reserved. Strictly except in conformity with the provisions of the Copyright Act 1956 (as amended), no part of this book may be reprinted or reproduced or exploited in any form or captured or transmitted by any electronic, mechanical or other means, whether such means be known now or invented hereafter, including photocopying, or text capture by optical character recognition, or held in any information storage or retrieval system, without permission in writing from the publisher. Any person or organization committing any unauthorized act in relation to this publication may be liable to criminal prosecution and civil action for damages. Colin Mackay is identified as author of this work in accordance with Section 77 of the Copyright, Designs and Patents Act 1988. His moral rights are asserted.

A CIP catalogue record for this book
is available from the British Library

ISBN   1-872988-46-6

The publishers gratefully acknowledge
subsidy from the Scottish Arts Council
towards the production of this volume

For Robin Denniston

Prologue

In the white nights of midsummer the river Neva gleams through Saint Petersburg like a seam of old silver, and people saunter the city streets in the pleasant twilight, unwilling to waste any of it in sleep.

That afternoon I had met my old friend Johnny, whom I had hardly seen in more than seven years. We had had dinner out in a place on the Fontanka embankment, and gone on to a nightclub which boasted a pretty wild strip show and an even wilder audience of *mafiya* gangsters lounging around with cigars in their teeth and guns in their trousers like hoods from old Chicago.

Johnny and I had both been Russian students at London University back in the days of the dinosaurs when studying Russian was a vaguely subversive thing to do. Since then we had gone our different ways. I had taken up computers and used my Russian to sell software to men from various ministries when this city was still called Leningrad. Johnny had joined the BBC and associated with androgynous people who called each other 'darling' and wore gold medallions. Then, round about the age of forty, we each, independently, underwent a sea change. I was now using my Russian to restore old buildings in post-Communist Saint Petersburg. Johnny was using his as an aid worker in Moscow.

After leaving the nightclub we wandered along Liteyniy Prospekt in a state of post-prandial benevolence to the

Liteyniy Most – Smelters' Bridge – which spans the Neva. At the northern end is the Finland Station where Lenin arrived on the eve of the revolution in 1917. At the southern stands Bolshy Dom, the Big House, headquarters of the security police when a third of the city's population disappeared under Stalin. There, leaning over the parapet of the bridge and looking at the dark waters passing underneath us to the sea, we reminisced as men do who have known each other for a quarter of a century, from the age of acne to that of sagging muscles and the first grey hair.

The changes we had seen! Remember, we had both been born in the shadow of what was once called The Bomb, and had grown up with the Cold War, the sputnik, and Yuri Gagarin. We talked about the events of '89, and where each of us had been when the Berlin Wall came down. We talked about the hopes we had had, and the calmer resignation we shared now that many of those hopes were destined to be disappointed. Were strip clubs really the sort of benefit we had wished to confer upon people longing for the joys of freedom?

'At least they've pulled down a few thousand of these Lenin statues,' I said. 'I was getting sick of looking at the old sod everywhere I went.'

'Same in Moscow,' said Johnny. 'They have a dumping-ground lumbered with statues – granite, marble and bronze. Someone should write a poem about it.'

'Or make a film.'

'Or something.'

I felt sorry for Lenin. He had not wanted any of it. In his will he had asked for his body to be buried in the quiet corner of the Petersburg cemetery where his mother lay, but his successors had mummified him like an Egyptian pharaoh and stuck him in that brutal mausoleum in Red Square. He had said that statues were only good for collecting bird shit, but they had raised statues to him everywhere. Perhaps, I said, it was a horror story that should be written: something about how Lenin's ghost had prowled the country for seventy-odd years longing to be released, until the day came when they took him out of the mausoleum and laid him to rest beside his mother under the quiet earth.

Then Johnny asked me quite seriously if I believed in ghosts.

Of course at first I thought he was joking, serious face or not – Johnny was the sort of healthy sceptic who doubted everything – but as he continued to stare down at the river, I put my smile away and asked him if he had ever seen one.

'No, I haven't,' he said. 'But I've heard the strangest story. Do you remember what happened to the Red House in London a few years ago? Well, it's about that. The thing is, the man who told me it works with me in Moscow. He's getting on, and I would have said he had no imagination at all – certainly not enough to make up anything like this.'

1

London, Autumn 1989

It was in the beginning of that smoke-coloured season called autumn that Tam Burns came to the Red House. Well, his name was Thomas Burns, but everybody called him Tam. He was a widower, the only child of a couple long dead, and the part of town he had lived in had been smashed to the ground and redeveloped. It had, before the compulsory purchase and demolition crews took over, been the docklands, and Tam, his father, his grandfather, and God knows who else, had all been dockers working on the river.

That was a long time ago.

Now the industry was gone and the waterfront had been turned into expensive housing developments. Tam prowled there occasionally. Otherwise, he read. You might meet him in the reading room of the public library where quite a lot of late-middle-aged men who have hardly read a book in their lives come in to get out of the rain and read the newspapers. He was a big, heavy, solemn man of that age; intelligent, slow-spoken, and unfashionably dressed. His face was brown and lumpy as a newly dug potato, and he habitually smelled like a damp sack.

He was coming to the Red House to start a job.

At his age there were few jobs. His skills were as a welder working on the big hulls, but nobody wanted to build them any more. After the docks closed, Tam had been unemployed for exactly 108 months. Then he had wandered into a demonstration that had clashed with police, been recognized on film with an angry face and a brick in his hand, and spent six months in prison. Twice a month for the first 108 months he had signed on, and every day of the last six months he had slopped out – 216 signings and 177 sloppings. He found both experiences squalid and depressing.

Otherwise, prison hadn't been any Hollywood hell-on-earth, honestly. It had been just like being back at school again – only this time around on the merry wheel of life he was older, and a lot wiser, sadder and less vulnerable. Warders, like teachers, called him 'Burns' and expected him to say 'sir'; but, unlike teachers, they didn't beat him up, tell him he was useless, no good, and would just end up working in the docks like every other no-good cretin. If his pride had swallowed being treated like a brainless little boy again, prison wouldn't have been so bad, because what was sex at his age? But his pride refused to swallow it, and that made it bad.

He had got out nine months ago, lived since then in a hostel for homeless ex-prisoners, and signed on at the social security office where the cheesy-faced kid on the other side of the counter got annoyed with him if he was late or talked in the queue. He knew all the men in the queue; they had been in the queue for as long as he had – the unemployable middle-aged men. Some had worked with him in the docks; some had been with him in the epic strike of '68, up there on the stands shouting 'Solidarity, brothers!' at each other through megaphones. Now here they were, round-shouldered middle-aged men with nicotine skin shuffling their feet through the fag ends on the social security floor.

Afterwards in the pub they talked about football and football, and television and football. Tam tried to introduce some culture into the talk. 'I'm thinking of writing a book about the strike,' he said out of the blue.

'Ach, who would read it?'

Tam shrugged. 'Somebody might,' he said.

'Yeah, somebody and my auntie.'

They went back to talking about football. Tam listened to the horrible metallic noise coming out of the jukebox. There has got to be a better tune than this, he thought. He took it seriously. He went to a creative-writing class run by some celebrity he had never heard of to try and learn the mysteries of style; but you know what these things are. Anyway . . .

One day a few months later he was called to the supervisor's office in the hostel. There were two men waiting for him. One, the supervisor, a screw by any other name, was called Paterson and he wouldn't have fitted into any of those black-and-white Warner Brothers films where the warders are all lantern-jawed sadists with shotguns under their arms just waiting for the chance to drop gas grenades through the roof or shoot up the dining hall during a riot. Paterson was a plump, small, solicitous man with a long horsey face, big teeth, and ears like rhubarb leaves. He had an excess of saliva in his mouth and spoke his words wet.

He first-named Tam.

Tam raised his cheek muscles in a sort of smile and sat down. There was a faint but high-pitched whine which he could not place. The room was stale. Like all the hostel it smelled of ten thousand cigarettes. The table in front of Paterson was spotted with sticky black burn marks. Paterson's plump, prissy fingers danced around them, gesticulating, and playing with some of the eternal forms that lay there. The foil ashtray was already overflowing.

'Anyway, Tam,' he sprayed in an unusually loud voice, 'we have some good news. Mr Steele here – you know Mr Steele? No?'

Tam shook his head. So did the third man in the room. Tam had been trying to work out who he was. He had the look of authority, but not *official* authority. A thickset, heavy man, older than Tam, with a badly dented I'm-going-to-change-the-world-before-it-changes-me face; tweed jacket stretched tight over slab shoulders, curly mane of harsh grey hair, small eyes that looked at Tam shrewdly from a crow's-nest of wrinkles.

'Mr Steele wants to offer you a job,' said Paterson loudly, his fingers dancing. 'Not only that, but a job *with accommodation.*'

'You mean—'

'You live on the premises!' Steele shouted.

Tam winced. 'Okay, okay,' he said.

'I said you live on the premises!' bellowed Steele.

'I see,' said Tam, raising his own voice a decibel or two, as Paterson gestured discreetly towards his ear. Steele was wearing a flesh-coloured hearing-aid pitched too high.

'You met Finlay McRath at his creative writing class,' Paterson began, naming the unheard-of (by Tam) celebrity.

'You met Finlay McRath at his creative writing class,' said Steele, speaking in echoing exclamation marks and blowing the ashes out of the tinfoil tray. His voice was hard and thick and jarring as a piece of broken machinery. 'Finlay's editor-in-chief of *The Red Flag* newspaper. Know it? Good! I'm economic editor. Right! We need a night-security man. Some cleaning, just light stuff. Live on the premises. Basement flat. On duty nine hours each night, eleven to eight, seven nights a week, total sixty-three hours. Right! At £2.35 an hour weekdays, weekend £4.70. Total £190.35. Right? Good. Before tax, of course, but the accommodation's rent-free. Right? Good. Well?'

'£2.35 an hour isn't hellish much,' said Tam in his usual voice.

'What?' said Steele, cocking his head.

'Rent-free,' whispered Paterson.

'What, what?' said Steele. He fiddled with his aid and the faint whine turned into a straw-dry whistle. The emptied ashtray flew on to the floor.

'I said it sounds good,' said Tam for the deaf man. 'How big's—'

'Good!'

'Yes. I said how big's the—'

'Right! That's settled then.'

'How big's the flat?'

'What? Ah, yes, the flat. Living-room, bedroom, kitchen, bathroom. All furnished. Television. And a charming view from the window of the capitalist devastation of the docklands. Accept?'

Tam – who was currently living in one room the size of a cupboard, with a gas ring, a camp bed, dirty wallpaper, and a smoke-stained ceiling with gloomy corners around which a large spider swung like Tarzan – accepted.

Now, standing with his two battered suitcases at the exit from the Underground station on the opposite side of Leveller Street, he looked up at the Red House. 'Christ,' he said. 'Dracula's castle.'

It was an ugly building.

Built for some long-forgotten merchant company in Victorian times, it stood four-square at the corner of the main road and a nondescript side-street, a big rusty red-brick edifice showing five rows of dull windows, the uppermost row bricked shut, an uninviting door (painted red) with an attempt at a classical column on either side, and a roof that was castellated like a battlement with a slope of greenish slate rising to a small cupola that crowned the whole with a little gothic flourish. Between the second and third rows of windows THE RED FLAG was spelled out in large red fluorescent tubes fastened to the brickwork. The lights of THE were not illuminated, and the F of FLAG was burnt out. Tam knew there was another similar sign round the back of the building, because the Underground ran in the open there under its windows for a hundred yards or so before disappearing into a tunnel, and coming east from the direction of the City you could see THE RED FLAG looking dingily down on you in daylight as you plopped out into the open, and, at night, its flawed lights yawning a vicious smile.

There it stood, between the financial palaces of the City to the west and the helter-skelter constructions that crowded the redeveloped docklands on the eastern horizon. Between these two islands of affluence – a mile on all sides of the Red House – stretched a ruinous collection of dwellings, shabby genteel stone houses, seedy brick terraces, squalid concrete estates, as though each era had tried to brand the place with its own unique character, only to give it up as a thankless task. Now small, dark, mysterious houses lined flyblown streets raddled with litter. Stumpy blocks of flats stood amid wasteland, and grey terraces backed on to demolition sites.

The station where Tam stood being on the eastern side of the road, the Red House appeared to him with the sun behind it. Dark and terrible it looked against the early evening sky. He had passed it many times in the course of his life, but paid it little heed. The Underground was too expensive for local journeys, and Tam had seldom made any other sort. So when he travelled, he travelled by bus, and no bus stopped within sight of the Red House. Looking at it – *really* looking at it now, for the first time ever – Tam saw how it stood and glowered there, and a shiver of fear went through him.

'Christ,' he said again.

Then he picked up his two suitcases and forced his feet forward over the running gutter and across the road, into its mighty and dismal shadow.

2

Finlay McRath

The great Finlay McRath, editor-in-chief of *The Red Flag,* and winner of innumerable literary prizes, was a big, florid man of seventy. His bush of white hair was thick and unruly, his shoulders broad, his chest deep, and his clothes had the shabbiness of genial eccentricity. He had a kind face and mellow voice. A firm handshake and confidential pat on the back put people at their ease. They felt honoured that such a man should treat them as his equals.

And yet . . . That scarlet face was also sad and wary. Faint brown pouches accumulated under the eyes, and from time to time he would sigh unconsciously, as though from world-weariness. He had a habit, increasingly pronounced as years went by, of turning abruptly and looking over his shoulder, expecting to see God-knows-what walking behind him. If he were talking to someone at the time, he would do this without interrupting the flow of his speech, which was always coherent and mellifluous, but it was an unnerving habit and it caused whoever he was addressing to lose track of what he was saying.

Finlay had lost his left eye in a childhood accident and wore a glass one in its place. In the Second World War this kept him out of active service, to his great disappointment, and in a munitions factory instead. He kept an old Remington typewriter in his room with the legend *This machine kills fascists* painted across it in red, and he spent his evenings banging away at it, producing belligerent stuff for the socialist and pro-Soviet press (he had joined the Communist Party after Hitler attacked the Soviet Union in 1941) demanding ever heavier bombing raids on Germany, and social revolution at home.

Finlay McRath had a desperate, lurching desire for recognition. After the war he had written much journalism in support of the Welfare State, nationalization, and the Soviet Union, but it had not led him to the editor's office of *The Times*. He worked as a newsreader on BBC radio, and was sacked for doctoring scripts about Suez and the Hungarian Revolution. He became a scriptwriter for television in the dawn of the sixties, and was one of the golden generation who contributed to *Armchair Theatre* and *Z Cars*, until producers grew tired of the sameness of his scripts and turned to younger writers.

He wrote reams of long declamatory poems on socialist themes which earned him honours east of the Berlin Wall, and toleration west of it. Latterly he had taken to writing stage plays – long plays, bad plays, *dozens* of plays – in which ridiculous pantomime capitalists and rebellious workers leapt across the stage in false noses delivering a mixture of textbook speeches and one-line quips at each other. This, at least, hit the financial jackpot. BBC2 and Channel 4 commissioned him to fill up their idle hours, and various agencies paid him the sort of money of which the government of Guatemala dreams in vain.

It was back in the sixties, when his TV career was on the slide, that Finlay McRath accepted the editorship of *The Red Flag*. He found it a dull little sheet given over to the minutiae of trade union meetings, notices about miners' galas, and reprints from *Pravda*. He made it into something at least comparatively smart and snazzy. He hired a staff of agony antis, paid-up anti-American Americans, and other sad people. Each weekly issue made peremptory statements about the joys of socialism from Leningrad to Hanoi, and the evils of everything else, everywhere else, at great length and in very dense prose.

There was also a good-food guide to progressive restaurants, and a lonely-hearts column.

Once upon a time *The Red Flag* had been the official organ of the tiny but influential British Communist Party; but these were dreadful days for the Party and it was its official organ no longer. The leaders of the Communist Party were, Finlay suspected, pleased. They were now very, *very*, embarrassed about ever having had anything to do with dictators and concentration camps, they said. They had never even *heard* of any of these things, they said.

It was all terribly confusing and depressing.

Finlay thought that if the Communist Party were a person it would be wearing dark glasses, travelling under an assumed name, and claiming to suffer from amnesia as well.

3

The Interview

Tam gave his name to a bulldog-faced commissionaire who reluctantly put down the sports pages, fumbled along his desk for some notification of Tam's existence and expected arrival, and, failing to find it, mutteringly exited through a blond door into a blond office. Left alone in the foyer, Tam parked his suitcases and looked about. It was well lit and cheerfully furnished with marble-patterned red linoleum and walls painted biscuit and pink, several red upholstered armchairs and a small table whose cover (red) reached to the floor. The whole was dominated by a huge lurid painting called 'V.I. Lenin Addressing The Petrograd Workers'. V.I. Lenin reminded Tam of someone, but he couldn't think who.

Tam was still looking at it and wondering when the blond door banged open and Joe Steele shot out.

The commissionaire followed.

'Tam. Evening. Got here, I see. Good. Excellent. Finlay would like to see you. This way. No, leave your stuff here. Bill'll keep an eye on it. Right, Bill?'

The commissionaire nodded. Steele's hearing aid was silent.

'Good. Excellent. This way.'

He stretched out an arm and steered Tam in through the blond door. The office suite was the neatest thing Tam had seen for a good long time. The short internal corridor was lined with glass-fronted rooms full of efficient-looking people doing efficient-looking things; electronic typewriters puttered silently, VDU screens cast out columns of rippling green letters, and the glow of the overhanging fluorescent tubes was as golden as Aladdin's lamp. The last office Tam had seen looked like the place where Humphrey Bogart hung his shoulder holster. Steele opened the door at the end of the corridor and admitted him to the Presence.

Finlay McRath raised himself from his desk, smiled radiantly at Tam, pumped his hand, patted him fondly on the shoulder, and fixed him with his piercing eyes, one of which was glass.

The creative-writing class that Tam had attended for the short duration of his literary ambition was full of drab, defeated people who briefly glowed golden as the fluorescent tubes in the presence of Finlay McRath. Tam also glowed – just a little bit – as they exchanged pleasantries.

'Pleased to meet you, Tam. And how is the writing going? No? – Oh tush, tush, mustn't say that! Sit down, man, sit down. Drink?'

No employer had ever offered Tam a drink before. McRath poured impressively. The office was warm and comfortable with blond furniture and maroon-papered walls. V.I. Lenin, in a head-and-shoulders photograph, stared down.

'Scotch. Or should I say Irish? Did I hear the trace of an accent?'

Tam smilingly confirmed that his grandfather had indeed crossed the Irish Sea.

'The reason I asked', McRath continued, 'was that my father was born in Ireland. Commandant of the Tyrone Flying Column, 1920. Up the rebels!'

They drank, and McRath talked on while Tam toyed with his glass, and Steele emptied his in a few loud gulps and poured himself another.

'Impressive,' thought Tam of McRath, as he had thought of him in the dim hall where the class had met.

Impressive, but . . .

Tam noted the desire to make an impression, the weariness, the false joviality. What did it all mean? Ah well, live and let live, he thought.

'So you were there in '68?' McRath was saying. 'That was a good strike. It had very important consequences.'

'We lost,' said Tam.

'Only in appearance,' said McRath. Then he laughed. 'The bosses lost. They just haven't realized it yet.'

Tam grunted non-committally.

'I'm not in your Party, you know,' he said.

McRath laughed again.

'That doesn't seem to matter much these days, alas! There are supposedly loyal party members buying shares and talking about God. No. When the situation became vacant, I thought of you. You had mentioned something about being unemployed and being a widower in our getting-to-know-you session. You made a change from all those middle-class ladies who want to write like Catherine Cookson, and jumble-sale students who think they're going to be the next Jimmy Glasgow. I want somebody who doesn't mind working at night while the world sleeps, and sleeping during the day instead – and whose imagination isn't going to run away with him in an empty building. Do you watch horror films? Stephen King stuff?'

'Eh . . . yes – sometimes.'

'Don't take it seriously, do you? Don't see vampires looking in the window, all that sort of thing?'

'Christ, no,' said Tam. 'It's rubbish, but it's harmless. Just a bit of fun.'

'Like the nine o'clock news,' said Steele.

Chuckles all round.

'The fact is,' said McRath, 'I've got a particular reason for asking. You see, our last caretaker – he killed himself. We don't know why, exactly. He was having domestic trouble, there had been a divorce – you know the sort of thing.'

Tam knew.

'We kept it out of the papers, of course. The left-wing press, such as it is, wouldn't want to print anything discreditable, and the right-wing press mustn't be allowed to – they invent enough lies as it is. So keep it under your hat, if you don't mind. I'm telling you this because, well, you'll be alone in the building until the cleaners arrive at six. Does that worry you?'

'Hell, no,' said Tam. 'I've got a good conscience.'

'Good, good. Excellent.'

Ten minutes or so of small talk followed. Tam realized that the interview was at an end. He drained what was left in his glass and set it down. McRath was standing, his round red face wearing an all-purpose smile. They exchanged the pleasantries of dismissal.

'I'll show you where your bunk is,' said Steele. 'Then Charlie – our engineer – will show you the job. Okay?'

'Grand.'

They left McRath beaming benignly at them from behind his desk.

Twenty minutes later Joe Steele re-entered the office. He didn't knock. It was one of the bourgeois conventions the workers of *The Red Flag* did without.

'Finlay—' he shouted at the empty chair beyond the big desk.

The great Finlay McRath was standing to one side of his desk staring out the window as though the darkening city were a leper colony in which he had a morbid interest. He turned hastily and fixed his good eye upon his subordinate. Steele saw the instant flash of fear fade away as recognition replaced it. His own cold, blank, harsh eyes never showed fear of anything.

'Well?' he said.

McRath nodded and pulled the red Venetian blind down on his window.

'He'll do . . . I think. I want a man with staying power – *this* time.'

'As I recollect, we thought we had one *last* time,' said Steele. He found the glass he had used and refilled it. 'Just shows you. Everyone makes mistakes.' He tossed his drink down and poured himself another. 'Tenth time lucky!'

McRath looked at him with distaste. 'Joe,' he said, 'you're drinking a hell of a lot.'

'I always drink a hell of a lot.'

'Don't get arseholed and start seeing things, that's all.'

'You've never seen me drunk, my friend, and you never will. I don't get drunk. When Ronnie bloody Reagan was prancing round Moscow, I was the only one in this building sober. The rest of you – you were guttered something suicidal—'

He halted in mid sentence.

McRath heard the whisky glass clink against his teeth. 'Nice choice of words,' he said.

The two men stared at each other in silence for a moment, then Steele turned away angrily, drinking and muttering and slurping his drink in consequence. He put the empty glass down.

'Finlay, who are you afraid of? If it's the fascists, the National Front, the British National Party, or whatever – they're pathetic, they're nothing, man, nothing.'

'At my age, Joe, do you think I'm scared of some spotty hooligan spraying a bit of racist aerosol on the back wall?'

'Then what is it? If you seriously think someone's going to torch the place, get the police. It's what the buggers are there for.'

'It's not a police matter,' said McRath quietly. 'Nothing they could handle.'

He glanced at the photograph of Lenin on the wall and his eyes had a supplicating look that was pitiful beyond words.

23

Steele's anger left him at once. Jesus – things must be rough if the old man was taking it like this.

'Look, if you're expecting something heavy—' he began.

McRath interrupted him:

'There are a lot of changes coming, Joe. Bad times – worse than the fifties, worse than '39, worse than either of us can remember.'

He sat down heavily in the seat where he had chatted so jovially with Tam Burns less than half an hour before. He put his elbows on the desk and rested his chin in his hands.

'I hear more and more rumours,' he said, staring at the fax machine that was positioned to the right, where his good eye could light upon it. 'Our friends in the east are worried. Germany, the Czechs, those – those *stupid* Balts! They've got balls, the bastards, hand it to them, they've got balls. The People are going to have to nerve themselves for trouble, but have the People got the nerve for it any more? They had it in '56 when they crushed the Hungarian fascists like flies. That's what Gorbachev should be doing now. Why isn't he?'

'He's yellow.'

'He's lost his nerve. The People won power in the streets, and they will have to defend their power in the streets. Nerve, that's what matters, nerve! Not sentimentality!'

Quotation from *High Noon In October*, Selected Poems of Finlay McRath, Burgess & Maclean Ltd, Cambridge, 1968; Winner of the Blunt Prize for Poetry, 1969.

> Ah Lenin, you were right!
> Sentimentality is the undermining tool
> of the fascist bourgeoisie
> and must be resisted with all the counter tools
> of the working class.
> For, as you wrote in September 1918:
> 'Secure the Soviet Republic against its class enemies

by isolating them in concentration camps,
and carry out merciless mass terror.'
Lenin, only a mind such as yours:
soaring above the rotten petty bourgeois concept of freedom,
can reach the true freedom
of working class experience . . .

And so on, for pages.

4

The Tour

The engineer was called Charlie Feaver.
Every institutional building has its engineer living underneath it. Some are big beefy beer-gutted men with brown skin and hairy arms, who eat heartily, talk obscenely, and are married to outrageous women with figures like melting ice-cream. Others are pale reptilian creatures who are silent, unmarried, and lean strongly towards fundamentalist religion and men's magazines. In common they have the job and the sports pages. Charlie Feaver looked like a very thin ape that was suffering from some wasting sickness. His small, lined face was hollow and covered with grey bristles, and he kept wiping a long yellowish hand across his mouth with a rasping noise, then stuffing it back inside his boiler suit where it jangled at a bunch of keys. His eyes were active, humourless and feral, and he talked incessantly.

'Okay,' he said, 'let's go up to the top and start there. Special tour. We'll use the lift, all right?' He punched the wall button.

Deep in the lift shaft, machinery wheezed asthmatically.

'Was that put in with the bricks?' asked Tam.

'Imphm – you'd better believe it. I wouldn't use the lift when you're here on your tod – not if I was you, I wouldn't. The whole thing's fucked. It never has packed in, but if you're in it when it does – boy, you'll be there all night.'

'I'll make sure I have the crossword with me,' said Tam,

smiling.

Feaver didn't smile back.

'You'll notice I didn't punch Four,' he said. 'That's because Four's all closed up. For good. They closed it, oh . . . about '62, it must have been. Put concrete blocks across it. Look, I'll show you.'

The lift stopped at Three and the door cranked painfully open. Lenin's photograph grinned down from the wall. Feaver pressed the Four button. The lift shunted up, stopped, and the door cranked open once more. But instead of open corridor, they faced a solid wall of concrete blocks, light grey and dusty, with cement runs in between. Feaver held it with his finger on the button.

'Like the Berlin Wall,' said Tam.

'Right. It went up about the same time too – or a little before. '62, like I said. Nope, I wasn't working here then, there was this other guy, old guy, no damn good, emigrated to Australia and opened a chip shop or something. Anyway, he told me about it when I joined, oh, twenty years back now. Built like the Anti-Fascist Wall, he said. Though whether this one's to keep something *out* or to keep something *in* I don't know, he said. What do you make of that, eh? You got to watch out. Comrades who lose their belief in Socialism start believing in astrology or some fucking thing. Like the stupid cunt cleaners we got here – religious maniacs, all of them. Got their cupboard looking like the Pope's bedroom, crosses, pictures of Jesus – make you want to throw up just to look at it.'

'So why do they work here?'

Feaver shrugged.

'Live in the neighbourhood, don't they? Got to use what you can get, and they do the job all right, I'll give them that. Anyway, you'll meet them in the morning. They opened this floor here only once, and that was back in '68, year I joined. They had cockroaches and rats and God-knows-what up here, you could hear them down in the Third Floor, getting into the air conditioning and squeaking and scraping around. So they got this pest-control firm to come and gas 'em. Worked too, least for a while, even if one of the poor sods managed to gas himself or something and fell out the window. Brained himself on the pavement. Anyway, they walled it back up again, and it's been walled up since. Windows bricked up too, in case anybody else fell out, I suppose. Don't know how they managed it, but these bugs and things got back in. You can hear them in the Third Floor, in the maintenance space between the ceiling and the floor above, having a regular disco to themselves. Anyway, that's enough of Four. Let's go down.'

The lift opened on Three, and there was Lenin's photograph on the wall.

'Everything up here's closed too,' said Feaver, waving an arm. He wiped his mouth, then pulled out a huge bunch of keys and carefully opened a door. 'All the offices locked – see. Two toilets. Two each on Second and Ground floors. Four on the First. We'll get there later. These two are used for cleaning cupboards.

'Used to be two flats here, one either end of the corridor. Day caretaker in one, night caretaker in the other. Use them for storerooms now. Used to be the engineer lived in as well. That flat you got downstairs at the back used to be the engineer's flat. I never used it, don't fancy living on the job, and the ceiling's noisy like I said, so they gave it to the night man. That was, oh, that was in '68. There's only been the night man living on the premises since then. 'Course, I mean there's been several. Jimmy – he lasted till '77 – then Terry – he lasted a couple of years – then Des. Des was the last one – before you.

'Nothing else to see up here. Just sweep up and lock up. Make sure no mice or rats or anything get a hold. Noisy ceiling – don't let it give you the creeps. Jesus, look at the state of those cobwebs! It's always cold as fuck up here. If you know a brass monkey, don't bring him up or he'll need a welder. Jesus,' Charlie said, wiping a low-hung cobweb out of his face, 'one day these buggers'll reach the floor. Keep meaning to bring a ladder and long-handled brush up and clear all this shit away, but what the fuck, always things to do, try to run this place by myself.'

Wipe, rasp, went his hand across his mouth.

'C'mon, let's get the flock out of here, as the first shepherd said to the second. These are the stairs, right? You got two flights, one at either end of the corridor and the lift's in the middle. Gets a bit dark at night. They only put sixty-watt bulbs in the lights, would you believe it? Sixty fucking watts! Might as well light a candle. You need a hundred and fifty if it's going to be any good. Sixty – tsch!'

They went down a spiralling staircase with worn cement steps. Its green handrail was chipped and spotted with rust.

'You've met Comrade McRath?' Feaver continued. 'Well, he's a wanker. Between you, me and the wall – right? Got the job in '65 after Stan Grady jacked it in. Not that he was much better, little prick. Went off to become a *meedja* personality. See him on the chat shows late at night, him in his posh suit sitting there chatting up dopehead rock stars and rich whores, and loving it all like a pig in shite, fucking traitor. Joe Steele should have got it, got some fire in his guts has Joe – and that's why he didn't get it, need I tell you. Party's gone soft as a wanker's prick. You want to know what's wrong with it – I'll tell you what's wrong with it. There's too many of them pink yuppies running the shop, that's what's wrong with it. Dead down on Stalinism, as they call it.

'What did Stalin do that was wrong?

'Put some fascists up against a wall. That's what we need in this country. There's too many of them fascists and racists and money-raking capitalists and all them walking around needing a bullet in the head and not getting it off any bugger 'cause they're all too scared to do it. Me, I cried like a baby when Brezhnev died. Now there was a man who knew the stuff! Christ! What's revolution about if it isn't putting a bullet into a cunt that needs it? Anyway, this is your Second Floor.'

'Cleaner,' said Tam, though it was dark and dull. There was a Lenin painting on the wall.

'Cleaner'n'greener, brighter'n'lighter. Now your lino here's got to be buffed. This is where the printing works is, okay? Hiya, Pete!'

'Hi, Charlie. Doing the guided tour?' said Pete, a long cylindrical man wearing a dirty bib-fronted boiler suit and a face like a melancholy borzoi. On one of the bib-straps was pinned a large white lapel badge saying 'Solidarity Solidarioscz' in red letters. He smelled like a garage.

'That's me, guided tours. I'll be doing fucking kissograms next. Pete's the printer,' Charlie said to Tam. 'Would you believe it? Peter the Printer, we actually got one. Don't talk to the toerag, he's a fascist. Backs them Polish cunts.' He poked at the printer's lapel badge.

Pete grinned a full graveyard load of big teeth and gave the clenched-fist salute. 'Solidarity!' he said.

'Solidarity my arse. Fascist cocksuckers, that's all they are. Paid by the CIA. Just like everybody else. Cocksuckers!'

'It's sad,' said Pete gravely, looking at Tam and tapping a forefinger to his temple. 'Fell on his head when he was a nipper. Doctor's trying to help him.'

Half a minute of utterly obscene profanity passed between the two men, Pete grinning away like a lugubrious undertaker, Feaver showing not a glint of humour anywhere in face or voice. It was a strange act, but Tam had seen stranger. He stood and smiled silently.

'Charlie's a tanky,' said Pete, turning to him again. 'Know what that is? One of the mad old sods who want to send the tanks in whenever anyone has a fart.'

'Yeah, well, they should have done a Prague on your

Solidarity, that's what they should have done. Shooty-shooty, bang-bang, savvy Polak?' Feaver asked, triggering a finger at Pete's chest.

'Maddo, maddo,' said Pete, shaking his head.

'Anyway, less of this subversion. Tam here's the new night man. Don't want him getting bad ideas about the place before he's over the door.'

'That right?' said Pete. He looked at Tam, and something drained out of his face. 'Rather you than me, squire. Know what happened to Des?'

'I heard he killed himself.'

'Yeah. Yeah. Well, that wasn't all that was heard. *I* wouldn't spend the night here. Gives me the horrors just thinking about it. Stay away from that Third Floor.'

'Why?'

''Cause that's where he done it,' said Feaver. 'In one of them unused toilets I told you about. Pushed his little girl out the window and strung himself up from a pipe.'

'Jesus!'

'Yeah, it was pretty grim. Reckoned he'd done it about – oh, what did they reckon, Pete? One, two in the morning, somewhere about there. Anyway, nobody found the little girl until daylight was up, on account of it being the railway line out there and nobody going near it. They found her first, and they was waiting for us at eight o'clock when we got here. It was me and a copper found him in the men's toilet. He'd gone and locked the door on himself, and he was hanging there from the pipe, neck broken and stretched out about two feet long. Pete here came along and helped us cut him down. None of them fat fucks downstairs would do it.'

'And his little girl – what was her name?'

'Rosemary,' said Pete.

'Yeah, Rosemary. She'd landed on her face on the Underground line out there. All smashed in. Then a train went over her, but she was dead already. Six years old she was. Pretty kid. Face all red and bashed in as a bad apple.' Feaver wiped his mouth.

For a moment they were all silent.

'Let's change the subject!' said Pete boisterously. 'We're putting the man off here. About to quit on the spot, ain't you?'

'Aw, I'm not that soft, pal,' said Tam in kind. 'This lad here's worked in the docks. Every shipyard's got a couple of stiffs in it, welders getting welded into the hulls they was working on, guys taking falls off the scaffold, guys getting burned up with the acetylene torches. It happens, man, it happens. Never had any kids dead around the place though. That's a shame, that.'

'Yeah, a real shame . . . ' said Pete. 'Anyway,' he said, his voice rising again, 'on that cheerful subject, gentlemen, I'm finished for the night. Off for a pint, my dinner, and the telly. And my missus. She makes the dinner and keeps the telly clean.'

'Garn, good riddance,' said Feaver. 'In here,' he said, wiping his mouth again, 'printing works. Pete switches off all the machines, if he's doing his job, which I doubt—'

'Up yours,' from Pete.

'—so all you need to do is sweep the floor, clean all the dirty bastard's fag ends up, and empty the bins, right? Don't bother about the shelves or surfaces. Pedro likes to keep it all to himself. And if you find a wad of chewing gum sticking to the back of the door, just leave it. Dirty bastard'll be using it again tomorrow.'

'Don't you listen to the old tanky,' called Pete from a far corner of the long printing room where he was climbing out of his boiler suit beside an open locker. 'His brains got purged a hundred years ago.'

'Fascist bugger!'

'Bollocks! Hey, Tam – do us a favour, son! Burn the fucking dump down before tomorrow!'

Tam laughed.

'Course he's not really a fascist,' said Feaver, after he had shut the door of the printing room behind them. 'I was just doing a piss-take, know what I mean? You got two toilets here: don't bother with the sinks or pans or anything, just sweep 'em out, and the cleaners'll mop and bleach them in the morning. Let's head down to One.'

After the dirty Third and the dingy Second, the First Floor was like a high-street show window. On either side of the corridor was a continuous row of glass-walled offices and conference rooms equipped with blond wooden doors and blond wood and metal furniture. From side to side the floor was carpeted in pleasant soft springy pink, and the interior of the outside walls was painted pastel yellow and hung with pretty paintings, travel posters – and Lenin in various poses, paint and photo. Representatives of nine-to-five humanity were pulling on their coats, messing about, and generally preparing to leave. Feaver dropped his voice, and his profanity:

'You don't have much to do here, 'cept security. Cleaners do all the rest – the hoovering, the toilets and bins and that. All carpet, see? So no buffing. Here's the maintenance cupboard. You got a key? No? Shit, I'd better give you mine. Here,' he handed a small latch key over. 'Don't go and lose the fucker. Christ knows when I'll get another one. Night, Sam,' he called to a Neanderthal-looking man who strode past them, jaw clenched. Sam flashed a smile like a grimace of pain and said nothing.

'Closing-up time, folk are going home. Five-thirty, end of the day. Eight-thirty, start of the morning. Course nobody expects you to be here all the time in between,' he added in a confidential whisper. 'Down the pub for a couple of pints, who's any the wiser? You don't need to haunt the place. Just live in and keep an eye out, know what I mean? Day caretaker used to be here till eight at night, but no day caretaker now.'

'Are they hiring another one?'

'Nah. Recession, innit? It's your cuts and that. Now this First Floor is where most of the work is done. The four sub-editors all got their offices here. There's the Economics editor, that's Joe Steele – the Women's editor, Janis Ulman – the Arts editor, Harry Haytor – and the Peace editor, Jack Straw. You'll meet them all in time. Course, you've met Joe Steele already. We'll skip the Ground Floor. Seen it already, right?'

'McRath's office—'

'Yeah, that. Empty his bins, carry off his empties. Lecture Theatre and Library. Nothing to do there except make sure some stupid sod (mentioning no names) hasn't left his window open. Same everywhere. Check the frigging windows. No security alarms, see? Keep checking, keep moving, that's all you can do. Sometimes some fascist puts a brick through one of the windows. Run through quite a bit of glass in this place, I'm telling you. Just make sure there isn't a fucking bomb attached to it, that's all. Any doubts – dial 999, okay?'

'Is it as bad as that?'

Feaver wiped his mouth.

'Yep,' he said. 'So why don't they put alarms in? 'Cause anything heavy happening won't happen in office hours, that's why; and if it isn't in office hours, these prickheads don't care. Get the picture? Way of the world, my son, way of the world! See the commissionaire's desk? There's always someone on duty there in office hours. Two men now, used to be four. Everything's cut back. The commissionaire is the last one out the building at five-thirty, unless someone's staying on late, which doesn't happen often. You lock the door after him – and I mean for Chrissake lock it! Right. Down here's the basement. They've shown you your flat?'

Tam nodded.

'Used to be the engineer's flat. That's why it's down here beside the boiler room. But I've never lived in, like I said. Wife didn't like it, and . . . and things,' he added, glancing at Tam furtively.

They went through a door and down a spiral metal stair (red) that Joe Steele had shown Tam down an hour before. Two doors, both locked, were at the bottom of it. That on the left led into Tam's flat (he had the keys – front and back doors – in his pocket and his bags were inside). Feaver unlocked the one on the right and gave Tam duplicate keys – front and back doors – with much profanity.

'I've got so many keys I'm jingling,' said Tam.

'Last stop.'

The boiler room was a long rectangular aerodrome of a place that seemed to stretch for miles. Half a dozen fluorescent tubes way way up flung a golden glow over the four big boilers that sat like cylindrical vats; each on its concrete bed.

'You don't need to come in here at all, 'cause I *always* lock up,' said Feaver. 'But you got to have the back door key as well in case of God knows what. Come here.'

He led Tam through a doorless archway into a small, bright, and incredibly dirty office stagnant with cigarette smoke. A lurid-covered paperback called *The Shining* was upside down among the fag ends, and a couple of pin-ups of outrageously big-breasted women decorated the walls.

'Makes a change from Lenin,' said Tam.

Feaver grinned, and it made his small withered face look like a leering gargoyle:

'I'm not into it much – just put 'em up to annoy Comrade Ulman. Janis from upstairs, see? Thinks sex was invented by Hitler. You got to watch out. She'll do a snoop on you sometime looking for porno mags and bum-and-tit calendars, just so she can bend your ears about women's rights. Got to get her kicks somehow, poor cow. Right, here's the back-door key. How many's that you've got?'

'Quite a pile.'

'Need to see about getting you a padlock key for the gate outside. You seen the gate outside . . . ?'

The back door was opened briefly. An unusual gust of cold night air rushed in from the back alley carrying particles of soot from the railway line. Then the men returned and recrossed the room, the small one talking all the way. He switched the light off at the door and the four big boilers sat in darkness. Only the little security light in mid-ceiling still gave its wan bluish shine, enough to show the four big boilers with a phosphorescent glow around them.

Then, slowly, other shadows began to accumulate in the room.

5

Alone

Upstairs, on the Ground Floor, the humans were leaving. One by one the went: the editors, the office staff, Peter the printer, and then the commissionaire. Charlie Feaver was last to go. He wished Tam well, told him that the cleaners would arrive around 7.00 a.m., this being autumn and dark in the mornings. ('In summer, if you're still here, it will be nearer six, see?') And then he left.

The sun sank beyond the City, beyond the gleaming glass and steel cliffs of the banks and insurance buildings, beyond the dwarfed spires of the highest churches, and darkness came wading across the sky sprinkling stars. On the skyline, the torn ridge of tower blocks began to glow with light: houselights, headlights, tail-lights, streetlights, whole silver and golden necklaces of light dotted with drops of ruby and emerald. Even the mean dereliction that wallowed around the Red House looked like a spilled treasure chest.

The street outside was husky with going-home traffic. A full moon was rising over the roofs on the other side of the river. Somewhere close at hand a dog began to howl at it.

Tam stood on the step above the pavement. The pavement was a river of people with homes to rush to all rushing to them. They paid Tam no more heed than the lampposts.

Tam stood there for a few minutes, then hitched his trousers and turned back into the Red House. The gloomy maw of the building swallowed him whole.

6

The First Night

That first night on the job Tam spent with his hair prickling. It was dry out there in the darkness, but windy. He could hear the wind – boy, could he. It got into the air conditioning and made it rattle; it got into the lift shaft and made it bang; and above each of the corridors the maintenance space between the chipboard ceiling and the concrete floor above it, through which the pipes and wiring ran, made enough weird noises to sound like a symphony orchestra playing the work of a very avant-garde composer with a German name.

At 11.25 p.m. the lighting in the foyer, the stairs, and the four corridors was automatically put on to night switch by a timer in the wall that only the engineer had access to. The offices, the printing room and the boiler room had their own individual on/off switches inside their doors, but in the public areas the light was regulated by a dial that said off/lo/hi, and at 11.25 the timer arrow clicked from hi to lo and stayed there for the next eight hours, so that the building was never entirely dark. Yet it was never more than dim in those corridors. The security lights that shone from their ceilings every twenty paces or so did their job with a ghastly gleam that had no more strength in it than a candle. The echoes rang up and down the staircases, and when Tam walked there a shadow came sweeping up after him, while another fled before him into the twilight beyond.

* * *

Tam locked the wooden outer door. He locked the glass inner door. Then he went down to the basement, and, beginning with the back doors, he did a complete circuit of the building, checking every door and window in the place as he came to it.

The Red House was silent as an empty church, which is to say it was full of tiny stealthy sounds. The first night on a new graveyard shift is always a bummer because of those sounds. Tam had sometimes worked nights as a docker, moons ago in the shadow of great ships. He had worked in deserted engineering rooms amid silent machines, and patrolled the perimeter fence of a building-site when the rain was lashing the rubble and car headlights were dancing like witches on the distant highway.

He knew.

'Master the sounds, Thomas,' the gaffer had said to him those many moons ago when Tam was but a lad with a past as bland and innocent as a baby's bottom. 'Master the sounds and you'll do.'

So Tam did his work and got so used to the sounds of the night that they seemed to become part of its silence.

Having locked the front doors, both the wooden and glass ones, he went down to the basement to lock up the back. There were two doors, the outside doors to his own flat and to the boiler room, and they sat a few feet apart in the back wall, in the L-shaped alley that wound down from the level of the street halfway round the building. The alley was all of eight feet wide and smelled like a public toilet. A brick wall topped with rusty barbed wire separated it from the railway line, and a mesh gate, topped and criss-crossed with more wire, stood at the L-bend to prevent access from the street.

Tam went out into the dark to make sure the gate was secure. It wasn't. It was supposed to be padlocked to an iron post that was bolted into the wall, but the chain which was there to secure it was looped in the mesh and padlocked to itself, while the gate creaked backward and forward in the wind and banged against the post at monotonously regular intervals. Tam got out the key he had been given and struggled to get the padlock open. There was no streetlamp in the alley, but there was just enough moonlight and city glow reflected off the walls for him to see by. He got the key into the padlock and tried to turn it. It made a dry screeching sound and refused to budge: it was rusted solid. It didn't much matter anyway – the mesh had holes in it big enough for a donkey to get through.

Tam re-entered the building through his flat (his own back door worked, reluctantly, with a key big enough for the Tower of London, but there were ugly cracks in the joints) and went next-door into the boiler room. He had checked it from outside and found it firm enough, but he wanted to check it from the inside as well. He snapped on the boiler-room light and walked down the central aisle between the big boilers. Suddenly he stopped and looked about.

Nothing.

Nothing at all.

Yet he felt

`There's something wrong with this place`

he felt watched. He turned round slowly, scanning the floor, the shadows round the boilers, the ceiling. Nothing. Yet the feeling remained.

Someone watching him.

From the shadows.

'Oh come on, lad!'

He walked quickly towards the door, his head swivelling owl-like all the way.

Nothing happened.

Of course not.

The door had the long handle of a floor brush wedged diagonally between its wooden frame and the metal pushbar so that it was tight. Tam looked at it in puzzlement and then carefully dislodged it. He turned the handle and the door swung open. Cursing to himself he tried the key Charlie Feaver had given him. It turned and turned smoothly contacting nothing.

The lock was broken.

'Christ on a bike!'

From the looks of it, it had been broken for a long time. Tam looked at the brush handle and saw that it was dented where the pushbar pressed into it, and worn at the end where it rubbed against the post.

Muttering a choice selection of curses he jammed the brush handle back in place. Great, just great, I've got to spend the night in a building whose door locks are broken! A brush handle is all that's preventing a hooligan – a gang of hooligans – from breaking into the place! Oh fan-bloody-tastic!

He kept cursing and swearing determinedly to himself until he had left the boiler-room and was in the stairwell again. Then he leaned against the door and realized his legs were shaking. Also that he was listening.

The sounds.

The bronchial cough of the boilers on automatic and the old-man wheeze of their breath accompanying it.

Something creaking in the ceiling above the stairwell. Remember. Identify. Harmless, normal sounds. Don't panic the next time you hear them.

The sights.

Nothing.

There is nothing standing waiting for you round the corner at the top of the stairs. None of the Evil Dead with cadaverous jaws and red staring eyes. No leatherface with a chainsaw. No Shape. No nightmare Freddy with razor hands.

So relax.

Tam climbed the stairs cautiously, keeping his eyes on the corner and his shoulder to the wall opposite. He turned the corner with a little spurt of speed, ready for an ambush.

Nothing.

Of course not. I wasn't scared. Of course. Not.

He was under a security light. It gave him two shadows – one black beast that lay crouched at his feet, the other a long grey phantom that spilled back down the stairs. Tam looked carefully in both directions like a child obeying the traffic code. His shadows twitched and readied themselves.

Tam set off.

One shadow padded silently before his toes, the other followed behind his heels.

Out of the chasms, now on the level of the street, Tam's nerves improved. He checked the Ground Floor without incident – it was an area pleasantly free of creaks and groans – and went up to First.

The first office on the First Floor that he came to, he unlocked the door, switched on the light – and there was a pale face staring in at him right up against the black window. *Thump* went his heart, even though he knew that the spectre could only be his own reflection. He glanced round the office, made sure no masked bandits were lurking, snapped the light off, and the room instantly flooded with moonlight, picking out everything in vivid black shadow or silvery illumination.

Tam was about to close the door when he took a last look, and stopped abruptly. At the desk in the corner, where he was absolutely sure no-one had been a moment ago, a caped figure had risen and now sat crouched, like an animal ready to spring. For maybe fifteen seconds Tam stood rigid, staring at the figure. Then, blinking his eyes, he switched the light back on, only to discover that his figure was a VDU screen over which a plastic hood had been pulled. Tam laughed crookedly, restored the room to darkness, and locked the door.

'Got to do better than this, sunshine,' he said to himself. 'Spooks at your age? Get a grip on yourself, man!'

He walked confidently down the corridor, whistling. And his eyes crawled from side to side, scanning the shadows that walked beside him . . .

Up to the Second Floor he went with his shadows.

And up to Third.

God, the Third!

And, for the hell of it, up to the dead end at the top of the stairs where a concrete wall blocked off the Fourth.

He went down to his flat in the basement, put the kettle on, and waited half an hour before venturing out again.

That was how he spent his first night in the Red House.

7

Nothing Was Done

Tam got up early in the afternoon, went out and bought himself a transistor radio. He spent his next shift with the hum of night-owl music massaging his ears: old-time rock-and-roll, ballads, bubblegum pop from the charts, and disc jockeys all chorkling like idiots.

'Rubbish,' said Tam.

But he listened anyway.

He complained about the broken locks, *and* about the missing bolts, *and* the rickety gate, *and* the rusty burglar snibs, *and* the lack of a security alarm, *and and and* – to the bosses. Yes, he went right on in there, into the middle of an editorial meeting in Finlay McRath's big office, and told them how it was, and all five of them sat and listened, and agreed that something ought to be done—next week, next month, within a fortnight, before next weekend—and Tam, for a week, a fortnight, and even a month, was foolish enough to believe them.

But nothing was done.

Finlay McRath listened to his complaints about broken locks, patted him on the shoulder, gave the old red-faced jolly Santa Claus laugh that went 'Yo-ho-ho-ho', and promptly forgot all about it.

8

The Wall

So the nights passed, turned into weeks, and Tam got used to the Red House, the ceilings that creaked, and the broken door propped shut with its brush handle. He locked the doors and swept the floors, emptied litter bins into a black polythene bag, polished the linoleum with an electric buffing machine, and tried not to talk to himself. Then the night drained away into dawn, the sun rose over the city and turned the windows into a blaze of glory, the cleaners arrived, the first members of the day staff began to trickle in; and Tam yawned, made himself some breakfast, read the morning paper, and thought about bed.

The cleaners Tam soon knew. The editors he knew more slowly, putting names to the faces, and characters to the names, of the five who bossed the House on Leveller Street.

There was Finlay McRath, of course, editor-in-chief, red-faced, white-haired, eccentric and benign (in Tam's estimation), and bullet-headed Joe Steele, in charge of Economics.

Then there was the Peace editor, Jack Straw, a small school-masterly man in tweed with round granny glasses, and the friendly face of a harmless rodent. He apparently was, or had been, a clergyman of some sort, and was in the habit of telling people confidentially that Jesus had been the first socialist, and would certainly be leading a campaign to embargo the import of Outspan oranges from South Africa, were he to live in the world today.

The Arts editor, Henry Haytor, looked like a man whose favourite occupation was sucking raw lemons. His mouth was sour, his eyes cold and ironic, and his dress was thirty years younger than his age. He specialized in directing plays in the subsidized theatre by Finlay McRath, and the friends and protégés of Finlay McRath, which were little more than bullish tirades against the capitalist system which paid for them. His sarcastic abuse of all those who made that point gained him the reputation of being a witty controversialist on television.

Janis Ulman, the Women's editor, had a broad, very serious face softened by sweet, kind eyes. She normally wore a sardonic smile which turned into a furious frown the moment she detected any criticism of what she termed her 'Marxist-feminist sexual politics'. She dealt with such criticism in an angry, despairing voice which suggested that any unwillingness to censor nude models was on the same moral level as Auschwitz.

In more enlightened days – when the Americans were still cringing over Watergate and Vietnam, and progressive people could walk tall and proud with their chins up – the five had called themselves, as an in-joke, the 'politburo'. Officially they were the 'Friends of *The Red Flag*', since *The Red Flag* was not owned or edited by authority figures, as *bourgeois* papers were (grrrr), but was *co-ordinated* in *the collective exercise of class responsibility.*

There are people who really do talk like that.

The Five were not the only friends of *The Red Flag*. Far from it. The published list of sponsors had numbered some three hundred names, including several Labour members of parliament, a peer of the realm, a score of assorted academics, numerous full-time trade union officials, a Church of England bishop, and a whole chandelierful of glitterati from the lesser ranks of stardom – television scriptwriters who had been at university in the sixties, alternative comedians who had been born in the sixties, and forgotten actresses whose heyday had been in the sixties.

There were other friends of *The Red Flag*. Pupils of the school of Frederick Forsyth wrote conspiratorial thrillers about them.

As for the Red House itself, it was British *art totalitaire*. Its resemblance to the Grand People's Study House in Pyongyang, or the People's Palace in Bucharest was that of a pale watercolour painting to a rich vivid oil.

Into this building trudged hard-faced Communist men and owlish Communist women. Their brains inhabited a glum fantasy world of chanting crowds and marching children, where the Market was replaced by the Plan, and the government won 99.8% of the votes in every election. They were *not* robots, they *were* capable of seeing that socialism didn't always get it right, and they did – occasionally – condemn its mistakes. Thus:

'We totally condemn oppression wherever it occurs, in
AMERICA
NORTHERN IRELAND
SOUTH AFRICA
CHILE
TAIWAN . . . *blah blah blah* . . .
and, er, ehm . . . Russia.'

At such times the Soviet Union was always 'Russia'. That way its naughtiness could be dismissed as the backwardness of a barbaric people who wore fur hats and lived near the North Pole, and the brilliant Soviet system (sigh with rapture) would not be brought into disrepute.

All this was in what still seemed like the warm summer of socialism, when Berlin was divided by its wall, statues of dead dictators stood in the streets, and power sat safely upon the Kremlin's domes.

* * *

But then an uneasy rumour crept out of the east. Everything which had been stifled for decades began to move and ferment. The mighty Soviet army began to draw itself in. The appalling treason of Reykjavik happened. Then unbelievable film showed the American president in Moscow, and friendly people milling about Red Square in their shirtsleeves eating McDonald's hamburgers. The enormous stone dictators shivered on their pedestals. What was happening? Hairline cracks began to appear around the feet of the big granite men. Concentration camps began to close. Security police commandants suddenly faced unemployment. Czechoslovakia began to pull down its barbed-wire borders. In East Germany people swarmed across the Berlin Wall – and the guards did not shoot.

Generals upholstered in medal ribbons stared at each other with scared-rabbit eyes. Party officials began talking about democracy on television, staring at the autocues and stumbling over the unfamiliar words.

And the people – who for so long had been instructed to decorate their windows with red flags on the dictators' holidays and promise to work longer and harder – came alive with something that was more than the life of a zombie, poured out into the streets, clambered on to the big stone dictators, and toppled their monstrous monuments to the ground.

There was a tension in the Red House as autumn turned into winter, in that year 1989 – something electrical in the air, as though the building itself was wakening from a long lethargy and slowly beginning to struggle back into life. One day a large television was set up in the Library, and when Tam came on duty he found the room full of people he had not seen before, and cigarette smoke rising like dry ice in a cabaret.

Amongst them, of course, the familiar faces. But there were dozens of others, some (he assumed) daytime office staff who worked while he was asleep downstairs. The rest, the ones with the refined voices, must be some of those upper-class left-wingers the tabloids kept going on about. When he opened the door and looked in, a few of them turned disdainful faces on him for a moment, then looked away. And when he asked the nearest one what was going on, he wasn't answered. Tam, whose ancestors had been tenants on someone else's estate, was a severe critic of such things.

The next night the room was full again.

And the next – and the next.

'Look at that Judas!' snarled Joe Steele, as some new Czech or Pole, or even Russian, came on to denounce tyranny. 'So what? So fucking what?' Steele shouted, hitting one palm with his fist as Communist crimes were recounted.

Pushing midnight, Tam met Janis Ulman coming out of the women's toilet as he was going in to sweep it. Tam was embarrassed, and mumbled an apology. Janis stared at him desperately, and Tam apologized again. Then he realized that she was staring right through him. 'You okay, love?' he asked.

She shook her head stiffly and took a couple of steps past him. Then she turned.

'How old are you, Thomas?'

'Eh, me – er, fifty-seven,' said Tam. 'Why?'

'I'm forty,' said Janis.

'Well, we're none of us getting any younger,' said Tam.

Janis wasn't listening.

'*Almost* forty,' she said, looking somewhere into space. 'Forty next month. Just thirty-nine and eleven months really, if you look at it . . . ' She gave a flickering, ghastly smile. 'No, I *am* forty,' she said. 'Forty, and I, I feel . . . you understand? I'm too *old*, too settled in my ways, to change my entire view of life!' And to Tam's dismay a large tear formed in the corner of each eye and trickled down her broad face. He reached out a hand to comfort her, but with an inarticulate cry she brushed it away and strode off down the corridor, shaking her head fiercely from side to side, and wiping her cheeks with her palms.

Tam watched the six o'clock news on his own little set when he woke up the next evening. He walked about in his underwear eating toast and marmalade and waiting for the kettle to boil, while the screen showed pictures of rioting Czechs and rioting Germans. Communist troops in broad-crowned caps stood around looking scared. A tank appeared, people pelted it with things, and it drew off again.

'Looks like the shit's hitting the fan,' said Tam to himself. He no longer tried not to talk to himself – he just made sure no-one else heard him at it. After breakfast, about 7.00 p.m., he went out to do his shopping at the late-open supermarket a couple of streets away. He met Charlie Feaver coming back along Leveller Street looking like death warmed up.

They went to the pub.

Tam didn't normally drink this soon after getting up, but the peculiar atmosphere of instability was getting to him. He took a pint. Charlie took several, and launched into a weird diatribe. The fascists were needing a lesson, he said. We were going to have to teach it to them again like what we had done when Hitler was at the head of 'em. It was weird. It got weirder. Freemasons, Zionists, and the people who put fluoride in the water supply, all paid visits to Charlie's troubled head.

Tam said yes and no alternatively till his ears echoed with balderdash. Eventually he managed to break loose. When he got back to the Red House, he looked into the office. Finlay McRath was wandering around touching familiar objects with a haunted look on his face.

'How's it going?' said Tam.

McRath jerked his head up, then smiled sheepishly and said he was just tidying up before going home. Tam nodded and walked across the foyer to the stair. There was a sudden scream and Janis Ulman came running out of the Library. She screamed again, and this time it was less of a feminine scream than an animal howl.

McRath barged clumsily out of the office. 'Janis! What – ?'

Janis clawed at the air with both hands:

'Quick, quick!' – the voice was a harsh falsetto – 'They're going to pull it *dooown!*'

She turned and rushed back into the Library with McRath lumbering after her. Tam hesitated a moment longer and followed them.

The main evening news bulletin was showing in the room to maybe a dozen people. The atmosphere was foul with cigarette smoke. Tam glanced around, eyes smarting. Steele, Haytor and Straw were there. Some of the others he had seen before; the rest were strangers. Janis stood behind Straw, her hands grasping the back of his chair.

'Berlin,' said the television.

Tam looked sideways at the screen. What he saw made him turn and give it his full attention.

The screen was full of the Berlin Wall. There were crowds singing and dancing. Young people were sitting on top of the Wall with their legs dangling on either side. Then a section of the Wall fell backwards like a cardboard prop in a theatre. Two policemen, one from the East and one from the West, stepped into the breach and shook hands. The crowd roared. A boy started to dance on top of the Wall near the breach with a tape deck in his hands blaring rock music.

'Oh, oh, oh!' cried Janis, clawing at the chair back as though she wanted to tear it to bits.

'Shoot the fuckers!' barked Steele. 'Shoot the fucking bastards! We've been too soft!'

'Oh dear,' said Straw. He stared at Haytor. Haytor was leering at the screen like a voyeur. Straw craned his neck to look at McRath, but McRath was mesmerized.

'Oh dear,' said Straw again.

'Turn it off,' McRath moaned. 'Oh, please. Somebody, turn it off.'

Steele kicked his seat over, stamped across the floor, and tore the plug out of the wall. The screen fell silent. And so, as if on an unspoken cue, did everything. It was bizarre. The Red House was always full of sounds. Now, not one. Not a creak, not a groan. For a minute, no-one either moved or spoke.

It was Haytor who broke the silence:

'They do it rather well – professionally speaking, I mean,' he murmured, but in the still room his voice sounded jagged and false. 'The American agents, that is – the CIA – Of course, they're all American agents! – But they imitate the people rather well. Plenty of practice, of course. I think I recognized one of them.' And he glanced furtively from side to side, then stared at the carpet.

'I did see some young man with a baseball cap on back to front,' said Straw. 'You know, a lot of Americans do that. For some reason. Never understood why. Er . . . '

'And I saw a Pepsi Cola poster,' said one of the others. She stood up to make sure everybody saw the significance of the fact. 'A Pepsi Cola counter-revolution, that's what it is.'

Janis turned, walked to the far corner, and stood there with her face pressed to the wall and her shoulders silently heaving.

'Well,' said Tam unasked, 'I don't reckon I'd like a sodding big wall built through the middle of my home town. I reckon the Jerries are better off without it. I mean . . . '

Nobody answered him.

'Well, anyway,' said Tam. He gathered up his bag of shopping and made for the door.

McRath turned on him, shouting:

'That Wall stood for twenty-eight years to defend the peace-loving German people from fascism. Now they are defenceless. My God!' he cried, rolling his eyes to heaven. 'They don't know what they're in for!'

'Aye, well,' said Tam. 'Whatever you say – but I've got my job to do.'

He left. Steele swore and shook his bullet-head.

'Fascist!' hissed one of the disdainful ones behind him.

And as Tam went off to work, and screens all over the country filled with rejoicing people, the Friends of *The Red Flag* sat in the murky closed-off little room and began a slow litany of all the horrors that capitalism was about to unleash on the innocent socialist east, wreaking fire and slaughter . . .

'Unemployment—'

'Pornography—'

'Crime—'

'Baseball caps on back to front—'

Tam went upstairs to the Third Floor and began his tour at the top. He found—

9

On the Third Floor

He found the window open and banging in the cold night air.

Tam frowned.

He was in the men's toilet, disused for its native purpose (though all the fittings were still in working order, as though *The Red Flag* nourished the ambition of reclaiming its abandoned upper plain one day) and given over to the storage of cleaning equipment. There were three wash-hand basins and three cubicles on the left-hand side, and a row of six urinals on a raised black-tiled dias on the right.

And one window.

Straight ahead.

It opened sideways on a rusty metal catch which hooked on to the sill. Now the catch was unhooked and the window was swaying open in the wind, and then smacking shut against the frame. When it opened, an icy current came through and blew under the door (badly hung with a half-inch space at the bottom) and into the corridor. The corridor was colder than it should have been, and the toilet was like a refrigerator.

The odd thing was that the toilet door was locked and it required the master key to open it. Charlie Feaver had a key, and doubtless there was another somewhere, but why should anyone come up here to ventilate a cleaning cupboard?

I'll ask Charlie about it tomorrow, Tam told himself.

Oh hell, no – he'll start telling me about the Zionists in the

Stock Exchange and the American plot to take over the world. Stuff that.

Ask the Night of the Living Dead downstairs? Christ!

Tam pulled the window shut and turned the locking snib. He went out into the corridor, turned to lock the door – and stopped. The place was silent, none of the usual noises from the ceiling overhead. Come to think of it, it had been silent when he came on to the floor, and he hadn't noticed. He frowned again. He didn't like this Third Floor, he didn't like the way it was uninhabited and cluttered at the same time, or the fact that Lenin's photograph looked that bit uglier than the other Lenin pictures and photographs dotted about the place. He didn't like the fact that his predecessor had killed his daughter here, and himself—

```
It was me and a copper found him
   in the men's toilet
Rosemary
She landed on her face
   on the Underground line
All smashed in
```

He didn't like this place—

Clunk from the other side of the door

—at all.

Clunk *creaaak!* Then a dull *Bang!*

No sounds: then sounds he couldn't identify: then—

A cold draft began to play round Tam's feet. He pushed through the door and snapped the light on.

The window was open again.

Tam stared.

Bang! it went – *creaaak* in the wind – and *Bang!* as it smacked shut.

His heart began to hammer. Tam knew this film, he had been in it several times before in his life, starting with the bombing raid he had been caught up in when he was a kid and Hitler's air force had come over to demolish around his ears the quaint olde-worlde acre of slum that was his home. He leaned his shoulder against the wall and let it take some of the weight off his feet. He breathed deeply several times until the old ticker had slowed down to normal and the sudden white noise between his ears (the distinctive sound/no-sound of fear) had lost some of its frizz.

Then he walked to the window.

The snib he had locked a minute or two before was unlocked; the catch he had hooked into place was hanging loose.

The frizz came back.

Des.

He had gone mad in this pile and flung his own little daughter out of this very window.

`Six years old she was`

Tam stuck his head out the window. The cold wind smacked him on the cheek. Down below, in the black, the lines of the Underground came out of their tunnel and ran for a couple of hundred yards in the open behind the Red House. Immediately below him was the back alley. The little girl – what was her name? –

`Rosemary`

ah, yes – must have been flung out with such force that she missed the alley, went clean over the wall, and hit the lines. And the trains went over her in the dark, over her and over her, and they did not know. It was so black down there you couldn't see anything, not a bloody thing. God, how could a man *do* a thing like that to his own—

Tam got an itchy feeling, the feeling of being looked at, of being very closely regarded indeed, right in the back of his neck. It translated itself into a cold finger that pressed into the base of his spine and started to slide upwards. He glanced back over his shoulder as though some cell deep inside his brain expected to see Des standing there, dead and lunatic with staring bloodshot eyes and his hands clawing the air, and

Rosemary tumbling out into the night, arms and legs flailing in all directions and her mouth wide open in a terrible
SCREAM

He spun round and grasped the window frame with both hands. By God—
SCREAM SCREAM SCREAM SCREAM
went the cars of the train as it tore out of the tunnel and along the track a hundred feet below. Tam could see the flash of lighted windows, but the angle was too steep for him to see any passengers. And then it was gone. The lines shuddered back into silence.

Tam closed the window gingerly. He fixed the catch, smacked it down with the palm of his hand, fixed and tested the snib; then tested it again for luck. Right, I'm going to turn my back on this box of tricks and walk away. Are you listening? I'm just going – to walk – away

(who am I talking to?)

so try and stop me if you can. Go on – try it.

He turned and walked away with his ears pinned backwards, ready to burst if the window opened *creak bang* on him before he reached the door. He got to it, paused

(there's something waiting in the corridor!)

and opened it. The corridor was empty and silent as a

(tomb?).

He locked the door and leaned his back on it, waiting. For a long blessèd moment there was nothing from the building, and whatever noises the party animals were making, down on the Ground Floor weren't carrying beyond the nearest fire door.

Then something thumped softly in the lift-shaft down the corridor.

Tam prised himself away from the door and walked towards the lift indicator. The little green light was sitting at G – Ground – and the machinery wasn't operating.

Something tinkled beyond the metal doors like falling gravel.

(??)

Then, like an old man waking up in bed and stretching his joints, all the ceiling sounds from the maintenance space above his head started off together in a mechanical jumble of crashes, clicks and bangs: the night music he had come to know and love.

Tam took a deep breath and smiled. The Red House was coming to life again. He turned his back on the lifts and surveyed the corridor. There was nothing else to do here. He—

The photograph on the wall opposite the lift had been turned around.

He was sure it hadn't been like that when he came up here. I mean, a photograph turned against the wall, I'd have noticed it, right?

No, no, no, not right at all.

Tam righted the photograph. Its cord was old and long and it had lost all the tautness it once had, so it was just possible to hang it back to front, stretching the cord round its frame. Anyway, someone had done it. Tam turned it round and a piece of glass fell out of the frame and clacked on the floor at his feet. He looked down at it in alarm, and then at what was left. The glass in the photo was smashed in the dead centre like it had been hit by a bullet, and three long deep cracks ran right into the frame, dividing what was left in two. On the glass were several strange bloody-looking marks. Tam licked his finger and rubbed at them. Dirt came off the glass but the marks remained. The photograph underneath seemed undamaged. Lenin stood beside a desk bareheaded and wearing a three-piece dark suit. His right fist rested on top of a pile of books on the desk, his left thumb was hooked into his waistcoat pocket, and he was staring into the camera with an expression of baleful cunning.

'Tomorrow,' said Tam. He picked up the piece of broken glass. There were obvious answers, of course there were. His brain just wasn't working right just now. He would think of the answers tomorrow. Or another day.

He went to the east stairs

paused

and, instead of going down, climbed up to the dead end at the top, nineteen steps, turn, seventeen more.

There stood the concrete wall. The night-light on the wall where the steps turned let him see it. He narrowed his eyes and leaned forward. There were small cracks along the cement seams which he hadn't seen before, and one of them was leaking a tiny stream of silver dust on to the seventeenth step.

He listened. On the other side of the wall he could hear – he could swear he could hear—

    'Tomorrow.'

10

Vladilen

And in Berlin the Wall came tumbling down: block by concrete block it fell, and the people cheered.

The man switched off his television set. It was 8.30 in the evening in Moscow, in a flat, spacious by Russian standards, on the fourth floor of a block of flats owned by the Ministry of the Interior near Moscow River.

The man went over to the window. In the courtyard below, the statue (the one that, so he always told people, he had been the model for) glowed in the moonlight like a ghost. The statue was a heroic idealization of a Chekist – a Soviet security policeman – brave and vigilant, with a gun on his hip and a body like a god.

The man was paunchy and greying. His face had more lines than a road map, and his eyes were haunted. He too was a Chekist. He stared at the statue's granite head – and beyond it at the road glimmering with streetlights, the sharp angles of the buildings, and here and there the river. A mile away, where the river curved like a ribbon of white satin under the moon, he could see the luminous red stars on top of the Kremlin. Just below them, hidden from him by the Kremlin walls, was the comforting presence of Lenin's mausoleum in Red Square.

Vladilen.

His parents had called him that after the great dead man in the mausoleum, Vladimir Ilych Lenin, because Lenin was quite simply the most wonderful human being who had ever lived, and they wanted their little boy to grow up like Lenin, brave and wise and beautiful, a tireless fighter for the freedom of oppressed people everywhere, and especially of those who were being butchered by Hitler's fascists.

When he grew up, Vladilen went off to guard a concentration camp in Siberia where they were putting fascists who opposed freedom.

Ah, the wicked fascists.

Forty years had passed since the day when Vladilen had shot his first fascist in Siberia. Since then he had shot many fascists. But the fascists always came back. Their guile was appalling. Sometimes they came back as pretty young women, sometimes as doddering old men, sometimes – as children. He shot them all, without bourgeois sentimentality. He was a Chekist.

He never married. He said he was married to the Service, which they called the Cheka – 'the lynchpin' – because the security police and their concentration camps were the lynchpin of socialism.

He didn't go whoring either. Or gambling. Or do deals on the black market.

His colleagues, who did all three, called him 'the monk'. He liked the title. He was a warrior-monk. He had a calling. In the service of Lenin he had turned more people into corpses than an outbreak of cholera. He shot them and he shot them. There was a permanent red callus on his trigger finger.

And yet the fascists always came back.

Always.

Hitler turned into the Americans, and the Americans were even more dangerous than Hitler had been.

Once a week Vladilen went to the red marble mausoleum in Red Square. His identity card could have got him to the head of the queue, but he never used it. He was happy to stand in the open for a couple of hours with the other true believers.

He felt an overwhelming love for them. When he entered the presence of Lenin's mummified corpse, he wept.

Why? he asked Lenin. Why?

Why do I feel so dirty?

Why has it all gone wrong?

At night, after work, he would sit alone in his lonely flat surrounded by scrupulously clean furniture, with a glass in his hand and a bottle on the floor, and stare glumly at the television screen.

He couldn't believe what he saw there – the betrayals, the lies, the filth. Every night some atrocity was paraded, some attack was made on socialism, and the legacy of Lenin was reviled.

And then the Wall – the Wall they had built to defend the people of socialist Germany from fascism – they were knocking it down, and there was nobody there to stop them.

Vladilen got drunk. Very drunk.

For more than forty years, all his adult life, he had worked – and for what?

He went to his window, opened it, and breathed the cold dark air.

At night Moscow looked so lovely with all its lights, like spilled treasure. His Moscow! He loved Moscow. But nobody in it loved him.

The Service was ridiculed and Lenin was rejected.

And in a moment of absolute eerie clarity it came to him that all his life he had just been made use of by sadistic old men. That he had been keeping Hitler in his grave all these many years by killing people who weren't fascists at all.

Innocent people.

Vladilen put down his glass, gripped the low metal security railing with both hands, and swung his legs over it, one after the other.

The last thing he wanted to see was the red star above the Kremlin shining in the night.

The last thing he saw was the statue of the comrade Chekist rushing up to meet him.

And the open window banged to and fro in the cold night air.

11

The Monster Man

Next day, while the offices worked upstairs, Tam had a dream in his basement. It went like this:

He was in the men's toilet on the Third Floor, only it had got much longer than it was; it was about the length of a railway carriage with cubicles down the entire left side, urinals down the right, and no wash-hand basins at all. The toilet smell of bleach and urine hung so heavily on the stagnant air that Tam decided he would open the window and ventilate the place.

He began to walk towards the single window, but the room seemed to get longer and longer (which was when he realized that it was a dream) and he was walking with that soft-footed slowness that you get in dreams, as though the brown linoleum floor was a conveyor belt on which he was going the wrong way. He stopped, feeling perplexed, knowing it was a dream, and yet such strange dreamlike things had been happening to him that he couldn't be sure. He stopped, wondering if the moving floor would bear him backwards. That's when he looked into the cubicles. They didn't have any doors, he noticed, and they were filled, not with cleaning equipment, mops and pails and so forth, but with

guns.

Pistols. Revolvers hanging in holsters from the wall. Tommy guns propped up against the cisterns. Rifles lying across the toilet bowls.

Then he saw men sitting there on the toilet seats; men

in uniform with the wooden look of paratroopers waiting to jump, each one with a tommy gun across his knees, staring – not at Tam, but at something beyond him. Tam turned. There weren't six white china urinals on the other side, there were rows of them, rows and rows, stretching in serried ranks into the far distance somewhere beyond the wall, and in the cup of each one sat a severed head, its eyes open and bulbous as marbles and flecked with rotting blood, its purple lips pulled back in a grin over a stinking mouth.

Then the urinals flushed one after another, like a staggered volley.

Blood spurted out of the pipes.

And because the drains were choked with pulpy flesh, the blood flowed over and spilled on to the industrial black-tiled dais and down on to the floor.

Tam lurched away from it. He had the feeling that this blood was like acid and that it might burn his feet if it touched them; or that it would perhaps anchor him in this nightmare and prevent him from ever getting out. An eternity surrounded by the stench (the rapidly increasing stench) of blood and gun oil and putrefying flesh! Even in the depths of his sleep Tam could not contemplate that. He ran towards the window, and he was very nearly there when

suddenly

out of the last cubicle a man swung – *Des*, he knew it had to be Des – dangling on the end of a noose

```
   He'd gone and locked the door on himself
      and he was hanging there from a pipe
```
with his legs bent at the knee and his slippered feet dragging on the ground like some badly battered dummy
```
   neck broken and stretched out
      about two feet long
```
his swollen tongue bulging out of one corner of his mouth, and his penis stiff as a poker pushing at his trousers.

At least his eyes were closed, thank God for that.

Then the door from the corridor burst open and a little girl rushed into the room.

'Daddy, Daddy!' she cried. 'It's him! Daddy! Help me!'

At the sound of her voice Des's eyes snapped open. They were silver eyes with no pupils. The little girl ran towards him but she was already ankle-deep in the blood pouring out of the urinals. She struggled, slowing down, pulling her feet out of the ooze with loud slurping noises, her thin stick-like arms flailing ahead desperately. Des gave a low moan and his tongue lolled across his mouth from side to side. He stretched his big hands out towards her, but there was no strength in his dead muscles, and his feet scraped and twitched uselessly.

Then there was a single sharp *craaaak* and Tam saw that the door was made of glass and that something had hit it from the other side. It hit again. The glass was opaque and the shape on the other side of it was cloudy, ill-defined, becoming darker the closer it came. It hit the glass again – and again – and

the glass broke.

The overhead light exploded.

The thing burst through, roaring. It was the shape of a frog, only it was the size of a man, bald and naked with two baleful eyes that cast a pale ugly light over the room. The thing seemed to possess no skin; its entire body was covered in blood that hung from it in great torn clots. The lower part of its head was one huge slavering toothless mouth that stank of slaughterhouses. Tam screamed, but the sound fell back down his throat into darkness. He tried to move, but his body didn't answer.

Floundering in the same sea of gluey blood that held Tam fast, the little girl cried:

'Daddy! It's him! It's the monster man! Oh *Daaaahdee!*—

And then her cries were cut short as the thing swept her up into the air and lumbered with her to the window.

All the severed heads began to laugh . . .

* * *

Tam woke. He had twisted the bed sheets into an impossible tangle and his pyjamas were slimy with sweat. For a while he stood shaking in front of the wall mirror, running his fingers through his wild hair.

A horrible haggard mask stared back at him.

Outside, the hour of the day people was ending. The wind blew; the window was spattered with rain. Another train went screaming down the line as the shadows came creeping.

12

Winter

Winter came, the winter they shot Ceausescu. The nights were long, and wet, and windy. The doors creaked and banged, the ceilings wailed and howled. The city was deep black with lights gleaming here and there like feral beasts' eyes. And fear gripped the Red House in its long curling claws.

Officially, damage-control was the name of the game, and they played it remorselessly.

Finlay McRath remarked hopefully to Joe Steele that socialism would lose its fat in opposition. The best thing would be to forget that the Communist states had ever existed. That way they wouldn't have to apologize for the past. Concentrate on green issues and gay issues and women's issues and ethnic and peace issues; get back in there on the side of the angels.

Joe Steele nodded his head dubiously.

So *The Red Flag* came out in favour of reform. It condemned what it too now called 'Stalinism', but said in the next breath that it would be wrong to make 'a song and dance' about its excesses. Sang Finlay's word-processor all over the editorial page:

> True, there have been excesses, there have been those camps we're all hearing so much about; but beneath all that ash a diamond sparkles like the dawn star of victory. The Soviet Union beat fascism, the Soviet Union helped Cuba and Angola withstand vicious U.S. imperialism, the Soviet Union leads the

struggle for peace and disarmament, the Soviet Union pays lorry drivers the same salary as brain surgeons. The Soviet Union, whatever her faults, is the enemy of greed and selfishness. The Soviet Union believes in equality. In the last analysis nothing can detract from the magnificence of these achievements.

The paper began a cartoon strip which portrayed Gorbachev, the honest, brave socialist, standing up to the bad bastards of capitalist subversion – with a senile old Stalinist thrown in for good measure.

They played the game out there in the big, bad, bourgeois world; my, how they played it.

Janis, in a television interview, said that *of course* she had always opposed 'Stalinism', oh yes she had, but she was worried about the real danger of the socialist baby being thrown out with the Stalinist bathwater. The Soviet Union had been a great champion of women's rights, as for instance abortion on demand, she said, and glared at the camera. All her abortionist friends agreed with her and wrote letters to the *Radio Times* saying so.

Jack Straw, interviewed on television by a friend of his whom *he* had several times interviewed on television (they were both university graduates from the sixties), reminisced fondly about the good old days of Paris '68 and the Vietnam demos. He had always opposed 'Stalinism', he said, but the Soviet Union had been a consistent champion of peace, and 'Russian' nuclear missiles were much smaller and much nicer than American ones, he said.

Haytor, in *his* television interview, declared that, while Stalin *had* committed crimes, all that was many years ago, and besides, socialism was ultimately justified by its support for the arts. The BBC producer, over subsequent drinks, told him that he was *appalled, totally appalled* by the number of reactionary scripts being sent in these days. They were *ghastly*, he said, *utterly ghastly*.

Haytor agreed vigorously.

Television did a profile of Finlay McRath, the Great Writer. He declaimed some mystical verses about deer on Highland hills and mist on mountain peaks, and generally fumbled around endearingly in an old pullover with his trousers sagging. Slightly drunk, he gave an extempore rendition of the *Internationale*, and other bloodstained ballads, a nostalgic smile on his old, red, genial, merry, ravaged face. 'I only wish,' he said, 'that some Russian policeman would come over here and put us right about all these so-called atrocities people keep going on about!'

Steele's brutal jaw said *Sorry, gone to lunch. Back when we can blame the Americans for something.* He refused to be interviewed.

But inside the womb of the Red House, things were different. The proud totalitarians, who blew their noses over a million corpses, now crept round its haunted corridors like ghouls in a ruined crypt. Some were vacant and swollen-eyed from bouts of lonely weeping; others were frankly hysterical, tormented by visions of American marines hitting the beach at Docklands; others still complained of psychosomatic symptoms such as heart palpitations, stomach cramps, and outbreaks of nervous boils.

One young man from the editorial office took to his bed with the fall of the Berlin Wall, and that was the last he was seen in the Red House. Comrades who visited him brought back reports of a wreck, a pale, worn face, red-rimmed eyes that darted restlessly round the room searching for enemies, and ears that heard fascists whispering together outside the window by the light of a midnight moon.

Then there were the deserters – those who discovered that their hearts had, after all, always been with the Green Party, or the Labour Party, or who quit politics altogether and gave themselves up to social work among the needy.

But most coped, since it is amazing what the human mind

can cope with, and they went about their business as alert as ever, if deeply dispirited by the rising smell of rot.

At night Tam often found two or three of the Five, and sometimes all of the Five together, sitting in the Library – hours after their usual finishing time – talking, drinking, smoking, and watching films. They were the faithful ones. While government officials, generals and hangmen were deserting the Cause, they remained true. They all had homes to go to, but the world was so treacherous that there were nights when they were afraid to go beyond the doors and preferred the creaking horrors of the empty building. Besides which, the Library could be made to seem so cosy with its electric fire and soft armchairs; its shelves reassuringly filled with hundreds upon hundreds of volumes of unimpeachable orthodoxy; and its framed photographs of happy peasants, happy workers, sunlit tractors, and clean industrial sites.

So they sat there, sipping their nightcaps, and made enjoyably doom-laden pronouncements about the rise of McDonald's and the fast-food industry, equating free elections with Pizza Hut, and the closing down of concentration camps with the opening of Burger King franchises in Siberia. Then, to end on an uplifting note, they would watch the video of *Battleship Potemkin* for the 529th time, or some dire documentary from a Third World dictatorship, all hip-hip-hooray and waving flags.

And the fug of smoke, and the warm drink, the talk, the triumphal music, and the assurance of the silver screen – they made such a potent mixture that the Five wanted to stay there for ever.

Tam waited to lock up after them, and tidy up the Library, remove their glasses, empty their ashtrays, and hoover the carpet. They gave him a lot of inconvenience with their late night carouses – but none of them ever thought of that.

13

How the Statue Came

So Tam was left to walk alone along the ugly Third Floor corridor; then down to Second; then down to First, very conscious of being alone in the big building.

This is how morning comes to the Red House.

Forget the nonsense you have heard about the city sleeping. Night men know that the city never sleeps. When the sun is still over Australia the London streets are noisy with late-night taxis, early-morning milkfloats, newspaper vans leaving the printing works, lorries going to the wholesalers, cruising police cars, and the click-clack of some night-prowler's feet on the echoing asphalt slabs, going God-knows-where-or-why, while the wind hoots and howls about the roof of the House, rattles at its loose-fitting windows, and makes music in the ventilators.

And Tam walked alone there, like the ghost of some forlorn sentry, and heard it all.

Outside, a taxi strayed down the street with its orange hire light gleaming, and Tam, now on the Ground Floor, looked out at it sadly. Then he heard voices approaching. With the room in darkness behind him, he pressed his face up close to the glass and stared down at a gang of noisy youths who came swaggering along the pavement like bandits, swearing horribly. If he opened the window, he could reach out and touch the tops of their heads.

The real world was as close as that.

For hours Tam walked that shift alone, watching and sweeping, watching and polishing, watching and emptying bins, and watching, always watching, and listening. And all the time something seemed to walk at his back, watching him, awaiting an opportunity to do him injury. God, he was glad when the humans came.

The milkman first. He regularly delivered a vending-machine refill bag inside a cardboard carton. Because the front-door bell had broken down years ago and never been repaired, Tam had to sit waiting in the foyer round about 5.00 a.m. Usually the milk got there around 5.15; sometimes a little earlier, sometimes later. Tam had to take the delivery personally – not that the office had told him that; the office didn't seem to care one way or the other; but fifty-seven-year-old Tam was the sort of man who believed in doing the job properly. At first the milky had left the carton on the doorstep if Tam wasn't there, and Tam picked it up five or ten minutes later, no problem. But then the box took to disappearing off the doorstep, and maybe turning up ripped open and puddling in the middle of the road fifty yards away, or, on one occasion, splattered all over the wall – this being on the same night that a brick came through one of the Ground Floor windows with a message about 'dirty reds' attached.

Tam reported this to the police, who duly noted it, and to the office, who duly did nothing about it. A Council grant paid for the broken window, and for the milk.

Thereafter, Tam took to waiting in the foyer. He opened the wooden outer doors at 5.00 and kept the glass inner ones closed with a brush handle. The milkman dumped the carton inside the wooden doors while Tam pulled the brush handle out of the glass ones. The milky said, 'Morning,' and Tam said, 'Morning,' back. Sometimes the milky added, 'Fucking weather,' or, 'Fucking rain,' and went.

Neither man knew the other's name.

Around 6.00 a.m. the two cleaners arrived. Neither had a

key to the door, so Tam was there in the foyer to let them in as well. Their names were Pat and Alice and they looked like a funereal female Laurel and Hardy. Pat was the sort of woman who earns the name 'lady' said in a deep-down bass. She was substantial, she was vast, she was built like a beer barrel over which someone had draped a blue pinafore; not exactly fat, she worked too hard to be fat, but Rubenesque, with arm muscles that bulged like Popeye's, and a tongue that flapped like a flag in the wind. Alice was small, sallow, and economical as an X-ray, with eyes like pinpoint torches, blue-rinsed hair, and a smouldering cigarette permanently lodged in the corner of her red-slit mouth. Her ears were small and neat, with the receiving capacity of radar stations.

Pat talked, Alice listened. A conversation between the two went like this:

'And then there's Paul's birthday, you know, our Ellen's nephew, the one that's in the oil rigs—'

'Ayuh—'

'And he's always needing a change of clothes,'cause these rigs, you get so dirty working on these rigs you come out looking like a darkie with all the grease and oil and that—'

'Ayuh—'

'So I thought I'd buy a nice new jumper for him, and so I went into that new shop, you know, the one that's just opened on the High Street—'

'Perry's?'

'Ayuh, and they had one in the window that was grey and sort of navy blue with these pink sheep on it—'

'Nice—'

'So I thought if I could get that for him, 'cause I know our Ellen's getting this new video recorder, and Tracy wanted to go to the West End for it, but I said to her—'

'Ayuh . . . '

And the horizon was either still blackly indistinguishable from the mass of London, or streaked with antique silver moonlight that masked the coming dawn and dimmed the stars . . .

Sometime around 7.10 a.m. the post came. The postie wasn't jolly Postman Pat the local character, he was a grey apparition in colourless clothes with a bag over his shoulder. He always wore the same thin jacket and open-necked shirt no matter how cold it was, and he never spoke at all.

Tam stood inside the glass doors. The sky was now achingly beautiful. The horizon was a river of brilliant orange on which the splintered silhouettes of Dockland offices and surrounding housing estates stood out like black cliffs encased in gold, and their windows sparkled bright as a seam of diamonds. Tam viewed it quietly and lit a cigarette because, well, he had seen it thousands of times. He kept on looking at it nevertheless for as long as it took his fag to burn all the way down to the filter.

It was just past 7.30 on this particular morning when the special-delivery lorry he was waiting for arrived. It looked neat in the first daylight, all scarlet and gold, and the two men who got out of the cabin looked big as bears and fresh as daisies. Their shift was beginning. Tam looked and felt like a sack of potatoes. His shift was ending. On the worksheet that morning was the cryptic line *Receive delivery of special parcel c. 7.00* in Jack Straw's small handwriting. While Tam did his thing with the brush handle and the glass doors, the two delivery men opened up the back of the lorry and jumped inside. Tam stood on the steps waiting for them to reappear. It was January, it was cold, he was tired; he hunched his shoulders and stamped his feet against the chill.

One of the men stuck his head out of the back of the lorry.

'You got some people to take this?' he asked.

'No, just me. What is it?'

'Box – bastard weighs a ton. I mean, look at it.'

Tam came down to look at it. Several boxes of various sizes

were stacked inside the lorry, and one, tall as a door, bulky as a giant's coffin, was sitting on a rolling board out beside the hydraulic lifter.

'*Bastard* weighs a *ton*,' said the delivery man. He was black-bearded and square and lumpy; his companion was tall and wore a turban. They both had biceps like watermelons.

'What the hell is it?'

'Statue.'

'*What?*'

'Fucking statue. See.' Beard held out the invoice sheet.

Statue, granite, Tam read. *Moskva*. 'Moscow?'

'Careful. The Russians are maybe out to get you,' said Turban.

'Bet it's a pile of porno mags,' said Tam.

They laughed.

'Yeah, okay,' said Beard. 'Let's get this fucker out.'

The two men manoeuvred the box on to the lifter, grunting and swearing blue fire. Turban operated the lift, and when it was level with the street, Beard jumped down with a long-handled metal hook which he looped on to a ring on the rolling board and yanked it two-handed off the base.

'There you are, squire, all yours once you've signed the doings,' said Turban, holding out the invoice sheet.

Tam checked the address on the box, and the customs stamp for good measure, and signed.

'Got a rolling board?' said Beard.

'Nope,' said Tam.

'Well, where's this thing going?'

'I dunno,' said Tam. 'I've not been told a fucking thing about it.'

They stood round the box and looked at it.

'Well, we can't leave it here, can we?'

They stood and looked at it some more.

'Okay, let's do it,' said Beard.

He and Tam yanked at the box until it was rocking just

enough for Turban to hook the front two casters of the rolling board on to the pavement. Another five minutes and they had got the whole thing on the pavement. Then they looked at the steps.

Tam hoped somebody would turn up.

'We need some planks, and a rope and tackle, or something,' said Beard. 'You got – ?'

'I know this sounds really wet, but we've got bugger-all of anything in that place.'

Charlie Feaver arrived.

Tam filled him in.

Charlie nodded judiciously. 'Oh, sure,' he said. 'So what's the problem?'

'We need the stuff.'

'Oh.' Pause. 'Do we have the stuff?'

'I don't know, Christalmighty! I don't have the frigging keys to all the cupboards, do I?'

'No? No. Okay, I'll take a look.' He went indoors.

'Christ, what a place,' said Tam, shaking his head.

'Look,' said Beard, 'we'd like to help, but we got to be going, know what I mean?'

'Yeah, sure – thanks.'

'That's okay. Look, we'll need to leave the rolling board.'

'Pick it up next time you're passing.'

'Sure, okay.'

'Have fun,' said Turban.

They sloped off.

Tam heard them laughing. He felt like a pillock. It took Charlie a long time to take his look. While he was doing it a couple of secretaries turned up. Tam said hello, but they ignored him. The morning commissionaire arrived, grunted, gave the box the look which says 'Not *my* job!' and went in.

Eventually Charlie came back with a good length of rope dangling from his arm like a cowboy's lasso.

'Give it here,' said Tam.

He took the rope and stood dangling it speculatively. 'We won't get it up the steps like that – it'll topple over. We got to lie it on its face, then two of us pull from the front, and somebody else shove from behind. We need another pair of hands.'

'Who?'

'The commissionaire.'

'He won't do it.'

'Ask him.'

'He won't do it,' said Charlie. 'If you was lying burning in the gutter he wouldn't piss on you to put it out.'

'Ask him anyway.'

Charlie sighed, and walked into the building. Tam criss-crossed the rope around and along the oblong box and knotted it securely.

'He says for you to fuck off,' said Charlie, coming back.

Tam's strode into the building, and along the corridor to the ratty little staff-room.

The commissionaire was sitting with a teacup and a tabloid.

'We need a third pair of hands out there, you coming?' said Tam.

'I'm not on duty and it's not my job,' said the commissionaire.

'When are you on duty?'

The commissionaire looked at his watch. 'Five minutes,' he said.

'Right, five minutes,' said Tam. He marched back to the door. Charlie Feaver was standing staring at the box like a meditating yogi.

Another secretary appeared; pretty and talkative. She asked Charlie what he was doing.

'You could help,' said Tam.

She laughed. 'Rather you than me,' she said.

'All I'm asking,' said Tam, 'is that you give the rolling

board – that thing with the casters that it's sitting on – a wee pull when we tip it over. That's all, pet,' he said in his most imploring voice, switching on the charm.

'Oh, all right,' said the girl. 'Look what's written on it,' she said suddenly. She pointed. There, painted on the side of the box in letters so indistinct that Tam had missed them, were the English words:

ON CHRIST'S BIRTHDAY THE ANTICHRIST IS DEAD! FREE ROMANIA! FREE RUSSIA! FREEDOM!

'Charming,' she said, wrinkling up her nose.

Tam got hold of the box. He wrapped his left arm around it and pressed his right firmly up against the nearest side. Charlie imitated him with right for left.

'Okay, pull towards us, and mind your feet. Pet, tug that rolling board away when you can – and mind your fingers. Okay – heave it!'

They yanked at the box. It wobbled, settled back, wobbled again, and then began to tip towards them. The two men were soon crouching under it, holding it up with all their might. The rolling board tipped up, raising two casters into the air. The secretary pulled it loose, and, with the men shouting to each other to mind their fingers, the box settled heavily, lengthwise, on the pavement. Tam looped his rope round its newly exposed base.

'We each take an end of the line and pull it.'

'How do we get it up the steps?'

'With difficulty. Hey,' said Tam to the commissionaire who had appeared in the doorway and was looking down at them, 'on duty yet, are you?'

The commissionaire nodded.

'Lend a hand down here then, will you?'

The commissionaire leaned against the wall and put his hands in his pockets. 'Not my job, pal,' he said.

Joe Steele and Finlay McRath arrived almost, but not quite, simultaneously. Steele parked his maroon Astra near the mouth of the alley and came striding towards them at five miles an hour with his hearing aid whining. Charlie stepped behind Tam and said nothing. Tam asked (loudly) for a hand.

'Struggle, struggle, Stakhanovite,' said Steele mysteriously, lowering his brows and bulling his way past them.

'What the hell does that mean?' said Tam.

Steele's back vanished through the door. The commissionaire preceded him. The pretty secretary smiled and followed.

Tam turned to Charlie Feaver. The engineer was looking redundant.

'What does that mean?' said Tam.

Charlie shrugged.

'Is he coming out again or what?'

Charlie shrugged again.

Then Finlay McRath was crossing the street towards them from his parked Granada, dodging the traffic like a practised toreador.

'Hey,' said Tam, 'we need . . . ' and he told him what they needed.

McRath slowed down, laughed his frank man-to-man laugh, and patted Tam on the shoulder. Then he disappeared into the House.

Peter the printer and Henry Haytor got off the same bus. Peter volunteered to help. He shoved from behind while Tam and Charlie pulled on the ropes, and Haytor stood by grinning and said encouraging things. Jack Straw arrived on a mountain bike looking bustling as a boy scout leader, and he also said encouraging things. Janis arrived in her Volvo. She nodded to them all with a preoccupied air and ran up the steps.

Between them the three men got the box inside the foyer.

14

The Statue Revealed

'I'm on overtime,' said Tam. 'I hope somebody's noticing.'

The commissionaire was sitting at his desk looking at papers on a clipboard.

'Better open it,' said Haytor.

'I'll get a chisel,' said Charlie, making his first decision of the morning. He went. Tam and Peter sat down on opposite ends of the box. Jack Straw fussed about.

'It could be a bomb, it could be a bomb!' he said.

Haytor's grin slipped an inch. Neither Tam nor Peter said anything. Charlie came back with the chisel.

'Er – careful,' said Haytor. He and Straw went into the office.

'That's bosses for you,' said Peter.

'Even this lot?' asked Tam.

'Even this lot,' said Peter.

'Hmmmph,' said Charlie.

Lenin's big picture stared down. Charlie stood indecisively dangling the chisel in his hand; then, taking a deep breath, he snapped the two aluminium bands that were round the box and prised the lid open.

Joe Steele came out and stood looking down at the box with his hands on his hips. The commissionaire had disappeared. Finlay McRath and Janis Ulman came out and stood beside Steele. Haytor and Jack Straw showed their faces inside the office door.

'Bang!' said Peter dramatically.

Everybody laughed. Tam leaned over into the huge coffin-like interior and began to scoop out armfuls of white plastic-foam chips. Charlie and Peter helped him. The five editors came closer and stood round them in a circle. The commissionaire came back looking like a man who had been busy somewhere else. Three secretaries, including the pretty one, came out to join them.

The statue lay before them, glaring upward. It was of the sort that are made of in the factories of successful dictatorships idealizing loyal workers and soldiers, leaders and police spies. Some mason had hammered away to transform this rectangle of rock into a semblance of a powerful young man in military uniform, one hand hanging casually by his side, the other resting on the holster of his gun belt. The sculptor's chisel marks gave him a macho look, as though he had exploded from the side of a cliff. His face was stern and hard as the blade of an axe.

One of the secretaries gasped.

'What in hell – ?' said Steele.

They all stood in a circle and stared into the coffin-like box. McRath edged forward. He took the side of the box in his hands and leaned over it, staring down at the callous face. The eye pupils were single chisel gashes in the cold stone. Engraved on the base were Russian letters.

'What does that say?'

'Something something internationalism something,' said Janis Ulman.

Finlay McRath shook his head.

'Well, that's a damn weird thing,' said Haytor, his grin back in place.

The others echoed him. McRath was silent, staring at the figure with bewildered concentration.

'Hey, look at this,' said Janis. She pointed to the inside of the lid where a white envelope was taped. Tam bent towards it; she muscled past him and tore it off. 'Unaddressed,' she said, turning it over.

'Open it, Janis,' said Straw, but she had already done so.

'"To the author of *Granite Does Not Weep*,"' she read. She glanced at Finlay. (So did Haytor, Straw and Steele.) '"That which he admires so much. The Moscow Democratic Committee." What do you make of that?'

'Finlay – ?' said Haytor.

McRath suddenly jumped as though galvanized. He made a hissing dismayed noise somewhere in his throat and threw his hands up in front of his face.

'Christ!' he cried. 'It's that statue! The one from the square!'

'Eh? What?' said his colleagues.

McRath turned round and walked back to his office unsteadily, shaking his head. Steele followed him. Five minutes later Steele came back.

'Get rid of that damn thing!' he said.

'What – ?'

'But – ?'

'Where – ?'

'What is this Moscow Democratic Committee?' asked Tam.

'Huh? Oh, just some bunch of fascists trying to make us feel bad. Put it – oh, put it in the boiler room.'

'Do you want it closed up again?' said Tam.

'Yes, yes, better do that,' said Steele. 'Fascists!' he said. 'Stinking dirty fascists!' He turned and walked off again. The other three editors hesitated for a moment and then hurried after him, all deploring the fascists. The secretaries vanished. The commissionaire went back to his clipboard.

'I'm due forty minutes overtime,' said Tam.

'That's right about these fascists though,' said Charlie vehemently. 'See these fascists—'

'Aw, piss off,' said Peter. 'Have we got to move this bugger again?'

'Forty-one minutes,' said Tam.

Then they hammered the lid back on, roughly, and rolled the box over to the top of the boiler-room steps. Then, toiling like slaves and swearing like pirates, they slowly lowered it down – bump! bump! and bump! again – until its base was resting on the lowest step. Then Peter went upstairs for the rolling board, handed it to Tam, who passed it over the length of the box to Charlie, who put it on the ground and steadied it with his foot while they lowered the box on to it.

'That's it!' said Peter.

Charlie grunted. 'You're not leaving it here, not for me to fall over every time I go to check the dials. Let's get the bugger out the way somewhere.'

With the rolling board underneath, the box moved easily. They trundled it around the wall, past the four huge boilers, to the corner beyond the engineer's office.

'We need the roll-board out,' said Tam. 'Those guys are coming back for it.'

'Okay, let's get it up.'

They pulled the box upright and worked it back into the right angle of the corner. Charlie viewed it with distaste.

'Fuck!' he said. 'Looks like something out of *The Curse of the Mummy's Tomb* – and I've got to live with the bugger.'

'You'll probably meet him taking a walk,' said Tam ominously.

'Balls!'

'He'll have *your* balls,' Peter said. 'Probably *eats* balls, he does. Shuffles out with his shroud trailing on the ground behind him. He'll stand behind the door and grab you next time you come down.'

'Yeah, sure,' said Charlie, laughing uneasily.

'Bet he loves balls,' Peter continued. '*Thrives* on them, he does.'

'He's had all the balls off all the comrades in Moscow,' Tam added.

'And now he's come here—'

''Cause he's heard about you, Charlie my son—'

'And he's come to plunder your toy box.'

'And when he's finished, he'll dig your eyes out their sockets: *aaargh*!'

'*Aaargh!*'

'And munch 'em up, and then bend over and suck your brains out your nose like ice-cream—'

'Charlie's brains *are* ice-cream—'

'Oh yeah, very fucking funny,' Charlie answered. 'Least *I* won't be here at night. Unlike you, sunbeam!'

'Argh, don't remind me,' said Tam.

'Wouldn't do your job for a million pounds.'

'Neither would I if I had a million pounds.'

So saying, the three men left the windowless basement room and flicked off the light, and the darkness flooded in, and the noise of their too-loud laughter faded with their footfalls going up the stair, and the statue of the invincible young warrior

    `'Honour the Struggle for Internationalism!'`
      `(Finlay McRath)`

stood there alone in his box. Darkness enfolded him.

Quotation from *Granite Does Not Weep* by Finlay McRath, in *The Ballad Of Greenham Common, And Other Peace Poems*, William Joyce & Co., London, 1984:

> Comrade Chekists! Red knights of the proletariat!
> Raised fists of the working class struggle against
> the poisonous serpent of US imperialist aggression!
> Honour the struggle for internationalism!
> Ah Lenin, you were right when you said that Russia
> had to be purged of harmful insects.
> But the Buddha, too, was right . . .

And so on. Hundreds of lines later it ends like this:

> And when Britain is finally purged of its bourgeoisie:
> its Tories and worse than Tories, racists, Labourite traitors:
> concerned clergymen, bleeding-heart liberals:
> charitable old women of both sexes:
> reactionary workers who fail to see the true beauty
> of the great red Leninist path –
> when all this human detritus is cleared from the road:
> without bourgeois sentimentality:
> but with firm socialist purpose:
> then the song of William Blake's Albion will be heard:
> then the Red Flag will fly like a beautiful golden bird
> (for *Krassivy* in Russian means both red and beautiful)
> over the roofs of London, and the Workers
> will rise up
> and touch the sun!

It won a prize.

15

Charlie

9.10 a.m. that day.

Downstairs in his little flat beside the dark boiler room Tam washed, had a bite to eat, and looked at the morning paper. Round about 10.00 he set his alarm clock for 4.30 p.m. and climbed into bed.

Five minutes later he was asleep.

Next door, the boiler room was almost completely black – yet not quite. Thin lines of daylight shone through the rickety back door that was still secured – as it had been for the past ten years – with the long brush handle. Another thin line of light, electric, shone under the door at the bottom of the stairs. The gauges on the four boilers each had two button lights, one red and one green, and the dimmest of dim night-lights glowed in the engineer's office in its small alcove beyond the doorless arch. Together, these sources of illumination provided a pale eerie twilight against which the cylindrical boilers loomed black and massive as missiles in a silo, and hummed, and hummed, and hummed, and rumbled.

And the box from Moscow stood where the shadows were thickest.

At 10.30 a.m. Charlie Feaver dropped in for the first time since they had hauled that sodding statue into the place. He switched all the lights on – four switches, all of them – standing in the doorway. Only when the room was shining with yellow brilliance did he let the door swing to behind him. It clicked shut on its Yale – that lock was kept in working order – and Charlie walked smartly to his office to get a new packet of cigarettes out of the carton he kept in his locker. He dropped the cellophane on the floor, stuffed a fag in his mouth, and gave the place a quick check over to make sure the tubs weren't going to blow up.

The box was standing in the corner beyond the arch where he wouldn't see it unless he went looking, which he wasn't going to do. No way. It would take a special collection from the refuse department to get rid of the fucking thing, and you could just see those pink pansies upstairs paying for a special collection, couldn't you? Yeah. The bastard was going to stand in that corner until . . .

Until . . .

Shit, he didn't like it at all, even the way the thing was standing there it really did look like something out of *The Curse Of The Mummy's Tomb* – I mean, a statue of a heavy with a shooter in his paw, for Christ's sake! It was like sending a hangman's noose or a bloodstained axe or something. Why rake up the past and give people shivers and start getting the fascists all itchy, just because the Comrades popped off a few million of the cunts in Siberia or someplace? I mean . . .

And Charlie Feaver, cursing into the stagnant air, stamped out of the boiler room, smacking the door behind him. But this time he left the lights on.

11.00 a.m. Upstairs, Finlay McRath was losing his shakes by hitting the jungle-juice. His daily bottle – a taste for which was the one thing he did undoubtedly have in common with Rabbie Burns, the *other* great working-class poet – was already more than half empty. By 12.00 it was all empty and the second begun. It didn't make any odds. Finlay was one of those rare mortals whom drink does not appear to affect in any serious way. He sat with Henry Haytor and talked about his latest dramatic masterpiece, which Haytor had directed for theatre to tiny audiences and great media reviews on a generous grant, and was now, inevitably, adapting for television.

In the boiler room, inside the wooden box, Vladilen shuddered and woke.

He was on his feet, but then he was used to snatching some sleep on his feet. It was cold and black around him, utterly black – not a houselight, not a streetlight anywhere – and the air was stale. Inside, then. He stood perfectly still, the way only a trained soldier or policeman can be perfectly still. He couldn't remember getting here, just . . . just a vague depression, the tail-end of a nightmare he'd been having. He'd had nightmares before, especially after he had had some really heavy stuff to do on the fascists, and their screaming had woken him up in the middle of the night, so real he could have sworn they were standing round his bed looking at him with their sheep's eyes and bullet-riddled bodies. He felt the familiar taste of black copper in his mouth.

He couldn't even remember what his orders were. Damn, that was serious. He searched his memory but its various bits and pieces slid away from him like shades. Nothing for it but to wait. Sooner or later his contact would reach him – the person who would point him in the direction of the enemy, and he could take the rest from there. Since he could see nothing, he listened, and with his heightened senses he could hear the rippling current of the river, the traffic on the streets around, the click-clack of a woman's heels on the pavement overhead, the sound of people playing radios, throwing parties, having a good time while he was on duty, alone, in the dark.

It took a strong, brave man to be forever on duty like this. A socialist man.

He smelled the dust, the rancid plaster-and-damp odour of a cellar – mouse urine, faeces, stale noxious air, decay. The stink did not offend him. He had stood in endless dirty damp doorways in his raincoat, listening, watching.

And waiting.

Now deep in the foundations of the Red House he waited. He knew his orders would come sooner or later – they always did. And he listened – for the enemy who was to be destroyed.

Next door, Tam slept fitfully. His sleeping mind recognized the daylight sounds. *('Master the sounds, Thomas, and you'll do.')* The constant volcanic rumble of the four big boilers did not breach his sleep, nor did the rush and roar of the trains disturb him. But he turned, and twitched, and once he cried out incoherently and seemed to be fighting something.

On the dot of 12.00 Charlie Feaver left for his official lunch hour, which extended effortlessly to ninety minutes in the pub, talking about football. He picked up an afternoon paper on the way back and, after another hour, most of which he spent haranguing Peter the printer on the dangers of reform, he went back down to his office to read it. He tucked his small body neatly into the alcove, and soon he was shrouded in cigarette smoke like a martyr at the stake.

A couple of weeks back, Janis Ulman had ripped the pin-ups off the wall as Charlie had known she would do sooner or later. They had both stood nose to nose in this stale little office and yelled quotations at each other in a way which people who are not initiates of Communist ideology would not believe possible. The names of Marx, Lenin and other famous corpses, had gone whizzing about like ricocheting bullets. Their faces had turned red, they had drenched each other in spittle, and their eyeballs had bulged and threatened to explode out of their heads and roll across the floor.

It was a regular performance for them.

Janis had gone storming out, dramatically tearing Gorgeous Gabrielle 36–25–34 and Delicious Debbie 39–24–36 into tiny pieces and scattering them on the stair outside – where Tam would find them hours later and sweep them up, wondering what all the confetti was – and there wasn't an awful lot that

Charlie could do about that, short of use physical force, and she was – well, she was a woman, after all, besides being considerably bigger than him, and Charlie was thoroughly intimidated on both scores.

But when it came to his locker, well now Charlie's locker was his castle. It was padlocked shut. Janis had demanded that he open it – and would Charlie open it for her? Not on yours, pal! Janis did what women are supposed to do in these circumstances; she howled and raved, she clawed her hands and tore at the air, she sobbed with rage; but seeing that it was having no effect on him, she calmed down with remarkable speed and went storming out again, slamming the door and swearing vengeance.

A couple of days later Charlie found chips and scratches bashed out of it where Janis had been trying to break the padlock with a hammer and screwdriver.

He nearly had an apoplexy.

War!

Next day he bought a heavy double-action padlock with a reinforced inner tube that looked capable of tying down a Challenger tank. He also bought the securing chain for a bicycle and tied it around the outside of the locker. Right then! Next time she tried that door she—

The sound was just like a door creaking. Charlie sat forward in his chair, instantly alert.

Upstairs in one of the corridors he wouldn't even have noticed it, but here – it was out of place. The creak of wood was one of the few sounds the boilers didn't make, and he should know. His first thought was for the back door. Christ, had Tam forgotten to push the brush handle across it? Charlie picked up a heavy spanner and tiptoed down the alley between the boilers with the tool raised in his hand like a Red Indian's tomahawk, expecting to find some streetfighting fascist at the end of it with tatooed muscles and a petrol bomb. But the brush handle was still there. Charlie put his eye up against one of the cracks, and there was no figure blocking the daylight outside and nothing preventing the cold draft from getting in.

Imagination, son, he said to himself, padding nervously back up the alley; getting old, getting the jitters; like Des. Christ!

There were plenty of noises here, after all; things scuttling behind the plaster, things going bump in the night; this isn't a horror video, son, this isn't one of your Stephen King stories, this is the real world, know what I mean? Just a boiler room, it looks like one, it feels like one, it smells—

    It smells

The boiler room smelled all right, but Charlie was so used to that stale old stink of dust, oil and mice droppings that he didn't notice it any more. It was a grey smell and he smelled of it himself. That was one of the reasons why his wife (now dead) hadn't liked the flat next door – the smell that clung to everything and wouldn't go away no matter how hard you scrubbed. The other reason was—

No, better not think of the other reason. Not down here on my jack.

(If pressed, Charlie had a well-rehearsed line said with a laugh and a shrug. 'The missus? Aw, she got scared of *the things that go bump in the night*. You know what women are.')

Yeah. And he hadn't been here at night since.

But this smell, it wasn't grey at all, it was sort of *maroon*, a thick bitter coppery smell like the stench of hot iron or – blood.

And cold too, creeping tomblike cold.

(Christ, this fucking place is getting to me. No wonder old Des went barmy.)

I'm not afraid, I'm not afraid, I'm not afraid, he said. But he screamed even before the hand fell on his shoulder.

16

The Day Passes . . .

It was 3.30 p.m. and the winter day was passing. The eastern sky was beginning to fill with grey embers, and the first chills of the coming night were in the air.

The day was passing for Janis Ulman. Angered by her failure to break into Charlie's locker (she had sneaked down again and seen the new padlock and chain he had put on it) she was, with absolute seriousness, contemplating her next stage of militant action. This involved getting Finlay McRath to order Charlie Feaver to open his locker right there and then in front of Finlay himself and Janis, of course, and as many of the other comrades as possible, who would thereupon engage in active criticism of his sexist behaviour, and make him see – not by force, not by intimidation, but simply by *constructive criticism* – the error, the very grave error, he was making in treating women as objects of sexual desire. He would be made to hang his head in shame, and serve him right. He would mumble his apologies and confess. He would seek absolution. And they would forgive him, because they believed in the essential goodness and innocence of human beings.

Janis sucked her teeth with satisfaction.

3.35 p.m. The day was passing for Jack Straw. He was sitting looking sadly at his fax machine which was bringing in details of the proposed abolition of the East German armed forces. As Peace Editor he was genuinely concerned that the abolition of the National People's Army of the German Democratic Republic (to give them both their full and proper names) might cause a war. This was only a paradox to the sentimental bourgeois. The Marxist understood it perfectly.

3.40 p.m. The day was passing for Henry Haytor. He left the office, looked for a bus, and, when one didn't come, walked the distance of two stops to where he kept his Porsche parked in a small passage beside a shop selling curry sauce, brillo pads, men's magazines, and other sundries. He drove for ten minutes and parked in the vacant lot behind the film studio. His company, Right-On Films, owned what had once been a bus depot that had been bought and equipped as a spacious studio, courtesy of a large government grant, where it devoted itself to strident works attacking the government.

3.45. The day was passing for Joe Steele. Unremarked by anyone – since he had no-one, and was not a man to attract sympathy from strangers – the past weeks had broken a strand or two of his nerve, if not his unbreakable heart. He sat glumly at his desk immersed in the minutiae of admin, the brand of tea bags to be made available in the vending machine, and the colour of the toilet paper to be used in the staff lavatories.

3.50. Finlay McRath, rosy with drink, wandered from his office to the Library, where he touched and stroked the works of orthodoxy, and from the Library back to his office, where he sat doing no work, just looking at his big bony hands in their wrapping of leathery skin.

3.55. The commissionaire, who had spent the morning reading the morning paper's sports pages, and the afternoon reading the afternoon paper's sports pages, was now commencing upon the crossword while a radio played unremarked pop music in his ear.

4.00. The day ended for Tam half-an-hour too soon. His unrest had ceased in the afternoon and let him slide down into a land of sweet dreams. That's where he was now. He was living in the cottage in the country he had always wanted to live in, and he was standing inside the window looking out into the garden which was lacquer-black and hedged with a blaze of gold and crimson flowers. The faces of the flowers looked at him steadily without the slightest motion. A woman was standing in the middle of the garden, smiling to him with her soft mouth and her laughing eyes . . .

Then Tam heard the noise. He took his attention off the woman for a moment as he puzzled to identify it.

Soft and regular as—

Soft but growing louder like—

```
Footsteps
```

A pained expression came into the woman's eyes, and the smile froze on her lips.

The footsteps quickened and swelled up to a thunderous roar, and suddenly Janis Ulman, many times life-size, burst into the garden wearing a black parson's suit and a broad-brimmed Quaker hat, with a huge butcher's knife in one upraised hand and a massive bible in the other—

'Huh wha—' said Tam as his eyes stickily ungummed themselves and slid open.

Thud thud thud, he heard it, *thud thud thud.*

And his thoughts swam round and round in his head like goldfish in a bowl that had a little toy house at the bottom of it with a black garden and gold and crimson flowers and a mermaid, and he said:

'Door.'

And he shambled to it in his pyjamas. It was vibrating in its frame. Whoever was hacking at it . . .

He unsnibbed the catch and pulled the door open. Charlie Feaver's fist had been about to hit the wood. The motion of it pulled him forward right on top of Tam, and the two of them staggered some steps down the little hall like two strange men doing a dance.

'Hey, Charlie, what's wrong? What's . . . ?'

'Ticker,' Charlie whispered, his eyes huge and popping.

'Ticker?'

'Dicky ticker. Check . . . check . . . ah . . . '

'Check what?' said Tam. 'What?'

Charlie became a dead weight in Tam's arms. Tam went down to the ground with him.

Charlie's face was waxy-looking and yellow.

'Check . . . ah,' he breathed once more.

And then he died.

17

. . . Into the Night

They stood and watched the tail-lights of the ambulance until they disappeared round the corner of the street that was full of reddish evening light. Tam, Peter the printer, and Joe Steele stood on the pavement, Straw, Haytor and Janis Ulman stood on the steps, Finlay McRath stood in the doorway. Other faces were at the windows.

'I never reckoned him for a bad heart,' said Peter. 'Never did. I was talking to him just this afternoon, I was. Right as rain, he was. Now this. Dead. Charlie. Just like that.' He shook his head incredulously.

'He's a victim of capitalism,' said Steele. 'The capitalists killed him just as surely as if they had shot him.' He shook his head. 'He showed his solidarity', he said, 'to the end.' He turned and mounted the steps.

The other editors had already gone back in.

Tam went to the boiler room. All the lights were still on. The only thing he noticed about the place was that the front had fallen off the box and the statue was standing there inside it like a sentry staring out.

And that it was cold.

Tam shivered and switched the lights off behind him as he went out.

18

Rosemary

The day passed and the day people departed with it.

The rush-hour howled in the street and screamed in the railway tunnels as evening came down with a long winter's night on its heels. It lingered briefly, making a golden sheen along the serrated skyline, and then faded away as the stars came out. The wind rose, shouting, with a whiplash of rain, and punished the eaves of the Red House as the storm clouds rolled down in great blue-green waves under the cold northern moon.

Peter the printer made it home to his family.

'Charlie's dead,' he blurted. 'Heart attack – just dropped him stone dead, just like that . . . I never reckoned his number was up,' he said later on, pretending to watch the television while his wife sat knitting and his daughter washed the dishes before going out. He talked quite a bit about Charlie Feaver, whom he had always pretended not to like, and his wife listened patiently and said various obvious, well-meaning things to comfort him, and looked at him tenderly.

Joe Steele went home to his functional flat and put a supermarket chop into the microwave. He had not lived with anybody since 1968, when his wife died childless.

Janis Ulman had a man. Finlay McRath had a succession

of women. So had Henry Haytor. Jack Straw lived with his mother.

Joe Steele had the Working Class. He didn't give a shit for anything else.

Tam's night began.

He did his usual rounds without thinking too much about what had happened. Ground Floor first, secure the front door; down to the boiler room, make sure ye olde brush handle is in place ('Hiya, Fred, how's it going?' he said to the statue); up to the Ground Floor again; up the west stairs to First, check all windows – one left open and the rain blowing in, damn it – up to Second, ditto, rain now coming down in buckets, windows running water like a fishmonger's slab; up to Third . . .

The Third.

He still didn't like the Third Floor, the place was spooky. And that *toilet* – he went through it like the clappers, after gingerly sticking his hand round the door to switch the light on before the rest of him went in. (Some day the light's going to go blink, and I'm going to have to replace it in the dark. Boy, that'll be fun.) The fault, whatever it was, with the window had never recurred. Lenin's broken picture had been taken away and the hook hung naked. Some comedian having his fun, Tam assumed – at least, in daylight. Peter the printer didn't seem to mind working with the Ghost Train Floor over his head, but then he wasn't alone, and he was on the Second, and he was only here in daylight.

Alone and at night and on the Third, Tam did his job, quickly and unhappily, and then got the hell off the Third as fast as he could.

He didn't go up the nineteen steps, turn, seventeen steps, concrete wall that led to the Fourth. Why should he? There was nothing to see or hear there. Nothing. And he didn't want to see or hear it again.

99

He went down to First, got the polishing equipment out of the maintenance cupboard, and sent it up to Second in the lift. He followed by the stairs. This was his night for polishing the linoleum corridor of the Second Floor, and this was how he did it:

First he washed the corridor and let it dry. Then he worked backwards from the eastern stairs with a rag-headed mop and a metal pail full of liquid polish, soaking the mop, squeezing it in the drainer, then carefully spreading the polish from wall to wall, left to right, being especially careful with the corners and the base of the skirting board, making sure every last inch of the linoleum was covered. About halfway along the corridor, near the lift-shaft, he stopped, stretched painfully, listening to his shoulders crack, and admired his work – the clean wet shine of the area whose polish he had just laid, the dull glow of the drying areas he had laid earlier.

He continued, working rhythmically, side to side, left to right, until he reached the stonework of the western stair on to which he carefully backed, taking his mop and pail with him. He went down to the First Floor, disposed of the pail, and spent the next hour hoovering carpets and emptying bins in the offices from west to east. Then he returned to the Second Floor via the eastern stair, dragged out the buffing machine he had parked inside the printing room door, and began to push it over the now dried polish, left to right, side to side, raising it to a fine high shine. The buffer was a big thing, a sort of heavyweight industrial hoover with a revolving thick felt base that buzzed like a hive of metal bees.

Tam was snaking the big buffer along there, left to right and back again, humming all the time to the tune his radio was playing, when something, some movement perhaps, at the far end of the corridor made him look up, and there was a little girl standing right at the far end beside the western stair, staring at him solemnly.

All alone, and wearing a yellow frock with a red pattern on it, she looked perhaps six years old.

Tam gave such a start that the buffer swung out of control and bashed into the wall. It took him only a couple of seconds to master the machine and switch it off, but when he looked up again the little girl had disappeared.

'Hey, pet, it's all right. Don't run away!' called Tam, hurrying along the corridor.

He reached the stair and halted with his hand on the rail. Up or down? He neither saw nor heard anything. After a moment's hesitation he ran down past the First Floor to the Ground, checked the front door, and found it locked. He got out his keys, checked every street-level window, and found them all secure. Tried the doors into his flat and into the boiler room, and they were locked as well.

Puzzled, he climbed back up the stair to First and began to check every door and every room, looked under every desk and in every cupboard and toilet, and then went on to do the same on Second and Third.

Nothing. Not a thing.

He tried the lift, and she wasn't there.

Okay, there's only one place left . . .

One two three, he went up the steps at the top of the east stair that he hadn't been up since that night when – whatever. Seventeen, eighteen, nineteen; he turned on the landing – Christ, what a dingy gloomy *creepy hole* – he turned and:

One, two, three . . .

He saw it by the time he got to five, but his brain was too puzzled to tell his feet about it so they just kept on going. The wall . . . the cracks he had noticed back in November in the cement seams between some of the blocks . . . they were much larger; Jesus, one of the blocks about three feet from the ground was ready to fall out; it was actually standing slightly squint. Tam stopped on step sixteen, crouched down, and gently pushed the block with his fingertips. Nothing. Solid. He pushed harder. It scraped and moved back a few millimetres. It was big enough, just big enough for—

Something scuttered on the other side.

Rats. No mice could make sounds like that. And big rats, because they sounded like, almost like—

```
Footsteps
```

Tam sat down on the seventeenth step with his back to the wall and put his head in his hands.

Footsteps? There is no-one there. No-one. You're imagining it, he said.

(Carefully he pushed at the concrete block, and it scraped back the merest hair's breadth. No, it was too heavy for a little girl to have moved it – and she certainly couldn't have lifted it up three feet and put it back in the wall behind her!)

He laughed, rather hysterically.

'Christ, I'm going daft!'

Wait – think . . . She was wearing a summer frock – not jeans, not a jacket, not a playsuit or anything like that; a summer frock – in the middle of winter. No coat, no mittens, nothing – like she was living in the place, almost. Where did she come from? And where, please God tell me, did she go to? She wasn't even up here in dead-end alley

(that creepy feeling again)

or in the other one.

The other one?

'Hell!'

She would be in the other one, at the top of the west stair, sitting like he was now, with her back to the dirty concrete. Scared . . . lonely . . . It was the only place she could be. Tam shoved himself wearily up by the flat of his hand, and—

He jumped as though he had been stung. The scream ripped into his right ear with the sudden cold force of a Black & Decker power drill. It wasn't exactly the shrill scream of a child, more the whine in a headset magnified ten times. It faded into a series of heart-rending sobs.

Tam stood stock-still for maybe a minute until his leaping heartbeat returned to normal and the flutter in his leg muscles ceased. Behind the wall, he could hear, those damn rats were scraping again. He took a deep breath and walked quickly and steadily down the stair and along the corridor. He heard his footfalls on the linoleum sound very, very loud. Behind him the silence was singing, and Tam looked narrowly at each door he passed and turned round sharply once or twice, half-believing – in the subterranean part of his mind – that something was walking through the air close behind him; but of course nothing was to be seen. He looked up round the corner of the stair at the other end to the concrete wall, but there was no one there. The wall looked like it was . . . no—

He didn't set foot on the stairs.

```
You can't see me.
```

Of course not, there's no one there.

```
Then who are you talking to?
```

I'm not talking!

```
You are.
```

I'M NOT TALK—!

```
Ah-ha!
```

Tam went straight down the stair to the commissionaire's desk in the foyer, dialled one 9 for an outside line, then three more, and asked for the police. He leaned against the desk waiting for them, and smoked three cigarettes in a row, lighting the second from the glowing butt of the first, and the third from the second. He was still on the third, puffing quickly and religiously like a monk telling his rosary beads, when they arrived.

Two young constables, one man and one woman, came in shaking the rain off their caps.

Tam told them what had happened. Most of it, anyway.

They looked at him non-committally.

'If I was her father I wouldn't let her wander about like that,' he concluded.

The constables nodded. With Tam they went through the entire building. One of them even looked up the dead-end stairs to the Fourth Floor wall while Tam waited with the other on Third.

They found nothing.

19

The Contact

Vladilen felt confused. Mixed up. And frightened. He wasn't quite sure just what had happened back there. He'd wanted to interrogate the man in the basement, that was all, just jerk a few answers out of him *because he had to know*. Once he knew what was going on, well, then he would know what way the wind was blowing, he would know . . . well – *things*.

It was important to know things. Just because he was in the Service didn't mean he was stupid. He knew lots of things. He had some books back in the flat that weren't just pictures; they had some pretty deep words in them about philosophy, history and politics too; and even if he hadn't had the time to read more than a few bits of them, he was going to, he certainly was, maybe when he retired; and then – well, he might just get down to it and write a book himself, you know, about the Cheka, and his time in it right from the start.

No, maybe not from the very start, that was still too difficult; maybe from, say, his first assignment through to the last: and this book would tell all the smart-arse intellectuals, bleeding-heart liberals and do-gooders, about just how necessary the Service was in a world that still had fascists in it. Yes, he'd do that one day, just so everybody would know that he wasn't just some walking pistol in a coat. He was a man who knew how to make sacrifices for the Common Good.

Vladilen began to feel a bit better. It always made him feel better to contemplate the Common Good, and just a little proud of himself when he thought of the sacrifices he kept making for it. If only the guy hadn't died on him like that! Poor little shit – must have had a bad heart or something, just ready to pop off any minute. Ah well, that was tough. That's how it goes. No point in crying over spilt milk, as Lenin said.

And here's another thing that Lenin said:
You can't make an omelette without breaking eggs.

Too bad if you were an egg, of course. But then it was bourgeois to think like that.

He took up his position beside the statue.

He was dying for a cigarette, but of course there was no question of it. He could not give his position away.

The contact would come. Just a matter of waiting long enough.

Vladilen watched.

And waited.

Waited.

Suddenly he saw a thin crack of vertical light appear inches before his eyes. He focused on it intently. For a minute or two nothing seemed to happen, but then the light began to broaden until it had gradually taken the shape of a golden cone that shone down into the darkened boiler room, its base spilling around the feet of the giant statue. Within it, as his eyes became accustomed to its radiance, Vladilen saw a swirling spiral of dust. He watched as the motes began slowly to coalesce and form themselves into a pattern.

Before him stood a little girl in a yellow dress who looked at him seriously with her head cocked to one side.

Vladilen stared at her.

The little girl said nothing.

'Are you – my contact?' he asked.

She nodded.

'Well . . . what are my orders?'

She smiled. 'Orders? What are they?' she asked.

He told her.

She smiled again and shook her head as though he had said something foolish. 'Did it hurt?' she asked.

'Did what hurt?'

'When you died.'

'Died? What are you talking about, girl? I'm not dead.'

She looked at him compassionately.

'I'm not!' he said.

He brought his hands up to his face to touch himself. His face – ! His hands found high cheekbones and gaunt cheeks. The face he had shaved that morning had been broad and fleshy.

'I'm not . . . '

The little girl stretched out her arm and pointed to something over his shoulder. Vladilen turned around. The statue was behind him. From the top of its head a red splash was running down over its cold stone shoulders and dripping on to the floor. He recognized a pink froth of brain with particles of shattered bone, scalp and strands of shorn grey hair mingling with the blood. His mouth fell open.

'I was frightened when I fell through the air, so frightened, but it didn't hurt,' said Rosemary. 'Are you all alone?' she asked.

Vladilen nodded stupidly.

'Where are your friends?'

'I don't have any friends,' he said. 'Just comrades.'

'Poor man,' she said.

He drew himself up. 'I'm a soldier!' he said proudly.

'Poor soldier,' she said. 'Would you like to meet my friends?' She reached out and took his hand.

Together they rose up through the air. The ceiling lost solidity and they passed through it.

'I am dead,' thought Vladilen. 'I really am.'

No-one saw them.

They came to a wall. The blocks of which it was made were seamed with dazzling light. Rosemary stopped, still holding his hand, and he stopped obediently beside her. Phosphorescence seeped out of the seams and over the blocks until the entire wall was brilliant as a sheet of fire. Soon the shimmering light began to steady and their reflections came gliding out to them.

The little girl was sweet and pretty as a picture.

The man beside her was a monster with a face like a radium dial.

Vladilen screamed. This was not the face he had had when he was young! When he was young he had looked happy and wholesome. This creature with its sharp machine-like features was unfeeling and remorselessly cruel. Blood and gun oil were dripping from its long clawed fingers, and its eyes were silver discs reflecting nothing.

'That's not me!' Vladilen cried. 'Everybody loved me! My mother—

```
She died
```
'My girlfriend—
```
She killed herself
```
'My home—
```
You forgot it
```
'And that . . . that *thing*, that isn't me!'

'It's what you became,' said the little girl gently.

And then he saw them, the people he had killed. They came walking out slowly to meet him.

'My friends,' said Rosemary. 'The Night People.'

20

In Moscow

No, despite what bourgeois critics said, Finlay McRath's great poem *Granite Does Not Weep* had not been inspired by the sight of a horde of KGB interrogators torturing a dissident to death with electrodes. It had actually been written during Finlay's last-but-one visit to Moscow in the spring of 1980 as an acknowledgement of the revolutionary struggle to build socialism in the face of imperialist plots. The imperialists were so wicked, it was necessary for the revolution to defend itself, and if it had depopulated the country by several millions or dozens of millions of people, well, it was all the fault of the imperialists for being so wicked.

A lot of left-wing intellectuals flinched from admitting these necessary actions of the Boys from the Cheka. Jean-Paul Sartre, Bertolt Brecht, Hugh MacDiarmid and others, had all developed butterflies in the stomach when it came to dealing with the Boys.

Not Finlay McRath.

He admitted what he called 'the necessity of murder' and bravely invited the critics to condemn him.

The critics admired his honesty.

Finlay McRath had never witnessed the murder of anyone in the whole of his life.

Finlay loved the Soviet Union.

It was the place where people were almost perfect, the way

he had always wanted them to be perfect. He loved Moscow; it was his kind of town, he said (often). He had first gone there in 1946, after the Soviet Union had won the struggle against German fascism single-handedly, despite the obstructions of the British and Americans. He had taken part in the great parade that poured across Red Square carrying red banners and huge portraits of Great Comrade Lenin and Great Comrade Stalin past Great Comrade Lenin's mausoleum, on top of which Great Comrade Stalin stood, hand beautifully raised in salute like the progressive current of history incarnate.

One of thousands in that vast surge of people, Finlay felt utterly insignificant by comparison.

He took great pride in feeling utterly insignificant.

'We're utterly insignificant by comparison with *Him*!' he yelled at uncomprehending Muscovites, who nodded and smiled.

He had visited Moscow dozens of times subsequently, and though he could demonstrate his healthy open-mindedness by joking about the service in hotels, etc, he could honestly say he did not have a single bad memory of the place. In 1980 he had even had a party thrown in his honour in the Lubyanka Palace itself, headquarters of the Committee of State Security, at which the Director of the Committee, a stocky man who looked like Humpty Dumpty covered with medals, had presented him with a medal, and he read his great poem *Granite Does Not Weep* to an appreciative audience of stocky men with medals (it was translated simultaneously) who were all cultured lovers of poetry, laughed at his jokes, and showered him with great praises.

It was a night of music and laughter – and this was the place that right-wing reactionaries said was no better than a torture chamber!

But then right-wing reactionaries are notorious for their lack of culture.

* * *

Seven years passed before he returned. He was getting on, and not travelling anything like as much as he had used to.

What a change! There were ominous signs of capitalism everywhere. There was a McDonald's Hamburger shop (or 'joint', as he supposed the Yanks would say) selling those filthy dreadful things beside the haloed precincts of Red Square itself. People were wandering round eating pizzas, drinking Coca Cola, wearing baseball caps (back to front) and listening to awful music, all noise and shouting. Shops on Gorky Street were selling sex magazines and reactionary works by so-called 'dissidents' – who, if the Soviet Union had been anything like as bad as they had made it out to be, would all have been shot long ago. Even the bloody Bible was being sold openly!

Finlay was appalled.

In 1980 these same shops had been selling nothing but the complete works of Lenin in 67 volumes, thousands of works about Lenin, records of Lenin's speeches, photographs of Lenin's mausoleum, picture postcards showing you what a nice place Siberia was . . .

And the Collected Works of Finlay McRath in Russian translation, his name in gilt Russian letters on the cover.

Now? Nothing.

Nothing?

Nothing.

Finlay crept about like an addled Casanova returning to the scene of his hottest triumphs, and he wept – literally wept – with bitter disappointment, from his one real eye.

Another party awaited him.

He picked up in anticipation; a little. Only it wasn't being held in the Lubyanka this time: no, not the Lubyanka with its enormous windows and chandeliers dating from pre-revolutionary days. It was held in the amenities room of the Ministry of the Interior flats on the river half a mile away. And here Finlay McRath finally met Vladilen, the young camp guard. Only Vladilen was no longer a young guard; he was a general in his late fifties, heavy and melancholy. Vladilen showed him round the small concrete housing estate which existed for the officers of the Ministry of the Interior troops and their families, self-contained with its own special shops, cinema, school and parking facilities, and Finlay admired it.

It was nice, he said.

Then they went into the amenities room, where the comrades were waiting.

The amenities room could have belonged to a club house anywhere in the world. It had silver trophies on the walls, a big television screen, a bar, and bar-room furniture, horrible in plastic. It had a mural which was its own, however. It stood thirteen feet high, this mural, and it showed Lenin smiling at a handsome young security policeman on horseback who was stabbing the dragon of capitalism to death with a long red lance. The dragon looked very wicked. It had a hooked nose and managed to look rather Jewish as well. It had swastikas and dollar signs on its back. St George the security man looked like a boy scout doing his good deed. Lenin looked kind and happy.

The comrades, however, looked anything but happy. Most of the men were middle-aged or elderly, wore security-service uniform, and had paunches and double chins, medal ribbons and weak eyes. They were accompanied by massive women dressed in perfumed sacks with garish jewellery, inch-thick make-up, and the sort of beehive hairstyle fashionable in the west in the early sixties. There was a scattering of young death-squad ultras with twitchy hands and faces like fists, and one rather attractive young woman whom Finlay couldn't help noticing, but who turned out to be from a dreadful right-wing paper called *Moscow News* – and when she began to ask embarrassing questions about camps, mass graves, etc, Vladilen had a couple of the twitchy boys fling her out.

General Vladilen apologized. 'That woman,' he said – and his tone clearly said S-L-U-T, even if he didn't use the word – was typical only of the benighted minority who had fallen under the spell of the so-called liberal reformers. The masses, he shouted, flourishing his arms, were still true – loyal – dependable – salt of the earth.

The paunches and the chins and the perfumed sacks growled and roared. They all got drunk.

Later that night, Finlay, pissed as a rat, in the company of Vladilen (ditto), and various other blue epaulettes and green epaulettes and squint uniform tunics shining with stars, suns, moons, rhinestones and spangles, staggered back to Vladilen's flat for a nightcap. They paused to admire a granite statue in the forecourt below Vladilen's windows.

A slender, virile young tough standing with his hand on his holster and a look of death-squad orthodoxy on his chiselled face. On the pedestal the inscription said:

Slava Voinam Internationalistam.

'Honour the Struggle for Internationalism!' iterated Vladilen, accentuating each syllable with care. 'There never was a finer, more glorious ideal than that! And this statue – this statue here,' he continued, giving the granite heel of the granite jackboot an affectionate pat, as though his hand were a dog rubbing itself on its master. 'Do you know – do you know who this – is – was – was the model for this?'

Finlay pantomimed his ignorance.

'I was!' cried Vladilen. 'Am – I mean – this man! *Me!*' And he smacked his own chest, and the granite-booted heel, and spun an invisible thread between them.

The other stout and melancholy officers of the security service, the immortal Cheka, swayed around them like a Greek chorus assembled on the deck of a heaving ship, and all variously nodded and grunted and muttered and spluttered their assent.

Finlay capped it.

'There is nothing wrong with this country!' he shouted. 'This wonderful, glorious country! Few traitors – rotten elements. Scum – fascists. On guard! Vigilance! A few firing squads'll fix 'em! *Bang bang bang* – And then,' he continued, above the agreeable roar, 'come over to Britain and carry on the good work! Kill them all! Come!' he addressed the statue, towering over him. 'Come, comrade Chekist!

'Come!'

21

The Phonecall

That night, while Tam was encountering the strange little girl, Finlay McRath was at home sitting in his favourite armchair with a well damaged glass of malt whisky to hand, reading about his genius in a back number of a small magazine edited by an earnest woman who believed she was being persecuted by Scotland Yard. Old photographs of himself with various famous people hung on the wall, an oil portrait of himself in famous pose looked down from the shadows, and a shelf of his own books had pride of place in the glass-fronted case by the hearth. A real coal fire was burning, the stereo was playing soft classical music, and his housekeeper would not be back till next morning.

The phone rang.

'Hello?'

No-one answered him. He heard the soft click-bleep of machinery.

'Hello?' he said again.

A hoarse, gravelly male voice said:

'*Comrade* . . .'

'Yes?'

The line hissed and crackled. It sounded like the surf of a faraway sea. The voice echoed.

'I'm sorry,' said Finlay. 'This seems to be a bad line. Could you say that again?'

'*I've come,*' said the voice. The word echoed *come – come.*

The rest was lost.

Something somewhere deep in Finlay's memory exploded like a pistol shot. His eyes withdrew their focus. He stared at the photograph of himself pumping hands with some grinning totalitarian who had fifty medals on his chest, and didn't see it.

'Harry,' he said lifelessly, 'if this is a joke, I'll kill you.'

Silence.

'This is a terrible line,' Finlay continued in the same tone. 'It hasn't worked ever since the Tories privatized. It's all the fault of—' He proceeded to list several things and groups of people it was all the fault of. He spoke mechanically, not really listening to what he was saying.

Silence.

'Comrade,' said the voice. *'Comrade . . . I've come . . .*

'Granite does not weep . . . Remember . . . '

And then, very faintly, *'Comrade . . . '*

Finlay's conscious mind finally admitted the voice. His legs began to tremble violently, the receiver shook in his hand, and he couldn't get his breath.

'I've come.'

The voice trailed into a thin whisper and then faded away. Silence, this time total. No hissing, no beeping of electrical machinery, nothing. Finlay had used the phrase 'the silence of the grave' often enough in his career. Now, for the first time, he heard it.

He put the phone down.

He went to his drinks cabinet, got the bottle of malt and filled up his glass. Then he sat down and began to drink quickly and messily, his eyes filling with tears and incoherent gibbering sounds escaping his lips.

22

Pat and Alice

Morning came, Tam finished as much of the work as he intended to do – feeling, and looking, like a man who had been whacked on the head with a mallet and then propped up. His ears were zinging unhappily with the sort of sound that suicides must hear just when they tighten the noose and get ready to kick the chair away. About 4.30 he thought, sod it, opened the front door and sat down on the dry top step watching the rain hit the shiny roadway, thinking how beautiful it was when you saw the city like this, and throwing his cigarette stubs into the brimming gutter.

And once or twice he glanced over his shoulder and caught Lenin's glare.

At some time after 5.00 the milkman arrived on the hop, sprayed water across the pavement with his wheels, deposited the carton with a quick 'Morning', and dashed off.

'Morning,' said Tam to the rear lights.

Then he waited for the cleaners.

Shortly after 6.00 he saw them on the pavement: big Pat and little Alice, walking in step, each with a dainty umbrella up, each with a scarf over her hair and rubber boots on her feet, Pat's broad mouth opening and shutting, Alice's glowing fag screwed into the corner of her silent dentures.

'Hello there,' they chorused in answer to his greeting. They went to punch their cards in the clock cupboard behind the reception desk.

'Quiet night?' said Pat, interrupting herself in passing. She always said something like that, and Tam always answered: Yes, sure, oh aye, nothing doing – an exchange as unvarying as a masonic ritual – before the women went upstairs to their cupboard on the First Floor and disappeared into it for the next half hour.

'No,' said Tam.

It took one split second for them both to turn on their heels and come back to him, their eyes bright and avid for the gossip.

Tam told them there had been an intruder and that the police had been called, and Pat was so desperate to get the details that she kept her mouth shut for nearly a whole minute before—

'Oh, that's happened before. In fact, it's happened regular. Hasn't it, Alice?' she recommenced.

'Ayuh,' said Alice.

'The last time must have been two years ago, no I tell a lie, it must have been nearly three years ago, no, more like two years 'cause that was just before Sheila left, and Des, the night man who was before you, he caught this man in the foyer here with an aerosol can in his hand, and you never would believe it, he had broken in the office window – you remember, Alice?'

'Ayuh.'

'And sprayed all that whatdyacallit graffiti stuff all over the place, all them swastikas and things, so they came and took photographs of it and got a lot of money, so that was all right I suppose, but all the same I wouldn't have your job, not for anything—'

'Me neither.'

''Cause my nerves just wouldn't stand it, know what I mean? – and that's what I said to Joe Steele, 'cause he asked me once if I would do overtime nightshift, he fucking did! – and you can ask Alice if he didn't, he did, didn't he Alice? Nooo—'

'Ayuh.'

'Way, I said, noooooo way I'm going to be here at night with men getting into the place as easy as a tart's knickers, pardon my French . . . ' She rattled on.

Eventually, with the desperation of a man trying to stop a runaway bus, Tam cried out:

'But this *wasn't* a man . . . It was a little girl,' he added, trying to overcome the rudeness of his interruption. 'I only got a glimpse of her, but she was alone and she couldn't have been much more than five, and the thing is I don't know how she can have got in because none of the doors or windows were open, and the coppers couldn't . . . What's wrong?' he asked, because the two women were looking at him as though his face had begun to sprout green fungus.

'Well, this isn't getting the work done,' said Pat.

Tam waited for her to say something else, but she didn't. It was the shortest statement he had ever heard her make.

'Ayuh,' said Alice after a moment.

They both moved towards the stairs.

Tam followed them up to the First Floor, talking all the way. They both kept glancing at him uneasily as though they thought he had lost his reason. Then they disappeared into their cupboard, from which Tam was excluded as rigorously as a young man from a convent. He was perplexed and walked away hearing the low babble of their voices sounding together like a kettle boiling behind the door.

He waited for them to emerge, but rather more than their usual half hour passed before they did so, wearing a strong scent of cigarette smoke and with their eyes patrolling the shadows on either side of the long corridor. Alice, as usual, took her cleaning cart down to the foyer. Pat remained on the First Floor.

Making sure not to startle her, Tam tried again, asking Pat several pleasant, utterly insincere questions about various members of her enormously extended family, whose doings she habitually recounted with the length and detailed accuracy of a tribal bard. She seemed pleased to have his company (he noticed how her eyes kept darting here and there into the dark places) and talked about her family – all the Nellies and Jessies, the Jimmies and Johnnies, the birthdays, the quarrels, the babies and funerals – and Tam smiled and prompted and nodded and heard hardly a word; but when, on some opportunity or other, he raised once more the matter of the strange appearance of the little girl in the yellow dress, Pat fell suddenly silent. Even some of the normal sprightliness fell away from her big body, and as she rolled along on her swollen legs she looked to Tam for the first time like a tired old woman.

'No, I dunno,' she said. 'Dunno anything about that. Got to do my work now. Scuse.'

And she switched on her noisy hoover and busied herself with it in such a way that Tam couldn't possibly ask her anything else.

Alice, by the time Tam went looking for her, was on the Second Floor, pushing her yellow cleaning cart with its two mops and its bottles of liquid detergent and toilet cleaner amongst the clutter of the printing room. She looked, with her parenthetical legs and quick stick-like body, like a sparrow picking crumbs off the ground. There was no point in wandering into a conversation about Alice's family. For all Tam knew, Alice had been born in a test tube, and lived as a hermit ever since. So with her he decided to come straight to the point, hedged, and talked about Charlie instead.

Alice plied her mop and listened to him, occasionally saying, 'Ayuh.' Then he couldn't think of anything more to say about Charlie.

'Alice,' he said carefully, 'why was it that when I talked about that little girl somebody seemed to be stirring your stomach with a stick?'

Alice tapped her cigarette into her pinafore pocket and replaced it in the paralytic twist of her mouth.

'Oh, just – things,' she said. She rubbed at her faded pink cardigan where it had three brown burn holes near the top button.

'That doesn't tell me much, Alice.'

'Ayuh.' Shrug.

'Look, Alice, I could get into trouble. If some little girl has gone missing, and she's hiding in this building somewhere, or she can get in and out of it somehow, I could end up being called a child molester or something, and who's going to believe me? Even if I don't end up in the nick, I don't want the stink. I mean, can you imagine what Janis Ulman would make up about it?'

Alice took a deep breath and turned to him with an air of grim determination.

'I've never seen her,' she said, 'and I never want to. But I've seen some things that I'd rather not have. There's something awful creepy about this place. You can feel it even in daytime when the sun's streaming through the windows, even then. It lurks about, in the corners, in the cupboards, behind your back no matter where you turn, and sometimes you feel it so strong that you don't dare to turn. No, don't ask me what it is. The job's handy, and I haven't done anything wrong, so I don't think anything bad'll happen. Now I won't say another word about it, so don't ask me. No, not one word.'

Nor would she.

23

Haytor

Haytor had spent the day in his film studio making life miserable for everyone, and it was dark when he got into his Porsche, after a restaurant meal and the final statutory visit to the pub, and began the long drive home. He wasn't a fanciful man. His attitude to life was severely material, concerned with power, and his own ability to perform the role of manipulator, guardian, and teacher of the masses. But in recent years something impalpable and ill defined had stepped between him and the solid reality of the world. He put it down to three terrible events – his fiftieth birthday, his divorce, and the accession of the traitor Gorbachev – coinciding in the same fateful year. Thereafter the greying of his hair kept pace with accounts blunt and horrifying flooding in from the east.

Many things pained him.

A brooding sense of oppression dulled his days, and hateful nightmares terrorized his sleep. He felt the need to sit close to people and feel their glow about him. He filled his big empty house with a succession of young women, mainly ambitious actresses and script writers. He cultivated the complacent pessimism of an émigré of the *ancien régime*, admitted ruefully that socialism was now a matter of damage control, and reminisced about the glory days when serried ranks of the happy faithful had marched and danced with flags in Moscow and Pyongyang. Ah, the glory that was Greece and the grandeur that was Rome!

Now even Albania was talking about democracy.

Shit.

Haytor shuddered and fixed his eyes narrowly on the road. He was within legal limits for the Breathalyser, his speed was not excessive. The dual carriageway led him out of the city and gave on to a motorway, empty and ghastly with the glare of arc lamps. The feeling of unease within him grew. He remembered that his current woman – 'girlfriend' seemed such an absurd word at his age – was going to be absent overnight at some junket. By the time he had turned into the winding country road that formed the last lap of his journey, the prospect of his cold house was odious to him. He stared dismally at the cat's eyes running ahead of his lamps. Once or twice he thought he glimpsed other eyes, to the side, in the bushes; red feral eyes that shone in the dark.

Imagination, he said to himself; bourgeois imagination.

When he got to the commuter town where he slept, he stopped; not at his own house, but at the local snooker club, which would be open until midnight. There he was somewhat cheered by meeting several people he knew – though the oldest was little more than half his age – and playing a good frame which, of course, he won. At last, however, the place emptied. He was the last customer. He lingered as long as he could. When eventually the tired manager and yawning barman ceased to answer him, he took his leave and drove the last few hundred yards home.

Within a few minutes he was indoors. He wandered round the big house making sure the doors and windows were secure, then made himself some peanut-butter sandwiches in the kitchen, though he wasn't really hungry, and watched a bit of a video. He got tired of Woody Allen in fifteen minutes flat and went back to the kitchen for a nightcap.

The thrice-a-week cleaning woman had been in that morning and the place was gleaming. Immaculate rows of bright-bladed Kitchen Devil knives hung from magnetic racks.

A dazzling pyramid of Amway steel pans stood by the cooker. (Haytor inspected the cooker, ran his finger along the surface, and inspected his finger.) The cupboard-sized Hotpoint fridge-freezer unit purred and clicked to itself and made mysterious little plastic snapping noises. Haytor selected his brandy bottle, checked the plimsol line, and poured. The cleaning woman's list of chores done was on the bunker beneath the knives, and he glanced down at it.

Ching!

One of the knives, a four-inch thin blade, was trembling.

Haytor stared, then put out his hand and touched the blade. It was vibrating slightly, like the fridge. But the fridge had a motor. He lifted the knife from its rack. The kitchen was a smart yellow room full of silver light. Haytor turned the knife this way and that until it shone like Excalibur in the silver light. Like a fire. Like cold white flames.

Hissing. Spluttering.

Cold fire.

Haytor shuddered. Then he realized that he was holding this damn dagger like Lady Macbeth or somebody, and stuck it back. Squint. He straightened it and backed away, managing – just – not to spill his drink.

Come on, comrade, get off this bus.

He turned.

Clang!

The knife had fallen. It was lying handle towards him.

Several long seconds passed.

Haytor breathed deeply, in and out, in and out. He kept it up till his heart returned to normal. Then he crossed the floor jerkily, back to the bunker, picked up the knife and reattached it to the rack. Okay. He prised it a little loose with one finger and let go. The magnet held and it snapped back, metal-on-metal. He tested it again. It was holding fast. Good. A–okay. He walked back to the door sideways like a crab. Go on: drop, you bugger.

Nothing happened.

Of course not.

Bourgeois shit.

Seen too many spook films. Fucking right-wing decadence.

He recharged his brandy glass (how many have I had?) still eyeing the knife rack.

Nothing. Nada. The big no-no.

Haytor grinned, turned to the door, and snapped the light off.

There was a sudden slithering metallic sound behind him, and—

Clang!

He snapped the light on again. The knife was lying on the bunker. Point towards him.

He left the light on, turned and walked away with that same jerky stride. His face was twitching and a flutter was making his left eyelid jump. He went down the hall, step by leaden step, to the video room – wondering what he would do if the knife came flying through the air after him, because he was only making it in slow slow motion.

He got into the video room, arranged the screen so he could look at it and the door without moving, and put on *Apocalypse Now* to check out the horrors of American imperialism. He stayed with it till the Yankee helicopters had finished blowing up the Vietcong village to the tune of 'The Ride of the Valkyries', and that made him feel a bit better – knowing who the enemy was. The US of A.

Knowing who you had to fight.

Hate.

Kill.

Haytor's big posh house was full of expensive paperbacks that said mass-murder was okay so long as it led to socialism; and posters, once crisp, now sadly ageing, of angry revolutionary people waving machine guns and screaming *hate!* and *kill!*

He switched off the video and tiptoed to the door. At the other end of the dark corridor the kitchen door was open and the light was shining. Nothing was moving in there. No sound.

Haytor sighed, decided to forget about that kitchen light, and moved gingerly upstairs to his bedroom. A few minutes later he was in bed with the sheets pulled up to his nose.

Quiet.

He lay listening.

The town was a real early-to-bed place; the street outside a cul-de-sac. There was not a sound, neither of car, bird, nor human being.

Haytor sighed again, with nervousness and bravado. The bedside light was on. His eyes roamed from end to end of his lavish bedroom looking into the shadows. Scraps of the day came unbidden to his mind; an argument in the studio which *he* had resolved, a discussion in which *he* had upheld the faith, a despicable attempt to sabotage his plans and dissipate money which *he* had exposed, the universal admiration this had earned him.

'Satisfactory, yes, very satisfactory,' said Henry Haytor as his eyes darted here and there among the shadows of the room.

At last he put out the light and closed his eyes for sleep.

Minutes or hours?

What time it was when he woke he did not know. He had his own inbuilt alarm clock, and his wristwatch was not luminous. There was a faint glow of streetlight through the curtains, but not enough for him to see by. He lay and stared up at the invisible ceiling conscious that something had woken him. But what? There was no sound. In fact, there was an unnatural absence of sound: no cough from a neighbouring house, no owl, though there were trees around, no step on the pavement, no hum of a distant car motor, no sizzle of tyres on the wet street.

126

The emptiness began to oppress him.

He was completely awake, though he could only have been in bed an hour or two, and there was little chance of his getting back to sleep. He threw off the covers, went over to the window, and pulled the curtain back. Even outside the night was mute; there was no rain, nothing moved; in the pale light every detail stood out as though cut in metal with copper-plate perfection. Yet the perfection of it oppressed him even more. There was an awful creepiness about it. He wanted something to happen. Nothing did. Haytor had never felt so desolate and utterly lonely in all his life.

Then at last he heard something. A big car, by the sound of it, and moving very slowly, was passing along the street out of his sight. Strangely, this sound did nothing to cheer him up; on the contrary, it was as if the oppression of the night were connected with this sinister vehicle, and he willed it to pass on without stopping. The engine rumbled slowly closer and closer, changed its tone as it swung into the cul-de-sac, and then he saw it.

It was a long black limousine, of some foreign make he didn't recognize. The side windows were unusually large and beyond them he could see a gleaming silver rail supporting a polished wooden—

It was a hearse.

And it slid to a stop outside his door.

Haytor stared down at the vehicle. Of course it had no earthly right to be here at this hour. It was a joke, he told himself resolutely. Actors were a notoriously childish lot. This was an actor's joke. The driver would turn out to be someone he knew. Every detail was perfectly clear, of the car, as of the street, in the pale light. He was looking at the driver now, the only person who seemed to be in the car – indeed, the only living soul in sight.

As he did so, the man opened the left-hand door and stepped on to the pavement. His face was hidden by a peaked cap of some muddy brown material with an unusually broad crown to it, a long hooded rain cape of the same dark colour hung from his shoulders to his knees, and his lower legs were sheathed in high boots that made harsh scratchy sounds on the asphalt.

For the first time Haytor began to doubt the nature of what he was seeing. The driver looked up at him. He had a sallow face with broad cheekbones, a cleft chin, and eyes expressionless as black holes. He raised his fingers to the peak of his cap in salute. His fingers were fearfully long and crooked and the light of the streetlamp shone through them. He stalked up the path to Haytor's door and rang the bell.

Haytor turned quietly away from the window and sat down, shaking violently, on the bottom of his bed. Again he heard the bell ring quite distinctly downstairs, and then, after a time, the locked front door creaked open and shut. Slow heavy feet began to climb the stair . . .

Haytor crawled back into bed, pulled the sheets right over his crown, and lay there, trembling and sobbing silently (for he dared not make a noise) with the sheets bunched tightly in each fist, and his teeth fastened on to the end of one. He lay there for a long time
> *It's nothing, just your imagination.*
> *A bit too much booze, maybe?*
> *No, I saw it, I heard it.*

listening.Those heavy feet. They had come up the steps; he hadn't heard them go down.

It was standing outside his bedroom door!
> *Just booze, that's all – just . . .*
> *No. It isn't!*
> *It isn't!*

Haytor lay in the stillness and silence of the room, his body wet and cold with sweat, the chewed end of the sheet soaking with saliva, and knew that if *It* made a single sound out there he would go mad.

There was a telephone sitting on the little table beside his bed.

He dared not risk it.

He dared not move.

It was waiting.

After an unknowable time, Haytor began to sense a difference in the light. Dawn was breaking and the pale glare of the street lamp was being softened by the natural light spreading over the sky. Still he lay, and only after he heard the unmistakeable hum of the milk float and the clink of bottles on the doorstep did he eventually draw the sheet down over his eyes and stare into the room. Seeing nothing, he got out of bed and crept to the window. There was the usual array of parked cars, but no hearse in sight.

Shame rather than courage made him open the door of his bedroom holding a harmless replica pistol in his hand, instead of phoning the police as he had intended. A gust of cold air blew around his damp pyjamas and made him shiver. He crept downstairs holding the plastic pistol (a stage prop) before him, for all the world as though it were the real thing. He examined each room, and each cupboard; he entered the bathroom and pulled aside the shower curtain. With a sense of physical shrinking he went to the front door and found it locked and chained. Last of all was the kitchen. The door was closed, the light was off, and the knife was in place on the magnetic rack.

What had happened?

I wasn't stoned, was I? – He examined his stash in a discrete cupboard. He was only a recreational user. There was none missing since the day before yesterday.

Drunk? – On a couple of brandies?

Did someone spike my drinks in the pub?

But I drove home all right.

Daylight.

He listened.
Birds were singing in the trees outside.
He waited.
Nothing.
He wept.

24

The Rocking Horse

During the next week Tam contrived to put the strange appearance of the little girl, and the even stranger reticence of the cleaners, as far from his mind as possible. He had gone over every inch of the building and satisfied himself that no-one had forced an entry. Everything was as it should be, except for the continued widening of the cracks in the walled-up entries to the Fourth Floor, both at the top of the two staircases and at the top of the lift-shaft – and even this was not as inexplicable as it first seemed, because the concrete blocks had evidently been laid hastily and clumsily, and the vibration of the trains passing outside was simply causing poor workmanship to crumble. At least that was Finlay McRath's theory when Tam reported it to him, and it seemed quite plausible.

As to the little girl – well, nothing else had happened, no harm had come. Mentally, Tam shrugged his shoulders.

He told himself he had forgotten it.

Of course, he hadn't.

Early one afternoon he woke suddenly from a deep sleep. For some moments he lay immobile, blinking, wondering where he was, and suffering that strange feeling of being outside his body, floating near the ceiling, and looking down at himself lying in bed. Then he stretched out his arm, touched the alarm clock, and saw that it was not yet 2.00 p.m. The room was full of the sepia glow of afternoon daylight muted by thick, heavy curtains. It was hissing with the white sound of the daylight world, the constant rumble of traffic, the occasional jarring cry from the street, the throb of the boilers, the regular rush of the trains. Tam knew that none of this had awakened him.

What had?

He lay and waited; then he heard it.

From the corner beside the door, a faint gentle bump.

Tam knotted his brows and tried to place the sound. It was a rhythmic noise of wood on some soft surface. Bump bump, it went, bump bump, just like a . . . *rocking horse.*

Tam had bought a rocking horse for his daughter when she was – what, three? four? The year before the big strike. Tam could remember the big strike in intimate detail, but he had forgotten his daughter's age. Five, that was right, he'd bought it for her birthday. He'd bought her a tricycle for her Christmas too. That was the year his Helen had died. The next year was the big strike that he was still determined to write a book about some day.

His daughter had been a frail, serious child with a pale face and her mother's long dark hair. She was now a pretty, but serious, young woman.

Come to think of it, she hadn't always been pale and serious. She had been bright-eyed and laughing those first years before his wife died. He had sat beside her and told her stories in the flat they had then. He had counted her toes, and thought that after all there was a God – she proved it. But then his wife died, and there was the trouble in the yards that swelled into the Big Strike, and he was busy – busy organizing the strike committee, busy attending meetings; and he didn't count her toes and think that they were a gift from God any more. He told 'that dratted girl' to 'keep the hell out my road!' – and he bought her the rocking horse and the tricycle to keep herself amused.

She needed more, thought Tam with sudden jarring clarity

as he lay awake in his bed and stared at the ceiling. She needed much more.

Once or twice he had tried to do something about it. He had taken her out walking. They tended to end up in the cemetery where his Helen was buried. He *had* meant to take her to the fun-fair – it wasn't his fault that an emergency union meeting was called. Or the time when he had arranged to meet her at the primary school gate so they could go to the zoo, and he suddenly had to go and address the strike solidarity committee, and he *had* meant to ask one of the lads to go down and pick her up for him, but somehow, what with one thing and another, he forgot, and – well . . .

He forgot.

And when he got home that night there she was, sitting on her little tricycle, pedalling it around the cold hungry house with a look of heart-breaking loneliness on her face, and *squeak* went the wheels, *squeak* . . .

And the other times when the strike committee meeting had ended up in the smoky back room of the pub, and he had staggered home drunk sometime near midnight, and found her up, sitting on her rocking horse; and *bump bump* went the wooden rockers on the carpeted floor, *bump bump*. And the sight of her tear-stained face made him feel so guilty that he hit—

He hadn't meant to – no – just meant to tell her to go to bed, just meant to lift her off the rocking horse and stop its infernal *bump bump*, that's all he meant to do. But the way it came out his hand *(bump)* on the side of her face—

Bump

He hit her—

Bump

Bump bump, bump bump, bump!

Tam jerked over in bed, stared into the corner beside the door, and there she was, on her rocking horse

BUMP

'I'm not dreaming this! I'm awake! This is really happening!'

BUMP BUMP

Tam stared. What was left of sleep evaporated out of his eyes. She was really there, his daughter, as she had been all those years ago, the long dark hair hanging down her back; and then she turned to face him, and . . . She was different. Her hair was golden. She was the little girl in the yellow dress—

Tam flung the clothes off the bed and leapt to his feet.

She was gone. There was no rocking horse in the corner.

Nothing.

Tam did not sleep another wink that day.

25

Haytor (discontinued)

That day Henry Haytor tried to go about his business as usual. He drove to the Red House and picked up some mail from his pigeonhole, then drove on to the studio. He seemed preoccupied, was untypically abrupt with people, angrily refused to hold a discussion on some esoteric side-alley of Marxist philosophy, ate seemingly without appetite and drank sparingly. Someone remarked that he looked as though he had been in his grave and dug his way out. He phoned home several times from late afternoon through to evening, and only when *his woman* answered did he leave the studio. He drove straight home and greeted her as happily as a young husband.

His woman, a theatre groupie who admired Finlay McRath's fearlessly committed writing, was joint owner of a crafts shop in a neighbouring village. 'Daddy' owned most of a merchant bank, 'mummy' bred some exotic type of dog, 'little brother' was an officer cadet at Sandhurst, and *her* name was Richenda, though she had trained everyone to call her Rikki. She had a mannish figure, wore ethnic smocks, dined as a vegan, drank ginseng tea, practised gestalt, and was 'very left-wing'.

She was also good at oral sex and submission, which was why she was currently *his woman*.

The evening passed.

Outside the house the trees and bushes were being threshed by a violent wind. Inside, it was soft and perfumed. Haytor was afraid. A superstitious and entirely irrational fear clung to him like a wet leech: in darkness and solitude *It* would return.

They smoked some illegal substance together. They shared an excellent meal and a bottle of wine. They smoked some more, and watched a conspiracy video about the Pentagon plot to spread Aids in the Third World for imperialist and racist, not to mention sexist and homophobic, reasons. As Haytor said.

Haytor talked.

And talked.

He talked over the film, and he talked after it.

Rikki listened.

'See?' he said, and stared at her with the face of an inspired robber chieftain.

Rikki stared back, because she thought this fifty-something man in clothes thirty years too young for his sour-lined face was indeed telling it the way it was.

'Gosh, yah,' she said.

And so Haytor droned on. But time passed, the night grew darker and quieter, and after a while he fell silent and took to eyeing like a cornered animal the shadows that were growing beyond the furniture. Rikki, who seldom noticed such things, wondered what was wrong. Then she smiled. 'Come on!' she said brightly. They did a check of the doors and windows together, then went upstairs to bed, where Rikki performed, with the obedient air of a well-trained geisha, that which was expected of her.

Given the nature of Haytor's proclivities, they were facing in opposite directions, he sitting on the bed while Rikki knelt on the floor in front of him with her back to the dressing table and her head moving up and down between his legs. Behind him, on the other side of the bed, was the wardrobe. Haytor stroked the back of Rikki's neck unhappily. He was not really enjoying it, just trying to tell himself that he was. And all the time his damp, frightened – yet still arrogant – eyes scoured round the room as though obeying a summons which his rational intellect refused to contemplate.

As Rikki beavered away, the idea began to grow in his mind that there was someone or some *thing* behind him, and that he would be more comfortable if he could put his back to the wall. He craned his neck round as far as he could without disturbing Rikki at her labours, but could only see a bit of the wardrobe door. Fortunately the dressing table had a mirror on it. He fixed his gaze on that. There was nothing behind him there, just the wardrobe. He grunted to show Rikki that her labours were appreciated. It made him feel very masculine, so he grunted again.

As he did so his eye caught the mirror. In that moment the wardrobe door sprang open and an arm came out and clawed the hair on the back of his neck. It was clad in coarse grey cloth, much worn and ragged, and its hand was broad, dirty and covered in calluses. With a scream Haytor was on his feet – knocking Rikki over in the process. He ran, screaming, to the door of the room, and wrenched it open. The corridor outside was huge and black. Then he suddenly remembered his woman there at the mercy of that *thing*. He turned. 'Rikki!' he shouted. 'Rikki!' He shouted other things too, called on God, and clung sobbing to the post beside the light switch.

'Harry?' said Rikki, shaking him. 'Harry? God, what's the matter? Are you totally freaked out? Harry?'

'Christ, girl,' murmured Haytor. 'Oh, Christ!' He was staring at the wardrobe.

She sensed what he wanted and went over to it. The door was already ajar. 'No – !' he cried, stretching out to stop her.

She pulled it open.

'Nothing, see? No bogeyman, okay? Jesus, Harry, you've got to give up smoking that stuff. I mean it!'

* * *

The next week and a day was a terrible eternity for Henry Haytor. Wherever he went he felt pursued, and he increasingly thought he heard steps – heavy, gravelly steps – that followed him remorselessly wherever he went. When among people he always tried to count their numbers, and always he miscounted, or found one more than he could account for, went back to the start, but had no better luck. When he went to sit down he could not be easy unless his back was to a wall, and then only fitfully so. In the street he spun round on his heel convinced that he had heard a particularly horrible lungless laugh behind him – but there was no-one there.

And during the eight nights he dreamt of cowled spectres and fingers that . . .

But let us talk no more about those eight nights.

That week the work in the studio progressed slowly.

Haytor drilled his crew. He drove them sternly. He hectored them, quoting many dead gurus and yards of Marxist theory, his sleepless eyes blazing, his fearful voice gulping with hysteria as he pled the cause of some battledressed Great Leader who lived by the graveyard door in a palace full of statues and policemen. And his actors looked at his haunted pale face, then at each other significantly, and mouthed:

'Drugs. Heavy drugs.'

And they nodded.

All this time Haytor said not one word of what was troubling him. Not to anyone.

The afternoon came when Finlay McRath phoned to remind him about an emergency editorial meeting that had been called in the Red House to prepare the Workers' answer to the latest piece of shabby treason being enacted in Moscow. Haytor went down to his Porsche. He felt, and looked, awful. Rikki was convinced he was on something wild – maybe even killer stuff like the mysterious crack and ecstasy the yobs took. But he wasn't. He was ill. Truth be told, he had felt ill ever since

Gorbachev had sold out to Reagan at Reykjavik – something that Shelley would have understood and written about, but that Finlay McRath seemed unable to comprehend now. He wondered if he was in the throes of a nervous breakdown.

The days were lengthening; it was still light; Henry Haytor had five minutes left to live.

He hit the car door, paused briefly to wonder if he was up to driving, or whether he shouldn't maybe take a taxi, or even slum it in the tube; but there weren't any taxis in sight, and the idea of the tube depressed him.

Four minutes.

He turned the ignition and pulled out. Maybe he ought to see a shrink, or just get away from it all to a socialist country with good room service

(three and a half)

like Cuba maybe. Or even a capitalist one, some place full of sun and sand where they played old Beachboys' records and served cocktails all day long.

He was thinking somewhat fretfully along these lines, and driving at a safe and steady speed with both hands on the wheel, when he noticed that the traffic in front of him was slowing down and pulling around some slow-moving vehicle. The only odd thing about this was that, from what he could see of it six or seven cars behind, the obstructive vehicle was not some lumbering lorry piled high with crates, or and antediluvian van with a black-belching exhaust, but a large saloon of stately appearance that was observing a thirty-miles-per-hour limit with magisterial indifference to the noisy vehicles by which it was surrounded.

He was only two cars away from it when he realized that it was, of course, a hearse. He had two minutes left to live.

Haytor felt a familiar bitter taste forming in his throat. Hearses depressed him. In the past he had merely laughed at the bourgeois sentimentality they represented, for he could scarcely believe that, in the year 1990, there was any real superstition left. Now, as he got older and thought of certain things—

Ah, the first car was swinging out to the right and passing the hearse . . .

And then, of course, there had been that dream, or whatever it had been, that hallucination—

The second car was swinging out now.

Automatically, Haytor followed it. He had thirty seconds.

The road he was on had been built for horse-drawn carriages two hundred years before; it was busy and narrow. Haytor's conscious mind was dull and distant, but the motorist in him was working mechanically, glancing at the oncoming lane inches to his right to make sure he had a safe passage there, glancing into his rear-view mirror to see if anyone had a mind to jump the queue, and glancing again at the oncoming lane. He drew parallel with the black vehicle to his left, and for no reason at all – a second's idle curiosity – looked into its driver's seat.

The driver – no, it had to be a coincidence – looked like one of his extras, a tall man who always appeared in the same dark overcoat and hood.

And the driver turned his face towards Henry Haytor, letting the hood fall back from his head. Beneath the hood was a peaked cap with an unusually broad crown to it, and the eyes below the peak were black and the face was sallow. The man smiled and showed his teeth, but his eyes remained black and hideous.

```
Comrade
```
said a voice quite clearly in Haytor's ear.

(BLARE of an oncoming horn)

```
Comrade
```
And Haytor gaped and heard, but didn't do anything about the blare of horns – several of them now – or the scream of a woman on the pavement who saw what was coming, or the ululating wail of the brakes in a builder's van, heavy with long

scaffolding poles, overtaking in the oncoming lane that Haytor had just let his car cruise into.

Shattering glass pulled Haytor's eyes back to his windscreen just as it collapsed and his car ploughed right into the van, jerking it backwards a pace with its rear wheels in the air. The impact made several of the long scaffolding poles shoot free over the roof of the van's cabin. One of them came right at Henry Haytor, straight as an arrow. He saw it coming, maybe a fifth of a second away, and tried to scream with his already open mouth.

The pole took him right through the teeth, tore open the back of his mouth, drove through his throat, and tore a fistful of red raw sinew out of his spinal cord an inch above the nape of his neck. It plunged on down through the top of his driver's seat and finally came to a stop deep in the foam padding of the back seat cushions. The Porsche shuddered and was still, and Henry Haytor's head rose forward and up, with its eyes popping incredulously, and its lips settled on the metal, blubbering red, and the last thought inside its ruined skull was of how bitter metal and blood taste together.

How very bitter.

26

Midnight

Finlay McRath spent the last week of Haytor's life trying to get his mind off the call. Obviously someone was trying to unnerve him. Whoever it was, he was doing a pretty good job. Of course, he had had threatening calls before – given the nature of his political views, that was inevitable – but they had never been so . . . ghoulish. The voice had been so exact. The speaker had caught the accented English and the strangely mechanical way of speaking that . . .

A thoroughly professional job.

McRath told himself it was MI5. Then it became the CIA. Then he decided that it was probably both combined – after all, Finlay McRath the Great Left Wing Writer was important enough for the capitalist world's two prime secret police forces to conspire against him. Wasn't he?

Finlay told himself this again and again over his whisky tumbler. For the rest of that week he was not sober. Yet the notion that a ghost from the past had spoken to him seeped into his brain and wouldn't leave.

He chewed his nails, walked to the window, and noted the numberplates of cars in the street. Several times he made up his mind to share his trouble with one of the comrades, but never did.

When the news of Haytor's death came, Finlay was in his Red House office preparing his next editorial. There was no doubt that Haytor had died as a result of a simple traffic accident, but the police had questions and the media wanted some quotes. Finlay left it all to Joe Steele, pled illness, and went home. Foreboding had made him sick to the stomach.

Again, as so often, his house was empty. He wandered from room to room fidgeting. Eventually he decided to eat, got out an instant dinner, and put it in the microwave.

He was picking his way through his food when the telephone rang. There was nothing unusual in this. Finlay led an active social life and was accustomed to hearing his phone ring three or four times of an evening. Yet now the most horrible despairing feeling took hold of him. He stood up reluctantly and crossed the room with slow unwilling steps to the little table where the instrument jangled. Trembling, he lifted the receiver.

'One,' said the voice.

'Please – who is this?'

'Comrade . . . '

The voice was stronger than before, and more intelligible.

'First liquidation – carried out – comrade.'

Finlay couldn't answer. His mouth had gone terribly dry. He coughed, tried to force himself to speak, and failed. His legs began to melt. He leaned on the table with his free arm, and shifted his body round until he could sit on it. The table groaned under his weight.

'Please . . . who is this?' he begged.

Laughter, deep, mirthless laughter, came at him through the phone.

Finlay closed his eyes and leaned back till the crown of his head touched the wall. He swallowed, and coughed, and then forced himself to speak again:

'W-Who are you?'

'You know who I am.'

'No, I—'

'Granite Does Not Weep. Remember the statue beneath my window.'

'Moscow,' said Finlay weakly.

'Moscow,' said the voice.

And Finlay knew: the reception, the general, the statue in the small square.

He ran his fingers through his wiry white hair. His hands were slimy with sweat.

'But why,' he said, 'why are you here?'

'You invited me, comrade. Remember?'

('We could do with a few of you boys in my country to . . .'

To what?

Re-educate – improve – instruct . . .

Liar, liar, liar!

To *KILL*, of course.)

'You mean . . . ?'

'Yes.' The voice was fainter now, like a radio station slowly fading away.

Then, just before the dead air came, Finlay heard that same final meaningless word:

'Comrade.'

He spent the next hour drinking. Cast by the fire, a monstrous shadow of himself crouched on the wall and mocked his actions as he poured and drank.

27

Through the Dark Hours

It was 2.00 a.m. that same night, and Tam was sweeping out the foyer of the Red House. He wasn't going to the crematorium the next day. He had gone to Charlie's funeral, but then Charlie had meant something. Haytor had meant nothing: pity about the man's accident, of course, but it was no reason for him to lose an afternoon's sleep.

Especially since he wasn't getting much. Tam's nerves were badly shot. He wondered if he was having a breakdown of some sort, and these hallucinations were a part of it. He had seen a documentary on the telly about nervous breakdowns, and he knew it wasn't just shaking hands and frayed tempers and such. Sometimes people got really weird, started talking to the wall, had fits of laughter and weeping, and acted like they were stoned. Some people had even seen ghosts – like the man who thought he had seen his dead daughter at the top of the stairs, and had had perfectly rational conversations with her, when all that had happened was that he had lost a few sandwiches out of his picnic box because of the stress he was facing in the office. Tam wasn't facing any stress in the office, but it was nice to know that he didn't necessarily need the Exorcist.

Perhaps it was all due to the Poll Tax.

Maybe he should start to involve himself in the activities of the Union, the way he had once done.

Or of the Labour Party.

Or the Communist Party. Or some Party.

Or take up golf.

Or something.

Tam worked nervously and kept on glancing over his shoulder. There was no wind, there was no pattering rain, it was not a night for ghosts – caused by the government, or otherwise . . . Caused by Communists, or otherwise . . .

Tam had never been a Communist, but he had always had respect for them. Back in the days of the Big Strike, when the Labour Party had welched out, they had always been there, the Comrades. They had made the boys who were out on the picket lines feel they were not alone in the cold and the rain; that they were part of a great worldwide movement that was sweeping forward, fighting for better conditions and pay for all workers. All the rest – the stuff about the killing and the camps and so on – he knew, but he couldn't really believe it. It was like discovering that your favourite uncle was a serial murderer, or that your dear little old auntie pushed heroin to nursery kids on the side.

Tam worked away.

He used a long-handled brush to sweep the dust and occasional cigarette butts and chocolate wrappers off the floor, carefully making sure he didn't miss anywhere. He walked around the commissionaire's desk, and the small table covered in red cloth where a pile of hate pamphlets was kept. He paused and glanced at some of them. They had names like 'Britain's Crime In Ireland', 'The Truth About The Malvinas', and 'The People Of Afghanistan Struggle To Build Socialism In The Face Of US Imperialist Aggression'. They would really have put Tam's mind at ease if he had got into them, because they said that it was all right to be a serial murderer if it helped the cause of socialism along a bit, and that piles of corpses would go away if you just didn't look at them.

And above the uplifting table, the portrait of the Great Teacher.

Tam looked at it. Suddenly he realized who it reminded him of. With his bald head and little beard, flapping jacket and bustling arms, V.I. Lenin addressing the Petrograd workers was a dead ringer for the manager down in the docks whom they had gone on strike against back in the days of the dinosaurs.

Tam leaned on his brush handle. The portrait stared back at him grimly. Strange he hadn't noticed those disdainful eyes before, that mouth set in a sneer of cold command.

'Well I'm damned,' he said.

Suddenly he jumped. Something had hit him in the back of the neck. A cold thrill ran down the top of his spine, and he knew that he had been stabbed. He spun round, his legs buckling slightly, clapping his hand to the place. There was no-one behind him, and there was no blood. Tam leaned against the table, causing a pile of the hate stuff to fall over and land on the floor.

I *am* having a breakdown. Christ, I *am*, I *am!* he thought.

In his big posh empty house full of monuments to himself Finlay McRath got ready for bed. He had drunk enough to poleaxe a pig, but he still felt stone-cold sober. Every word that had invaded his sanity over the phone was still there. Not one had slid away into alcoholic amnesia as he had hoped, not one. It had happened, there was no doubt of it.

Either that or he was mad.

Many people in his life had thought Finlay was mad, but he had never been one of them. He knew that he was both sane and right. Always. To think otherwise was bourgeois. If something had happened which reason had difficulty in explaining, then reason could be made to accommodate itself to the difficulty, given time.

Finlay had in his time reasoned away many difficulties, smelled roses instead of blood, climbed over corpses and not seen them, listened to firing squads and heard sweet music. He would reason this oddity away too.

It just took time.

Meanwhile the phone lay buried under a pile of cushions on the sofa downstairs and was damn well going to stay that way. He had a horrible vision of that phone taking life like something out of a horror film and bouncing upstairs, ringing all the way. The picture was so funny that he laughed. And laughed. And laughed. At last he managed to stop laughing and wiped the tears away with the palms of his trembling hands.

He climbed into his fresh, crisply pressed pyjamas. He had a dozen pairs in assorted patterns and wore a different pair each night.

He switched the ceiling light off, but decided to leave the bedlamp on. It had a pretty pink shade with little blue birds on it. There was also the nightlight on the wall above his bed. It burned there like an icon lamp. He got a small rubber torch out of a drawer and laid it beside his pillow, just in case.

Then he climbed in and pulled the neat, clean sheets up over his nose.

And lay awake and trembling for hours.

Tam sat down heavily behind the commissionaire's desk. He waited till his hands were steady, then lifted the phone, dialled nine – and put it down.

There wasn't anyone to phone, there wasn't anyone. His neck was still cold.

He picked up the receiver again and dialled the speaking clock.

The tape-recorded voice told him that the time sponsored by Accurist was two twenty-nine and thirty seconds, peep peep peep. He put it down. A minute later he dialled again. He found himself talking to the operator. The operator was a woman with a friendly middle-aged voice. She listened to him.

'I – I'm alone here . . . night watchman, you see, and . . . I think I'm maybe . . . I mean . . . This is stupid, I'm sorry—' he babbled.

'That's all right.'

'It's just that sometimes I think I hear things and see things, and, and . . . I mean, I'm not drunk or on drugs or anything, it's just . . . Maybe I've been watching too many of these horror films, or something . . . '

And so on.

Eventually he made a joke – about the horror films that he'd watched too many of – and laughed at it. The operator laughed too. Then they were silent for a while.

'Well, good luck, friend,' said the operator.

'Yes – thank you.'

'Look after yourself the rest of the night.'

'I will . . . thanks.'

There was another moment's silence, and then they both hung up.

Tam took a deep breath. His neck wasn't freezing any more, and his hair wasn't bristling. Whatever it had been, it was over. He looked up at the portrait. V.I. Lenin was staring straight at him, his eyes full of disappointed malice.

'Fuck you,' said Tam. 'Fuck the Party. I've got work to do.' He went to the cupboard where the equipment was kept, filled a mop bucket with water, and went to wash the abandoned bit of the east stair that led up to the Fourth Floor.

The cleaners never came anywhere near these dead-end staircases. Tam swept them occasionally. It gave him a reason for coming to look at those walls, so they wouldn't get on top of him. Not to mention what was behind them. He put his bucket down at the bend in the east stair. Even from there he could see that most of the cement between the slabs in the lower part of the wall was now missing. He brushed a shovelful of the stuff away from the top step, quickly brushed the rest, then soaked his mop and began to splash water about, smacking it from one end of the steps to the other in his hurry to be done and get out of the place.

He washed his way down to the bend of the stairs, then he plunged his mop into the bucket again and squeezed the excess water out in the drainer.

He was straightening up when it happened again, the stab and the cold stinging pain. This time it hit him under the right ear, just behind the angle of the jaw bone. The mop clattered on to the steps, and Tam leaned against the wall, frozen.

'I touched you,' said a voice.

A cold, rasping, gravelly voice.

```
I touched you
```

Tam's head turned slowly and looked back up the stair. The steps were shiny with water. Down the middle, leading from the crumbling wall that sealed the Fourth Floor, was a line of descending footsteps. Tam stared at them. Down the steps they came, on to the level where he was standing, large prints that left tracks like tyre treads. Army boots. The nearest were six inches away on the step behind him, the water bubbling between the treads.

Then on the step on which Tam was standing another footprint appeared. This time he actually heard the *squish* of the water. His tingling skin crawled into goose flesh, the short hairs on the back of his neck prickled and tried to stand up. Slowly he raised an arm that suddenly weighed a hundred pounds and tried to find something out there on the step beside him:

(It – he – is standing right beside me!)
but there was nothing there.

Tam moaned helplessly.

'Comrade,' said the voice in Tam's face.

The bucket fell over, the mop went hurtling down the stairs, and Tam lunged after it, half falling, banging off the walls in blind panic.

He was out in the street and two blocks away before he stopped running.

28

And Darker . . .

Nine o'clock in the fuckin morning, cuntin phone rings. Guy asks Scobie if he's the cunt with the greyhound.

Aye, says Scobie. So what the fuck?

'Cause I'm wantin to put a fuckin fiver on it, okay? says the guy.

Aye, says Scobie.

Wis you at the gemme Saturday? says the guy.

Aye, says Scobie. Fuckin crap it wis.

Better believe it, says the guy, 'cause there's this cunt says he's gonny chib your fuckin face.

Fuck, says Scobie.

Way it fuckin is, pal, says the guy. Phone goes dead.

Aye, fuck, says Scobie. Fuck fuck fuck.

Goes back into the kitchen. Kippers beginning to burn. Smell of burnt kippers all over the fuckin place.

Whit a cunt, says Scobie.

The pretty little cuckoo clock on the wall, a souvenir from the German Democratic Republic, struck three. Janis Ulman glanced up at it as the little wooden bird made her musical appearance and then retreated inside her little house that was made up of miniature wooden logs topped with wooden flowers. Sticking on top of the gable end was a pin with a tiny red flag on it.

Janis had woken up half an hour ago, haunted by the

unpleasant memory of a dream the precise details of which she couldn't remember. She was now sitting in her own nocturnal kitchen wrapped up in a dashing dressing gown, drinking a cup of steaming cocoa, and reading, with blurred eyes and anxious face around which the hair hung like tangled seaweed, a volume of Jimmy Glasgow's short stories entitled *The Game's a Bogey* which said that life in a contemporary housing estate was no better than life in a concentration camp, and probably much worse.

Jimmy Glasgow, friend and acolyte of the great Finlay McRath, was the most outstanding member of the school of subsidized Scottish writers who produced works of indescribable bleakness in which various terminally depressed and embittered men sat in pubs on rainy afternoons staring at half-empty pints and whingeing on about capitalism, women, the English, capitalism, the weather, etc., all of which were responsible for their plight, whatever that was. His books appeared regularly year after year and received orgasms of praise from reviewers, all of whom seemed to be English women with large salaries, and prizes sponsored by various Public Limited Companies.

Janis genuinely admired the stuff. She had been a social worker once, and recognized the life Jimmy Glasgow described – the boredom and alienation softened by drink, sport and rock music. It reflected working-class reality, she thought.

And it showed that socialism was still not just *important* and *correct*, but *more vitally necessary than ever!*

Despite the horrors of 1989.

About which she was sure she had just been having nightmares.

The little cuckoo clock ticked on.

Tam walked quickly.

Mirrored in the black windows he passed, his face had a

pinched, deathly look. Not at gunpoint would he go back into that building and be alone in it, no, not if his life were at stake. He recollected that he had left his radio playing somewhere, and perhaps the door was open. He didn't care. That infernal place had a better watcher than he could ever be. He was not going back alone! He could not tell the police because they would think him mad; he could not let the cleaners go in there either. He would meet them at the door (he glanced at his watch) in four hours. Probably they would think he was mad too; perhaps they thought it already. He didn't care.

He passed through the network of squalid streets that lay around the Red House, each decorated with the broken glow of streetlamps and an overhead ribbon of moonlit sky. No-one stirred on these streets, only an occasional car passed by. He heard the far-off percussion of a stereo, and from nearby someone coughed harshly in his sleep; one black window snored, most were silent; from streets away came the pitiful high-pitched howl of a dog.

Clack-clack went Tam's hurrying feet, *clack-clack*.

All else was muted.

The night was quiet. Occasionally the wind brushed around a street corner. Occasionally it sighed over some piece of dereliction. Once or twice other pedestrians passed, *clack-clacking* too, on the other side of the road. Once one passed on Tam's side, a tall intense man with chiselled features who glanced at him fiercely and hurried on. Nothing else moved in that bit of the city of twelve million souls, nothing.

He came to a main road. A few more cars, shops with neon signs burning all night, a bunch of noisy youths. Tam crossed over. The city was changing, the old tenements and stunted council flats thinning out, new housing estates replacing them. In a horrible new brick-and-metal confection off Wapping High Street his daughter lived with the man she couldn't be bothered to marry, who had shorn hair, an earring, red braces, and was something well paid in the 'leisure and recreation industry'. The two of them did things Tam could not understand. They were something called 'self-employed', used the services of an accountant, owned shares, and voted Conservative. His daughter admired the way Margaret Thatcher held her own in a man's world. It perplexed Tam. He passed on.

And came to the river.

The old docklands he had known? – Gone. Concrete and glass, now, and brick and glass, and concrete. The offices that looked like a creation from Legoland, the cramped expensive weird-looking houses down on the very waterfront with its creeping damp, where it was always cold and noisy and no-one in his right mind would want to live, but hundreds of rich people now did. This stretch – this very stretch beside the oily waves – where Tam had worked aeons ago with young men like himself in cloth caps looking devil-may-care and glad to be at war, and old men in cloth caps looking glass-eyed and prim as parsons, and the ships that queued like buses from Gravesend to the Isle of Dogs . . .

Empty now.

A wasteland . . .

On which his daughter's boyfriend planned to build amusement arcades and rollercoasters!

Tam stopped. In two hours he had walked miles. He laid his hands on a crooked safety railing that ran along the embankment and looked out over the water. There, as they had done forty years ago, the river barges rocked gently like gondolas on a sea of moonbeams.

'Am I mad, really mad,' thought Tam, 'because I don't understand any of this?'

He turned his back on the river, and stood still as he could, and listened. *It* hadn't followed him. Whatever *it* was, *it* wasn't here. All he had to do was keep on walking and be free of *it* for ever. Free of the noises, free of the nightmares. Oh, God – even people who slept in cardboard boxes didn't have his nightmares! To sleep for seven solid hours without—

He began to walk along the embankment beside the Thames. Westerly; for no particular reason except that that was where noise and people would be, and Cardboard City, the benches on Victoria Embankment, and an all-night café that he knew of at the bottom of Ludgate Hill.

Another hour went by in this fashion.

Walking slowly now, Tam passed through waste sites, down dingy roads lined with old warehouses whose windows were smashed and doors boarded, past sudden rows of suburban bungalows, an Edwardian terrace, blocks of new offices haloed with security lights that had uniformed guards sitting inside their glass-and-steel doors reading newspapers or staring blankly out at the night, past another waste-site boxed off with sheets of corrugated iron: *clack-clack* went his feet, *clack-clack*.

Suddenly he heard a woman's scream, and then the sound of distant shouting, male voices mingled in alarm and anger. He rounded a corner quickly, into a street lined with small houses, each with a tiny strip of walled garden in front, and a car parked by the kerb. At a distance of ten parked cars away there was a tussle in progress on the pavement. Figures staggered and reeled drunkenly in the unearthly glow of the streetlights, the woman screamed again and he heard the whinnying curses of men fighting. The prospect of physical danger brought his strength and determination flooding back to him, and he went rushing up the street to meet it.

Half a dozen youths, some white, some black, were milling around and a streetlamp caught the flash of a knife. A bottle had fallen and was rolling down the pavement towards him. He stooped as he ran, picked it up by the neck, and smashed it against a garden wall. The fight broke apart as he arrived and he caught a panorama of sharp malignant faces, and the woman who was screaming, her mouth open and her spiky hair in disorder. Tam had first had to fight for his life in the year of the Berlin airlift, and he had done it like this, with a broken bottle in his hand. A couple of hobgoblins came at him with the sheen of bloodlust in their flat eyes. Tam warned them off with the bottle, and they retreated a step and glanced warily at each other. He warned them again, advancing purposefully as he did so, and they turned and ran.

The rest of the fight fell apart. The woman was standing with a man who had one arm round her while the other dripped blood into the gutter. Another man was sitting with his back to a car and his face in his hands. Here and there window lights were coming on, and a man came out of a nearby door in his dressing-gown with a brass poker in his fist. Tam flung the bottle away and turned his back on the street. He was already a block away when blue lights passed him at speed.

He walked on, but the further he got from the place, the more irresolute he became again, his steps slowed, and the fear of returning nightmares oppressed him.

Suddenly he stopped.

He *had* to return to the Red House.

Pat and Alice would be there in (he consulted his watch) an hour – less. My God, what were they going to walk into?

They will think you are mad, said a voice. They will laugh at you, said another.

'Let them!' said Tam, and turned his steps back towards the fear and the darkness.

29

First Light

It was 5.30 a.m. and Joe Steele had fallen asleep in his chair fully dressed, snoring, with his mouth hanging open and his hearing aid round his neck. His small single-man's flat was very neat, its colours sober and respectable; you would have thought an old-fashioned church elder lived in it, or an old-fashioned schoolteacher of the sort that Joe Steele had once been. On the floor lay a Left Book Club volume from the 1930s, all blood and barricades. His elbows were on the armrests of his battered chair, his forearms hanging down over his thighs: occasionally they twitched and jerked violently, and he looked like a man being electrocuted.

Haytor's death hadn't bothered him in the least – far less than Charlie Feaver's, because Charlie had been that noble thing, a worker, one of the People. Haytor had been a wanker, a pink yuppie bourgeois, a mere educated hanger-on halfway to being a fascist, and people like that didn't count as People. In fact, most people didn't count as People in Joe Steele's opinion, and the only ones he ever felt really at ease with were white, British, male, inner-city-dwellers.

Amazingly, he also felt quite at ease with the few *genuine* fascists he had ever met – one of Oswald Mosley's old blackshirts from the glory days, a couple of British National Party members who shared his local. He regarded them as misguided workers, but workers nevertheless; he liked their accents and their guilelessness; he shared unpleasant jokes with them about Israel, women, dykes and queers. This, of course, didn't prevent him from eating fascists for breakfast. Oh no. He boiled them alive and ate them for dinner, tea and supper as well.

So it wasn't Haytor's death that was bothering him.

It was *everything*.

Everything was what had gone wrong in Eastern Europe and the Soviet Union: *everything* was socialism fallen in the gutter, capitalism triumphant, and fascists – oh those wicked fascists, marching in the street. *That* was what was happening in the world, and it was making Joe Steele ill. Sometimes he even thought . . .

Never mind.

He had got home from work when the lace-like meshing of television aerials was jet black against the pink and golden evening sky. He stood and glowered out of the window at the heartbreakingly lovely sight, and sighed. On the walls around him were sepia photographs of long-dead comrades in cloth caps with long judgemental faces. He paced about his cold lonely flat that no woman ever entered now, and he knew that he was hungry, but couldn't bring himself to make anything. He went out to the pub and made a meal out of a pint, a slab of cold pie left over from lunchtime, and two packets of Smith's crisps. Around him were workers – noble souls – talking about football. The pub glowed warmly amber like Aladdin's cave and resounded with manly conversation. With a feeling of warm benevolence creeping into him, Joe Steele, munching his crisps and on to his second pint, glanced up at the television set on the wall.

He watched, munching, for thirty seconds . . . forty . . . his munching slowed down . . . fifty seconds, sixty . . . it ceased. A crisp fell out of his mouth and landed in his pint.

The screen was showing a documentary about a mass grave recently discovered in a wood somewhere in Russia. Apparently there were hundreds of skeletons there. Now someone was holding a skull and pointing to a hole in the back of it . . . Now there was some old woman with a scarf on her head crying . . . Other old women . . .

Joe Steele turned to the barman and demanded that 'that fucking propaganda shit' be put off. The barman was busy and couldn't hear him. Joe Steele tried to reach the controls, but the set was too high off the ground. He jumped up and down but still couldn't reach them. Someone laughed. Joe Steele rushed to the bar and demanded the remote control. The barman still couldn't hear him. Someone else laughed. Joe rushed out, away from the accusing pictures, into the night . . .

The city is never dark. There are always plenty of street lamps, the occasional window, the headlights of a passing car.

But night in a darkened bedroom is something else. Joe couldn't face it.

He made himself a cup of tea; sat in his living-room chair beneath a 150-watt bulb; listened to cassettes of radical ballads, read a bit of one of his ancient much-loved books, and reassured himself that, yes, the children of light would once more be ready to man the barricades and fight the good fight against the legions of Satan.

And like an old warhorse hearing the trumpet, Joe Steele made soft whinnying noises in his throat; and stretching out his legs, settled down and fell gently asleep in his chair with the light on.

Comrades! (yelled his last conscious thought). *The fascists are swarming all over the street, pulling down our walls and statues, and the People in their uniforms and battle-tanks are doing nothing to stop them. Organize, comrades! Kill the fascists! Kill them all!*

And he slept.

And around his chair gaunt white faces clustered, skeletal with hunger; and his arms twitched, and his mouth gabbled and slobbered as the nightmare rode him.

30

First Light

They arrived at first light, big Pat and skinny Alice, when the black buildings were sailing along the sunrise like ships to harbour. They were walking side by side in their usual fashion, both wearing coats and headscarves with bags swinging from their arms; and Pat was talking talking talking, her jaws rattling loud as the lid of a boiling pot, while the smoke of Alice's cigarette steamed from her mouth like a kettle spout, and occasionally she whistled.

Tam was waiting for them, pacing in front of the door (which was closed) with a jaded anxious look on his face, and with his hands twitching and dancing nervously, now shoved deep in his pockets, now clasped behind his back, now fluttering in front of his chest as though preparing to ward off a blow. Occasionally he would run up the steps of the Red House and listen at the door; occasionally he would crane his neck and try to see in the lower windows; and all the time he smoked, puff puff puff, with furious concentration. It stopped the scream in his mouth. He had taken a taxi the last two miles. When he got out, the driver thought there was something wrong with him and asked if he could help. Tam didn't hear: he was too busy staring at the ground with eyes that blazed like torches. He had bought his fags from an early-opening newsagent's. After half an hour the pavement round his feet was littered with stubs.

Alice saw him first, as soon as they turned the corner.

She nudged boiling, rattling, puffing Pat with her elbow, and pointed with her forehead. She said not a word, and her sharp eyes never left Tam as he marched up and down stamping his feet and slapping his arms. Pat followed her gaze and, incredibly, fell silent. The two women exchanged glances.

Tam finally saw them as they crossed the entrance of the alleyway that ran round to the back door, and came hurrying to meet them.

'Women, listen, you – you mustn't go in there!' he stammered. 'God, if you knew what I've seen tonight!'

Briefly, he told them. Alice let her cigarette die down to a blackened filter, and failed to replace it. Pat looked from one to the other in alarm, and opened her mouth many times, but nothing, except breath, came out. Tam finished. Alice nodded grimly. Pat, after a second's delay, followed her friend and nodded likewise. Alice began to move towards the door.

'Don't you have the key?' she said. 'Won't you open it?'

'I know it sounds mad,' said Tam. 'I don't expect you to believe—'

'Oh, but we do,' said Alice.

'We do,' Pat echoed emphatically.

They both nodded.

'We've known about it for years,' said Alice. She paused for a moment. 'Come up to our cupboard,' she said.

'Alice—' Pat faltered.

'It's all right. We have to talk about it all. Come on.'

And gaunt Alice, like a stick woman put together out of yellowed pipe cleaners, pushed open the heavy wooden doors of the Red House with her knobbly nicotined fingers and went in.

The other two followed.

Everything was as usual. The lights were burning. No bloody axes lay on the floor. No severed heads. No slime, no chainsaws. Lenin stared dully down from his portrait. The hate sheets were back in a neat pile on the red table.

Alice led the way up the stairs.

Tam and Pat followed one step behind her. Tam was frankly terrified. He expected at any time to see *it*, and he searched for *it* with ferret eyes.

On the First Floor, the editorial floor, Alice produced a key and unlocked the door of the cleaning cupboard. She clicked the switch inside, and all three entered.

The cupboard was small in its floor area, but tall as the adjoining offices, so that it had the proportions of a rectangular box standing up on its end. It was lit by a naked 150-watt bulb hanging from the high ceiling, and the brilliance of this light – where 60 watts would have done perfectly well – reflected from the yellow-painted walls and the bright blue doors of the wooden wall cupboards, caused the little room to shine and glow like a shop window at Christmas. Tam blinked, dazzled. He wasn't prepared for it. Pat and Alice guarded their walk-in cupboard as jealously as two old misers would their treasure trove. Tam did not have a key, and had never before seen the inside of it.

He looked at the walls and blinked again. Taped to one blue door was a cardboard crucifix. Taped to another was a picture of Jesus. An embroidered cross hung from a tack on one yellow wall beside Mother Teresa of Calcutta. A framed photograph of the Pope sat on a shelf between several aerosol cans of furniture polish and a small Bible. The Pope seemed good-humoured and kindly. Mother Teresa looked like a happy prune.

There were two plastic seats. Pat and Alice both sat down and laid their bags on the floor. Tam leaned against the door and stared.

'All this . . . ' he said, gesturing weakly.

The two women made inarticulate sounds.

'Do they know?' asked Tam.

'They know a lot of things they say nothing about,' said Alice.

Pat grunted her assent, inhaled mournfully, exhaled a long whistling sigh, and being seemingly at a loss for words – an event as rare as 29 February – contented herself with settling her great weight more comfortably on the chair, shifting her thick legs with their swelling calves, and glancing furtively from Tam to Alice and back at Tam. She left it to Alice to do the talking.

'You know what you've seen, don't you?' asked Alice of Tam, leaning forward in her chair and looking up at him. 'Them footprints you was talking about, and that little girl – you know what they was, don't you? Course you do! Give it its name: *ghosts* is what you've been seeing.'

'That's it,' said Pat, and sighed. 'You hit the hammer with the nail there, Alice.'

'Ghosts?' said Tam. 'Ghosts?'

'Think there aren't any such things?' said Alice. 'So did we, once.'

'Once,' Pat echoed.

'Before we started working here,' said Alice. 'But not now. We may not have much money, but we do see life – don't we, Pat?'

'Ayuh.'

'We've seen things you wouldn't believe! Things we can't talk about, 'cause we'd be taken away and put in the loony bin if we did. So we keep this shut, we do,' she continued, pressing her index finger to her lips. 'And we wouldn't be telling you now, except for what happened to Des and his little girl.'

Pat groaned and shifted her feet.

'Horrible that was, horrible what he done to her! So we knew we was going to have to tell you sooner or later, but somehow – well, you know, we just couldn't get our tongues round it. Know what I mean? You'd have said we was two cracked old women talking about ghosts, and next day the van would be calling for us like it has for – others. So we kept it to ourselves and thought maybe Charlie would tell you. But he didn't.'

Tam thought for a moment. 'I knew he was uneasy,' he said, 'but he kept on talking about plots and fascists. He said he moved out of the flat because his wife didn't like the noises on the Fourth Floor.'

'That was Beth,' said Pat. '*She* knew all right!'

'She knew,' said Alice. 'Beth had been an orderly in an old-folks home that had been an orphanage years and years ago. She did night shifts like you. A couple of the old people said they heard children screaming and crying in the night. One of them said it was so loud he couldn't sleep: children crying in the corridor, he said. Children in the next room crying through the wall. Beth never heard anything, but she said it was kind of eerie. One old lady said that she woke up during the night and found a woman sitting on the bottom of her bed looking at her. She said the woman was wearing an old-fashioned grey dress and carrying a big bunch of keys. Turned out that was what the matron of the orphanage had looked like – and she'd been dead fifty years. So Beth didn't know what was going on here, up on the Fourth Floor, but she knew *something* was going on, and she kept an open mind about it.

'But not Charlie. Charlie knew there was something going on too, but he didn't have an open mind about anything, Charlie. Hate to speak ill of the dead, but that's how he was. He knew, but he didn't want to know. Beth took against the place right from the start. So they never lived here. Never. Since '68 there's only been the night caretaker, and I wouldn't do your job, not for a million pounds.'

In his house in the Chilterns Jack Straw kept on waking up – convinced he could hear horrible noises in the night.

Jack Straw had a heart condition, a private income, an invalid mother, a commitment to peace, and a nephew who was going through teenage torments in a boarding school in the West Country. These things were all important to him, and all tied together. He had a genuine, if inarticulate, love for his sister's family, and he didn't want to see her son dead on a battlefield, or his home incinerated. Even back in 1967, when he had stood alongside thousands of other students in Grosvenor Square and shouted abuse at the American Embassy, he had had the sense of doing it for yet-unborn children. But now, lying under his electric blanket in the dark lonely morning, his life came down to two words:

Heart Condition.

I have a bad heart, he said to himself. It's not my fault, I can't help it, it's just worry and – things.

Before he had a bad heart, Jack Straw had had soft soft hands, gentle hands, like those of a healer. They fluttered like wings. Sometimes they settled in his hair, and he would find himself stroking his own hair (he had fine, silky hair) as he sat at his desk. If he had a pen in his hand, that hand would sooner or later raise the pen to his lips and let his tongue caress it while the thumb and index finger slid up and down the barrel. If there was nothing to hand, his hands would fondle each other.

But most of all they liked to touch other hands. Jack Straw often found himself holding hands with complete strangers, clasping a member of his peace group round the shoulders while talking confidentially into his ear, and sometimes playing with children, patting their hands, stroking their hair, encouraging them like a kind teacher.

And he had been a kind teacher.

Perhaps it was the worry after his dismissal by the board of governors that had brought on this heart condition. He had sought to lose himself in his work for peace, yet in a way he was glad. He had originally joined the church to liaise between it, the Party, and the peace movement. It was only when his doctor diagnosed his condition that he felt a 'presence' there.

It was more of a gentle mist than a raging storm; a feeling that human perfectability (by which he meant a sort of all-round niceness) was not only desired by every right-thinking person, but was part of the order of the cosmos.

That thought gave him courage to face the fact that his own life trembled on the edge of an abyss within which lay he knew not what.

His body, dependent on stabilizing heart pills, was like Vietnam menaced by American bombers, like Russia coerced by American missiles. Like civilization threatened by barbarians.

Jack Straw was haunted by visions of tough men with full-blooded animal faces and hairy brown hands. They were the dreadful ones – the racists, fascists, warmongers, homophobes. Socialism, which was such a nice idea, had been overtaken by something malevolent. It was as if some kind of evil were abroad.

Perhaps they were what was keeping him from sleep, and not his bad heart, or the horrible noises, after all.

The cleaners' cupboard in the Red House.

Pictures of Jesus and the Pope. Crucifixes on the wall. Alice talking. Now Tam realized why Alice usually talked so little. She was one of those rare people who spoke only when something urgent had grabbed hold of her tongue and wanted out. She had plenty to talk about now.

'This trouble,' he asked, 'the sort of things I saw tonight, the little girl, the sounds . . . When did it all begin?'

Alice and Pat looked at each other and shook their heads.

'Before our time,' said Alice. 'There was a story that Lenin had lived here when he was an exile in London, but I don't think *that's* true. Old Flo that used to work here – you remember Flo, don'tcha Pat? – she said they had trouble in the thirties when they were killing all these people in Russia, and the people here in the Red House were pretending that they weren't. She thought all the lies were making the air sick. They renovated the whole place during the war after it got bombed back in, oh, '42, and that put a stop to it for a while. It started again a couple of years after the war was over.

'They renovated the place a second time in the middle fifties. Flo said they used to have a great big portrait of Stalin hanging in the foyer, and they took that down and put up one of whatshisname, Khrushchev, repainted the walls, and put in a new office suite, and that quietened things down for a while. When it started again they decided to close the Fourth Floor down in, oh, '62, because that's where all the trouble was, apparently. Flo said it was sounds, like somebody crying all the time, and the feeling of being watched. She never saw anything, she just had the feeling that something was seeing her. It got so bad that nobody wanted to go near the Fourth Floor, even in broad daylight, so that's why they closed it.'

'Were you here then?' Tam asked softly.

'No, neither of us. Finlay McRath and Joe Steele were both here, but I don't think anybody else was – eh, Pat? I didn't come till '69, and Pat came six months later. Charlie Feaver came in '68. They had taken Khruschev down by that time and put old Brezhnev up instead.'

'That's right,' said Pat. ''Cause Charlie was here when they opened the Fourth Floor up. He told us about it, said it was in the spring of '68. The bosses had decided that all the noise on that floor was made by beetles and things getting into the woodwork, so they opened the wall at the top of the stairs, and sent a firm of exterminators in to clear them out. One of the men got killed there – remember, Alice?'

'Ayuh. Charlie said the man fell out the window. Bloody lies. Beth told us what really happened. The windows were all boarded up, she said. Had been for six years. The man ripped the boards open and *jumped*, that's what Beth said. The other men heard him screaming in the room that he was in, but they were too scared to go and see what was happening. They said he sounded like a man scared out of his wits, pleading with somebody or something not to hurt him. So they said. They were afraid to go near, anyway. In fact they all clambered back down the stairs as fast as they could, and would they go back? No way! Not for time and a half, not for double time, not for nothing.'

'But there must have been an investigation,' said Tam. 'The police must have been all over the place.'

Alice nodded judiciously:

'Oh, yes. They would be. They would ask all their questions. But there was no trace of anyone else in the room, and the other men who had been on the floor all alibied each other. So they put it down as suicide. If you ask me, the coppers had a notion there was more to it than that – a whole lot more to it. But they kept it to themselves – just like Pat and me. Nobody wants to be laughed at. After that, they closed off the floor again, and bricked up the windows from the outside.'

'From the outside?'

'Nobody would go on to that floor again, not for any reason. The brickies put scaffolding up and worked from outside.'

'Must have cost.'

Alice made a dismissive gesture with her right hand:

'Nah. *Red Flag* was in with the union bosses. They were all real chummy in those days. Not now. A lot of the nobs who used to be downstairs having drinks with Finlay McRath all the time like to pretend they've never even heard of *The Red Flag*, but we know different – don't we, Pat? Anyhow, they kept it out of the papers and everything. But a lot of people weren't happy. A lot of the staff left about then. The old engineer who was here before Charlie, he went and emigrated to Australia. Opened a restaurant in Melbourne and sent us a card. Lovely place. Flo left as well. Said it was her nerves, they were giving her nightmares, and the doctor had to give her tranquillizers.'

'You knew all this,' said Tam, 'and yet you kept on working

here. Why? I mean, there are other jobs, and unemployment twenty years ago wasn't anything like it is now.'

'We didn't know,' said Pat. 'Not really. We'd heard stories that we didn't really believe. Everyone knows someone who knows someone who might have seen a ghost. Flo was just a cracked old woman getting her sleep out of a bottle of pills.'

'Besides,' said Alice, 'the pay's good. We're getting six pounds an hour. Six pounds! The Council only pays four, and we'd be lucky to get three in the private sector. I don't mind putting up with a ghost or two for six pounds an hour. And we're only here for four hours in the morning, mind, we don't live in or anything. It was the night men – the men in your job – they're the ones who saw it. Or felt it.'

Pat nodded in wordless agreement.

'There have been three since we've been here,' Alice continued. 'Jimmy, he was here when we came – remember him, Pat? He was weird. Don't know if he saw anything or not. He never talked about it. He thought the Americans were putting fluoride in the water supply to make his teeth fall out. *That's* what he talked about. Come to think of it, that's *all* he talked about. He once told us that Stalin hadn't been all that bad a man – at least he didn't put fluoride in the water to make people's teeth fall out.'

'He never went to a dentist,' said Pat. 'Said dentists were all Zionists who were in with the Americans. So his teeth got rotten and stank so bad it was awful to stand anywhere near him. Eventually he got blood poisoning from them and had to go to hospital.'

Alice resumed the tale:

'That was in – when was it, Pat? '77? About then. They took Brezhnev's picture down, put up another one of Lenin – the big one that's still there – and Jimmy took early retirement. Then there was a young boy called Terry. He was single too, like Jimmy had been. Too young for the job. I mean he was just twenty or something. Now he *was* scared of the place, that I do know. Used to rush to get all his work done in the evening, and then lock himself in the flat downstairs – your flat – all night with his radio playing. He stuck it two years and then he left. Used to say there were all sorts of noises, and he felt there were eyes following him everywhere. All those pictures of Lenin they've got hanging on the walls: used to say Lenin's eyes kept following him everywhere. He would turn the pictures round against the wall because he couldn't bear Lenin looking at him all the time.'

Tam felt as though he had just been given a transfusion of ice-water.

Eyes, he thought, *looking at me all the time.*

Alice saw that he was upset. 'What's wrong?' she asked.

'N-nothing. I don't like these pictures, that's all.'

'He's not a nice-looking man, that Lenin.'

'No, he isn't. Is that when Des joined?'

'Yes. About 1980, that must have been. The Russians had just gone into Afghanistan, and Maggie Thatcher was prime minister and Ronnie Reagan was president, and the people here were happy because things looked so bad. Finlay McRath said to Pat and me once that there was going to be a revolution against Mrs Thatcher, and the Russians would send soldiers to Britain the way they had to Afghanistan. I don't know if he was joking or what. Anyway, that's when Des joined. He was married, and he and his wife – Lucy her name was – lived in your flat downstairs. Rosemary, their little girl, hadn't been born then. She came along a couple of years later.

'At first everything seemed to be all right. Lucy and Janis Ulman didn't get on, but that was just one of those things. We'd told them about the noises and said that they were just drafts getting under the ceilings and vibrations caused by the trains, and not to worry. But Lucy began to swear she *saw* things. She said that sometimes when she came up in the middle of the night to tell Des that she was just going to bed and his meal was in the oven for him, she would see grey faces looking at her from the corners, and sometimes she would see these grey shapes, all rags, shuffling along the corridors.'

'Christ!'

Pat said:

'Nearly gave me a heart attack with those grey shapes of hers.'

'Me too. More than one. *We* never saw anything. She was expecting Rosemary at the time, and, well, you know, women get funny sometimes when they're expecting, so we didn't pay too much attention. But it kept on.'

'She kept on seeing things?'

'Ayuh. She got more and more depressed. Started acting all weird. We would meet her walking in the corridors laughing and talking to herself. Sometimes she would swear she was talking to *them*, you know, these people she thought she could see. Des couldn't see these people, and he got terrible upset by the way she was acting. The doctor said it was just nerves after her baby, and she should go away for a while and relax, so they went away for a fortnight, but—'

Alice paused and sighed deeply.

'It was a *Red Flag* holiday,' she said. 'They do special discounts for employees. They went to Romania. The night before they were due to come back she took an overdose of sleeping pills in the hotel. And died . . .

'After that Des lived downstairs with Rosemary, but he never recovered. He became stranger and stranger, and little Rosemary didn't have any friends or anything, she just played about by herself in the corridors.' She shook her head.

'Shame, it was,' said Pat. 'She was such a pretty nipper.'

'She was,' said Alice, and shook her head again.

Tam didn't want her to stop while she might still have something important to tell him. 'Did anybody else – see anything?' he asked.

Alice looked at him. 'She did.'

'Who?'

'Rosemary.'

'Rose—?'

'Rosemary. She told both of us.'

'She did,' said Pat, without waiting to be asked.

'We felt sorry for her, not having any friends, not having any other kids to play with or anything. And the people here didn't like her. I mean, Charlie and Peter the printer were all right, and I don't think Finlay McRath minded her too much, but Janis was always shouting at her, and the others didn't like her either.'

'Why?'

'Who knows? They didn't, that's all. Anyway, one morning we met her on the Third Floor. It was before she started going to nursery school. Des let her wander about the building, and Peter was keeping an eye on her. She was playing on the floor when we started mopping it, and we asked her if she wasn't lonely. And she said—' Alice paused for a few seconds, then continued:

'She said, no, the night people were nice. They kept her company and played with her. She liked them much better than most of the day people, she said.'

'Night people?'

'Those were the words she used.'

'You mean – ?'

'Yes. The night people. She's gone and joined them now, I suppose.'

Sometime during that night, that awful night, Finlay McRath crept out of bed and crawled downstairs to the phone. He didn't need to put any lights on, or at least he couldn't remember having done so. When he got to his living room he found it illuminated by a pale deathly glow that streamed out from under the pile of cushions on the sofa where he had buried the phone. Sobbing, Finlay removed the cushions. They were soft and feather-light, yet they weighed in his hand like lumps of cold hard metal.

The glow increased. The phone was waiting for him.

Finlay lifted the last cushion and dropped it on the floor. The phone rang.

He lifted the receiver.

The whispering began . . .

His next memory was a consciousness of being exhausted, and furthermore of being back in his upstairs bedroom. He lay down, shivering, and pulled the still-warm sheets over his shoulders. The bedside lamp with its cheery pink shade was still on, the nightlight still glowed.

Finlay closed his eyes. His body was stiff as a statue. When a floorboard creaked behind his back, he didn't move, didn't even open his lids, but held his breath for ten long seconds waiting for it to creak again. It didn't. Finlay lay petrified.

Unobserved, the moon and stars slid slowly across the dome of heaven. An eastern horizon appeared of buildings blacker than the sky. Shadows crept back into the corners of rooms and under beds; they edged across walls and ceilings, and slithered downstairs into secret places. The first notes of birdsong were heard among the streets of the metropolis and the trees of the Chiltern Hills: a long V of geese flew inland from the estuary of the great river, and their *honk!* was heard high up above Hampstead Heath.

Finlay woke. His face had a haggard, doomed look. His eyes were black and stunned. It was Saturday.

They had talked the sun up. Dirty grey light was beginning to filter through the windows of the Red House. Tam and Alice and Pat walked to the head of the west stair and stood there, unwilling to separate.

'We've never done them any harm,' said Alice. 'We've never said killing was good. No reason for us to be afraid. Is there?'

'I dunno,' said Tam. 'It's just—'

Then he heard it, they all did. Footsteps. Down the stair they came. At first he thought they were distant. Then he realized, no, they were the sounds of a big man walking softly, as though cushioned by a thick carpet.

The three backed away until their spines touched the wall. The footsteps left the stair and touched the corridor carpet. One, two, three seconds of silence. One, two, three impressions appeared on the carpet pile. Above them, a moving haze that temporarily soaked up six feet of the wall and obliterated part of the railing. Then the steps began again on the stair going down. The opaque haze above them vanished round the corner of the stair.

Pat slid down the wall as though her legs had been chopped away.

31

Funeral Rites

That day they burned what fear had left of Henry Haytor.

He had been well known in his profession, and many people, including those who had hated his guts in life, came to pay their respects to him now that he was dead. The crematorium authorities, warned in advance, assigned the Large Chapel, capable of seating two hundred, to the affair. It was solidly packed, with some people standing in the aisle, while others clustered round the door. Most of them were from the strange world of the Arts, some faces vaguely familiar from television, all looking sleek, spruce and dieted, with suntanned faces. Others were from the stranger world of Communism, and looked like salesmen at a convention. Each group regarded the other as exotic, dangerous and fascinating.

The air in the Chapel was thick with aftershave lotion and scent.

As Haytor hadn't belonged to any church, Jack Straw had volunteered to perform a secular ceremony. There were several large bouquets of flowers on the table, their perfume mingling with the other aromas.

Rikki was in the front pew wearing a dark blue dress and broad-brimmed dark blue hat with white polka dots on it. She appeared more embarrassed than heart-broken. A muted Finlay McRath, whose red face seemed to have had an overnight haemorrhage, sat on one side of her looking like a lugubrious small-town undertaker. A television producer sat on the other side looking like a television caricature of a television producer, down to the medallion, the Italian shoes, and the Rolex. Joe Steele sat in the row behind. Every so often he yawned and looked around, blinking and sucking his teeth. He caught Janis Ulman's eye and winked.

Janis smiled.

On the podium Jack Straw was delivering a panegyric that made the dear departed sound like a cocktail of Albert Schweitzer, Ivanhoe, and Spartacus.

Janis stared at the ceiling.

When the ceremony was over, and the coffin was being trundled into the oven on steel rollers, the audience filed outside into the cold, bright winter sunlight where the cars were parked, and a couple of uniformed chauffeurs lounged, smoking and talking about football. A good number of people came up to Rikki and murmured their condolences. The caricature television producer handed her into a Maserati and drove her off. A few people still talked about Henry Haytor and the circumstances of his death. Others began to talk about production schedules and money. A small, fat, babyish man kept saying 'forty-five fucking thou, darling!' in a querulous voice, and fluttering his chubby hands. Steele and another television producer were chewing the fat about perestroika and glasnost. The producer thought that Gorbachev was *cool, brill,* and *awesome*. Steele bawled balefully at him that the man was a traitor and ought to be horse-whipped. The producer, who regarded himself as *a man of the left*, nodded like a frantic metronome and hastily agreed with everything Steele said.

The cars drove off. The authentic wheels – the BMWs, the Volvos and Renaults, the Porsches and Mercs, a vintage Jaguar, a Rolls Royce or two. The street-cred wheels – dusty little Fiats, an old Volkswagen beetle, a sixties Mini. Finlay McRath climbed heavily into his Granada. The chauffeurs vanished, caps, buttons and all.

Janis Ulman didn't like chauffeurs, she didn't like the distinction of servant and master that the job implied. Above all she didn't like it when the character being chauffeured had the gall to call himself (*him*, always!) a socialist, feminist, man of the left, or some such rubbish. Finlay McRath and the other men were jokey and tolerant about it, but then men – even socialist men – often failed to see these things properly. As far as Janis was concerned, a socialist with a chauffeur was like a socialist with a mistress, a mirror on the bedroom ceiling, or a penchant for the sixty-nine position with the light left on – just plain WRONG!

One of the lackeys was still there, standing at the bottom of the exit drive.

Janis shot him a disapproving glance over the roof of her Volvo as she fumbled for her key.

He was in full rig too – broad-crowned upward-sloping cap with some sort of badge, riding britches and knee-high boots, for God's sake – that made him look like a Nazi officer in a war film. She couldn't make out his face yet, but she had the feeling that he was looking straight at her. Janis turned the ignition key and grasped the wheel. A couple more cars headed out in front of her. Janis followed. Both cars turned out into the main street, but Janis had to wait for a flow of traffic to pass her.

The man.

She could see his face now; gaunt and pale with staring, hungry eyes, he looked weird. Creep! Who was he waiting for? Maybe no-one. Most of the cars seemed to have left. Maybe he just got his kicks out of dressing up like that.

Maybe he is waiting for me.
Shit.
It's just like that dream I used to have.
No, it isn't.
Yes, it is.

No, it isn't. That was an alley in the dark, in the rain. This is a main street in broad daylight. Totally different.

No, it isn't.

Yes, it is.

'Oh, shit, he's moving.'

A big lorry lumbered past. Janis pulled out right behind into the vehicle's slipstream, missing another car by inches. The driver hit his brakes, then his horn. Janis got a glimpse of an angry red face. Then another horn blared – then another. Three little angry drivers in a row parping their horns at her. Janis took it for granted that they were all male. Stupid buggers. She looked in the rear-view mirror expecting to see the pale face staring after her, but there was no-one there.

Steady on, lady. Life's too busy to crack up now.

Forty. The big Four-O. Everybody gets odd. They call it the mid-life crisis. And sometimes they go weird.

Like that white-faced creep . . .

Janis shook her head and put it all behind her. 'Balls,' she said, out loud. Balls to the grim authority men and their uniforms. She delivered a whole gust of profanities at the windscreen, and smiled, which (although she was quite unaware of it) made her broad and so-very-serious face look sweet and pretty, even at forty, the big Four-O. She slipped a cassette into the player and flooded the car with soft golden jazz all the way home.

Nothing happened that night. Janis took her usual couple of pills and slept.

32

Janis

She dreamed.

When she was a little girl, Janis Ulman had wanted to become a nun. She loved to sit in the dreamy atmosphere of the church with the sunlight falling palely through the stained-glass windows. She liked to kneel on the worn red prayer stool and ask God to forgive her for all manner of things. When she knelt like that, with her gentle eyes upraised above her clasped hands, she looked very pretty, just like Audrey Hepburn in *The Nun's Story*.

Her mother was a pale, devout woman who kept a picture of the Sacred Heart of Jesus (looking rather like an illustration from a medical textbook) on the bedside table, and crossed herself before letting her husband make love to her. Janis's father was a kind-hearted boozy-faced drunk who snuffled and grunted like a pig at the trough. When doing *it*, his mating calls resounded around the darkened house, and were heard by Janis who lay crying in her room along the corridor with the pillow pulled over her head.

Although she never actually saw what happened in her parents' bedroom, by the time she had entered her teens Janis was having sex nightmares in which some hideous monster fell out of her insides and dragged along the ground behind her like an anchor tearing at her flesh and making her stagger and fall. She managed to deal with this, however. She didn't need to go and talk to any authoritarian man about it, just to learn that she was riddled with neuroses, angst, penis-envy and blah blah blah.

And eventually the dream faded.

She grew up, married, and had no children. She gave her love to metaphysical absolutes and sought among paperback books full of generalizations the many questions she wanted to her answers.

To promote these aims, Janis believed deeply, indeed passionately, that unnecessary people should be killed. If they had not actually been born, then there were no visible corpses, and it was really just like going to the dentist, getting *it* terminated. If they were fascists (and Janis regarded all people who emphatically disagreed with her as 'fascists') then it was a matter of social hygiene, and should be done humanely in a controlled environment.

She believed in abortion because babies were the handcuffs that women had to wear, and the process of revolution would mean nothing if women didn't achieve control of their own bodies. She ridiculed 'religious fanatics' who held that the womb and its contents were sacred, and hated racists who made life miserable for black babies. She did, however, have a certain sympathy with the Islamic fundamentalists because they were black, or brown, and hated Americans.

She believed in euthanasia because her father had died of Alzheimer's disease, and this was the real root of her murderousness. Every day Janis went to the hospital that her mother refused to enter. Every day she leaned over and kissed her father's apple-skin wrinkled cheek and tried to make some sort of conversation with him. After a while she realized she was simply surrounding herself with mental buffers – saying ordinary things to prevent herself thinking extraordinary ones – and that he probably couldn't hear her anyway. His eyes bulged and watered, his skin turned dirty yellow, and he rolled about in bed, played with his turds, and made pathetic mewling sounds. Soon he was little more than a skeleton, but his body wouldn't die. That skeleton walked beside Janis down the street, it leered at her at night in the midst of unlikeable sex, it haunted her the way it didn't haunt the arrogant male doctors, it knelt beside her when she prayed to the God she no longer believed in that this cup of life might pass from the man she had once loved. At last he died, and Janis wept and wept, and when her husband tried to console her she shouted at him.

After her father died, her dreadful dreams came back.

There was one dream that was particularly bad. In this dream she was walking down a long long wet dark street. She was all alone in this street, the dingy little shops on either side were derelict and the flats above them were empty and shuttered. Even the streetlamps were broken, and only a silver ribbon of moonshine lay down the centre of the street to light her path.

Janis stayed scrupulously in the centre of that ribbon, pulling her coat close about her. On either side she heard them – *men* – horrible men, hissing at her, fiddling with their flies, sometimes spitting or flicking semen, calling her a 'cunt bitch' in hateful throaty voices, or whispering, 'Mummy, I need you, mummy,' and staring out at her like pale-faced spectres from the ruins they had dabbled with their obscene woman-hating graffiti.

Eventually, though, she left the slum behind and now seemed to be walking between high walls that looked recently whitewashed. The moonlight reflected on the white walls and made them shine like graves. Then she came to a railway embankment with a tunnel running underneath it. She hesitated for a moment, but there was no sound, and she could see the moonlight at the other end.

She plunged in, walking quickly, alert for men.

Click clack, click clack, went her heels on the grimy road.

Then she stopped dead.

Click clack, came the sound behind her, and she knew that it wasn't an echo.

She started again, walking faster; *click-clack-click-clack*, from behind her.

He's following me!

She ran.

So did the steps at her back.

When she reached the moonlight she turned and raised her fists, ready to make claws.

'Who's there? I see you! Don't you dare come near me!' she shouted.

Her pursuer was a child, pale and naked, with a streak of black blood running from her throat.

'I – who are you? What's going on? What is this?' Janis stammered.

More children loomed up out of the darkness; they were all white as sheets and slashed with horrible black blood lines; and they all stared at her crazily.

Janis backed away.

They started to move in on her.

'Please . . . ' murmured Janis, holding out her hands. 'Please—'

She turned.

Behind her was a man. Tall, hard, marble-white. He held a long brush in his hands, and a huge tub of whitewash stood behind him. He grinned.

'Don't,' she whispered.

She woke just as they plunged her into the whitewash.

She told no-one about this dream, although it recurred in one form or another again and again; and in the editorial office, or addressing one of her innumerable 'groups', the day after having the dream, she would be bold, garrulous and violent; and no one would guess at the worm of fear and self-disgust that turned in her stomach.

* * *

Janis never actually said – *pace* Peter Simple in whose *Daily Telegraph* column she regularly appeared as 'Belinda Beria-Browne, Stalin's Rise, Gulag Gardens, Hampstead' – that she believed concentration camps were wonderful: though she admitted that certain restrictive measures might be necessary to combat all those fascists, racists, sexists, etc, whose poisonous policies might otherwise lead straight to Auschwitz. She saw Communist concentration camps more as educational centres than penal institutions, and believed that anything bad that had happened in Cambodia had been entirely due to the American blockade of that country. Anything bad which had happened in the Soviet Union was again due to the Americans, and the admitted misfortunes of those few thousands, or millions, or whatever, of peasants who had died of the cold in Siberia (a place where it was always cold anyway) was the fault of the Americans who had prevented them from getting the fur hats, boots and thermal underwear they needed to see them through the winter. After all, people died of the cold in London and New York too, whose slum areas were just concentration camps without barbed wire.

And the Soviet Union, Janis frequently pointed out, had done nothing like Hiroshima, the McCarthy witch hunts, men's magazines, or the Poll Tax.

She approved of Communism because it censored pornography. The KGB, she said, had doubtless done some unpleasant things, but it didn't allow calendars with pictures of naked women to hang in the staff-room. It was a no-nonsense creed that treated men and women, black and white, as equals.

Janis was quite serious about this.

Yet sometimes something seemed to be troubling this serious, well-meaning woman. Sometimes she would sigh to herself; sometimes she would turn in the street and look after young mothers walking with their children.

Someone might have noticed if anyone had cared, but no-one did.

Her big placid husband, through long and bitter usage, respected her independence to a degree indistinguishable from callousness, looked after his law practice and his property development business, and did the cooking.

They had no children.

Janis and her husband were quite happy to be without children.

So Janis always said.

33

The Mirror

In the living room of Tam's little flat a solid oblong mirror hung upon the wall above the mantelpiece. An electric log glowed comfortably in the bricked-up fireplace below, and the mantelpiece itself sported an old clock and two small vases left by the previous occupant (Des), and other assorted oddments. That evening, half an hour before his shift began, Tam, battered by events, was clambering into his boiler suit with his eyes fixed on the television screen in the corner. It was a good second-hand colour Ferguson that McRath had laid on for him when he moved in. On it cynical American criminals and cynical American policemen were noisily shooting holes in each other.

Tam rummaged nervously for his cigarettes, didn't find them in his pockets, and saw them on the mantelpiece behind him. He slipped one out, struck a match and, hearing a burst of television gunfire, saved himself the trouble of turning round by glancing at the mirror, where he naturally expected to see the set perfectly reflected.

The match burned down and stung his hand.

There in the mirror a brightly lit room was reflected, but not the room that was behind him. Tam's room was austere – two armchairs, a sofa, a small table by the window whose heavy curtains were closed. They were all there in the mirror in almost, but not quite, the same positions. So too was a large dolls' house on the floor beside the sofa, half dismantled. A

Sindy Doll sat on one end of the sofa and a ragged teddy bear on the other. A red tricycle with yellow handlebars was half hidden by one of the armchairs, and on the table was a scattering of picture books. The television set was a small portable black-and-white, and a Mickey Mouse lamp sat on top of it with a Snoopy shade. And in pride of place, a rocking horse.

Tam jerked around. Nothing like that here – no, *nothing*. No Snoopy shade or Sindy Doll or red tricycle. Jesus boy, hang on there, son, you're losing your marbles, they'll take you to the loony bin, how many have you had, tilting the old arm a bit much, doing the whaccy baccy? *(I'm not)* Jesus Christ on a bike!

Tam looked back in the mirror.

Jesus, it was still there.

His testicles feeling like shrivelled bags of crushed ice, his cigarette abandoned, Tam clutched the mantel feverishly with both hands to prevent himself from falling. He stared into the mirror seeing every detail with photographic sharpness. Suddenly he noticed two dull spots on the glass. He wiped them with the cuff of his shirt, but they did not move. Instead they began to grow and change. They turned into a pattern of motes, like dust in a sunbeam, coalesced into shadows of human shape, and finally emerged as two distinct figures.

One was a man, a big broad-shouldered man with a face that was flat and rather vacuous, and a nose slightly awry. He appeared to be in his mid thirties.

Sitting on his lap was a little girl with a freckly face and happy eyes and a cloud of golden hair. She was wearing a childwear pink playsuit with 'Rosemary' printed on it in blue letters.

Tam gasped.

Rosemary turned her face until she was looking straight at him. Then she half-closed one eye and motioned very slightly with her head in the man's direction.

'Yes, yes,' Tam mumbled.

The little girl smiled and turned back to her father, Des.

He for his part seemed utterly unaware of Tam and intent on her only, ruffling her hair and dangling some toy over her head. Rosemary began to laugh and kick her legs out, and reach for what was in his hand. He kept it just out of her reach and laughed in turn. Then he let her catch the toy, a plastic ball with small bells inside it, and the two of them laughed and talked together in a way which was touching to see.

Then the light began to dim and Tam saw various ill-defined grey shapes moving in the back of the mirror. Rosemary seemed to see something there that Tam could not, because she ran to the back and began to talk excitedly, stretching her arms out above her head as though taking some adult by the hand. Then she came forward.

Her father had turned to face her and consequently Tam could only see the back of his head. Now he turned round again and his expression was bleak. He cupped his face in his hands and let his fingers crawl up towards his eyes. The mirror darkened and Tam saw that he was no longer looking at the room but at a dark blue wintry sky against which the grey shapes shuffled. Slowly the light faded and went out. The mirror was perfectly black in its silver frame.

Tam couldn't take his eyes off it.

When the light rose again it was a reddish sunset glow as though a furnace were burning over the edge of the world. The five editors of *The Red Flag* were standing round Des in a semi-circle expostulating with dramatic flourishes and gestures, and spraying him with the blood that came out in slobbering mouthfuls every time they opened their teeth. And they glanced at each other over Des's head with eyes that were dark with suspicion, and grinned slyly.

Then they began to dance, and for the first time Tam *heard* the mirror. The music was grating and toneless and eerily unpleasant to listen to. Lenin appeared from the portrait in the foyer and began to conduct, with a gun instead of a baton. Four of the dancers now had partners. Haytor spun past with a pale, dishevelled woman who had a noose around her neck, followed by Straw waltzing with a skeleton child whose skull was pressed into his crotch. Then came Janis with a man-sized foetus that was bloody as raw pork, and Joe Steele with his arms round a young soldier who had two bullet holes instead of eyes. Finlay McRath came last, alone and naked, with a big erection and hysterical eyes that gleamed like headlights.

Des stared at each in turn as they passed him, as though hoping for some light to dawn in their darkened faces, but there was not a glimmer of comprehension there. The dancers joined hands and did a conga over the puddles of blood, and Lenin climbed down from his conductor's podium and joined in, firing his gun in the air. They danced out of the door and the music ceased abruptly. Faintly, as from a vast distance, came the sound of gunfire. Then there was silence.

The light rose in one corner of the room and Tam saw Rosemary. She was sitting on her horse in her yellow dress, rocking back and forth and singing to herself. She looked at him.

'What is it you're trying to tell me?' croaked Tam. 'What is it? What?'

Rosemary smiled sadly. Des was standing gazing at her with eyes like some dying hen. The little girl remained in the glow, but the rest of the room was slowly filling with an ugly green shine. Des suddenly jerked his head round and stared into it. Tam could see strange nightmarish shapes beginning to appear from behind the furniture, frog-like creatures but of human size with terrible teeth and claws and eyes that were silver blanks rimmed with red. Des cried out (no sound was heard), grabbed hold of his daughter, and stood hugging her fiercely with his mouth in her hair, while the creatures—

Tam could not look at what followed.

When he opened his eyes only seconds later the mirror room had become the toilet on the Third Floor and Des hung there from the cistern pipe, the rope still moving slightly with the effort the strangling man had made to kick and twist his way back into life. His eyes were closed, but his tongue was bulging out of his mouth, and the toes of his slippers were touching the ground.

Tam stretched out his hand and touched one of the hanging man's pale wrists. The skin was cold and damp, the blue veins had no flowtide in them.

A slipper fell off one foot: its heel slapped on the linoleum.

Tam backed away out of the cubicle. He felt cold air on his neck and saw that the window was open. He went to shut it.

Leaning on the sill he stretched out to grab the catch that was swinging loose in the brisk, steely wind – and Rosemary was staring straight at him

> Pushed his little girl out the window
>   and strung himself up from a pipe

suspended in mid-air with her arms and legs flung out like a swimmer's, and a look of desperate unhappiness on her face.

> She landed on her face on the Underground line
> All smashed in. Then a train went over her
>   but she was dead already
> Five years old she was. Face all red
>   and bashed in as a bad apple . . .

Her face—

Tam leaned right out of the window and tried to grab her arms – his fingertips nearly, nearly touched hers, but not quite . . .

And he saw her face, so small, so pretty and freckled, with its crown of golden hair . . .

> All smashed in

'Oh, God, oh lassie, I'm so sorry, I'm so sorry, please—' Tam pleaded without pause for thought or consideration, and already dangerously far out over the railway line he stretched just another impossible inch more, his fingers nearly, so very nearly, touching hers. 'God, pleeease – !' he cried.

And suddenly Rosemary smiled at him, a shy, happy, little-girl smile, and she didn't fall: instead she grew faint and faded away until she was no more than the vapour of his breath on the cold air.

A train screamed out of the tunnel.

Tam shuddered as though he had been hit. He was standing in front of the mirror, trembling. The room reflected in the glass was his own. The television was playing, and the upper half of his grubby boiler suit was hanging bunched around his waist.

His shift had begun half an hour ago. Upstairs everyone was gone and the front door was open. Out of the corner of his eye he caught a glimpse of a red tricycle, but when he turned round there was nothing there.

34

Janis's Sunday

Sunday morning was bright and windy and the forecast promised rain by the evening.

Janis and her husband circled round the house in different directions eating buffet breakfasts and reading bits of various upmarket broadsheets. A woman who had been to school with Janis had a regular column in one of them which she used to lash the 'reactionaries' who had annoyed her during the preceding week.

BEWARE THE SUGAR BULLETS OF CAPITALISM!

Isn't it just wonderful that Russia is ditching Communism? Gee folks, this sure is the best thing since ice-cream. Yessiree. Now the poor moujiks will get their faces rubbed in capitalism, and how!

No more watching classical opera and stick-in-the-mud productions of *Swan Lake* on the telly. Now they will be able to lie back with wall-to-wall soap operas, game shows, and glamour ads cunningly devised to maximize the humiliation and stereotyping of women and the macho aggression of men.

Instead of having to read fuddy-duddy old Tolstoy, Dostoyevsky and Dickens, Ivan can now turn on to the *Sun*, the *Daily Sport*, and the 57 other varieties of instant pornography produced by our super-duper market system.

And forget those dreary Sundays you spent wandering round the Hermitage gallery in Leningrad looking at impressionist paintings, comrade! Now you can sit in a traffic jam rotting your brains out with moronic pop music on the car radio. Just like us.

Gosh, isn't capitalism wonderful?

And check this out. How long's it going to be before TV evangelists (male) in electric blue suits start stomping out the old reactionary message about how the womb and its contents are sacred and only harlots would want abortions anyway?

When the single Russian mother has to put up with all this, and rocketing prices too, she is going to be hammering on the door of the Lubyanka asking for the KGB to come back.

And I'll be there with her. Yep, you got it.

Janis read reams of this stuff, and agreed with it all.

She was expected at a meeting of one of her several women's groups so she called goodbye to her husband and drove neatly through the meander of quiet side streets that led out of Hampstead into Indian territory.

By the time she had passed the last parked Volvo and seen the first rundown row of tenements with high-rises behind it, her eyes had adopted a feral alertness. This was the land of the Democracy, the striving working classes, God rot them, who wanted to *buy* their grotty council flats and *own* shares in something; the entrepreneurs with shorn hair and earrings who called people like her 'wimmin', read the *Sun*, drank lager out of cans, liked football, sex, cars, and holidays in Benidorm.

The patriots – *yuk!*

Janis approved of patriotism everywhere, so long as it was left-wing and not in Britain.

She narrowed her eyes and looked out for Apaches as she cruised down Caledonian Road and passed the cavernous building sites of future office blocks around King's Cross.

Suddenly there was a noise underneath the car.

Thump.

Janis frowned and looked in the rear view mirror to see if she had run over something. No, nothing there. She scanned the instrument panel, but there were no warning lights and none of the gauges was plummeting. She drove a block and nothing else happened. Then another – and another. Evidently the car wasn't going to fall to bits just yet. She relaxed.

Thump.

This time the car jolted, the steering wheel pulling out of her grip for a second. Janis spun the car round into a side street off Marylebone Road and stopped. For about a minute she sat still with her eyes shut, opening and closing her hands on the wheel until her heart stopped pounding. Calm, calm, she said to herself. Okay. She opened her eyes, checked the instrument panel again, and cut the ignition. The car trembled into silence.

The street had 1920s blocks of flats on either side of it. There was an occasional vehicle passing on Marylebone Road, but nothing in the side-street itself, and no pedestrians in sight. An alley ran behind the flats where Janis had parked that was grimy and smelled of cats' urine. Two big round metal dumpsters sat there like huge vats with crude sexual graffiti scrawled on them. Janis shot an apprehensive glance into the alley, but there was nothing moving. Besides, it was broad daylight. She took another look just to be sure, and opened the bonnet of the car.

Mummy . . .

Janis's head jerked up quickly, so quickly that she only just avoided cracking her crown on the raised bonnet.

Mummy, came the voice again. *Mummy, I need you, Mummy.*

`Cunt, bitch`

'Who's there?' said Janis, deepening her voice.

There was the sound of something – someone – moving beyond the dumpsters. Janis looked around desperately. There were still no pedestrians in sight. A small van rumbled by on Marylebone Road, a hundred yards away. Somewhere out of sight a motorbike began to rev.

Mummy, said the voice again, *I need you, Mummy.*

'No!'

Janis ran round the car and pulled the door open. She rummaged in the shoulder bag lying on the seat beside the wheel and pulled out the anti-rape alarm she always carried with her. It looked embarrassingly like a big dildo, but would let out a high-pitched metallic shriek if she hit the button on the base. 'Right, you bastard,' she said. I am not going to jump into the car and drive off. I am not going to panic. I am certainly not going to leave you free to attack another woman. I am not going to surrender my right to be on this street to anyone – got that, matey?

On that note Janis walked back slowly to the mouth of the alley. 'All right, whoever you are,' she said. 'Come out of there.'

Christ, suppose the bastard's got a knife? I wish I'd been more serious about taking karate lessons.

'Come out. Show yourself,' she repeated, walking forward and holding the alarm at the ready like a cosh.

He came out from behind the dumpsters, a tall strong bully of a man with his broad-crowned cap tipped back on his head, dark coat hanging open, sharp pale face staring straight at her, and boots – boots! – crunching up the broken asphalt.

Oh, my God, it's him! Him! The creep. The Nazi officer. Help me. Please, God. Someone. Help me.

'Mummy,' he said, smiling, in an adolescent, immature London voice. 'I need you, Mummy.'

No, *no.*

Don't take your eyes off his face. He's like a wild dog.

Dominate him. Control him. If you lower your eyes he'll attack.

Janis fumbled with her alarm but couldn't find the button. Her hands were shaking too much.

'Mummy,' he said. His teeth, crooked, rotten, yellow and brown. 'It's cold, Mummy. Make me warm, Mummy.'

Please someone come.

Janis threw the alarm at him and turned to run. His broad hands shot out and grabbed her by the shoulders. He spun her round.

'Comrade,' he said in a harsh foreign voice.

His mouth was inches from her eyes. She saw that his teeth weren't crooked at all, they were brutal and white.

He pushed her back. She fell against the side of the car. His face swung over her like the head of an axe.

Comrade . . .

'You orl right, luv?' said the anxious little man.

She looked at him, dazed. He had a blunted face with pouchy cheeks like a hamster's.

'Saw you fall. Come over dizzy like, did you?'

Janis only just stopped herself from speaking.

'But you must have seen him,' were the words on the tip of her tongue. But she didn't say them. He was a man, after all. She didn't want him, harmless mousy creature as he looked, writing her off as a neurotic woman, maybe telling his friends down the boozer about this hysterical feminist having hallucinations in the alley.

— *Fuckin swore this geezer was trying to rape her.*

— *Needs a fuckin shagging that's what she needs.*

— *All the same these fuckin lesbians.*

— *Yer right there. Fuckin slags, the lot of 'em. Fancy another, Fred?*

— *Don't mind if I do, Bert. Cheers!*

They would talk about her like that. They would, they would.

So Janis just nodded instead. She picked herself up and brushed the seat of her trousers.

The little man looked at her with his steady eyes.

'Thank you,' she said, then drove off.

The women's group was meeting in a spacious flat in a nice bit of town, not rich but comfortable.

Janis felt secure as soon as she got there. She knew all the women and knew they would approve of her and like her. None of them wore a boiler suit or had a cropped head. They were educated women in their thirties and forties who resented the high-heels and sexy-lingerie stereotypes. They sat and talked for several hours, and the woman who owned the flat served coffee and cupcakes.

The talk was all about the baleful effects of what they called 'porn', to make it sound ugly, and the need to step up their campaign against the 'porn merchants' to prevent them selling men's magazines with pictures of naked women in them.

The familiar pitter-patter of the words, which led to so little actually being *done*, had often irritated Janis and caused her to shout and smack the table with her fist; but today she found it reassuring because it gave her the sense that, despite all the terrible and inexplicable things that were happening in it, the world was still the same logical place whose quirks and inequalities were diminishing steadily with the forward march of progress. She needed reassuring because she couldn't get what had happened out of her head. When it came to her turn to address the group, she performed badly. Her speech was lacklustre and rambling, and she thought the women were looking at her oddly.

She was so disconcerted that she left early. She had left her anti-rape alarm lying in that wretched alley, and briefly contemplated going back to retrieve it. She decided not to. She didn't know if she was more afraid of seeing that man again, or of not seeing him.

197

(Hallucination? Am I cracking up?)

She drove home, and on the way she blew her horn viciously at some stupid bitch with a pram who was trying to cause a traffic accident – enjoyed the brief thrill it gave her – and then hated herself for enjoying it.

35

Jack Straw

Jack Straw spent the evening at home playing host to his peace group, munching shortbread fingers, sipping coffee, and blaming the Americans for everything that was wrong with the world.

Absolutely everything.

Then, after they had all gone, he went upstairs to his mother.

Mother was a stern, enfeebled old woman who had been a suffragette many aeons ago, and now lay in bed surrounded by paperback romances and shelves of china animals. Every day of his adult life, from the days when he had banned the bomb as a divinity student, Jack Straw had shared the world news with his 'Mummydarling', all one word. When the news was bad, she grunted with discontent; when good, she purred. In the seventies, when the Yanks were being chased out of Vietnam and the neutron bomb was scrapped, she had purred all the time. Latterly – grunt, grunt, grunt.

These past few terrible months, ever since the peace-loving Berlin Wall had fallen, Jack Straw hadn't had the heart to talk about world news. Instead, he would sit beside her bed and hold her hand silently, his heart (bad) full to breaking with the wickedness of men. Then his mother would pat his hand with both of hers and tell him that the ungrateful Russians, and the ungrateful Germans, and all the other ungrateful people, would come back to the cause of peace and socialism one day with their tails between their legs like naughty dogs. And he would smile and hope that it might be so before the capitalists blew the world up, but he doubted it.

He knocked on her door now and entered immediately.

'Hello, Mummydarling.' Jack Straw was fifty-one years old.

The old woman looked at him benignly. Her eyes shone like weak lamps behind dull glass shades. 'Have your nice friends gone?' she asked.

'Yes, Mummydarling. Were you all right?'

He sat down on the edge of her bed. It was covered with several layers of bedclothing, topmost of which was a thick hand-crocheted counterpane. He stroked the chunky white wool and played with the tasselled end of it. He noticed then that she had not answered his question, so he repeated it.

'Oh, yes,' she said. 'I was having such a nice talk with the dear little girl who was here.'

'Girl, Mummydarling? But there wasn't any girl here.'

'Oh, but there was. She was standing over there admiring my animals and saying it was such a pity they weren't real ones.'

Jack Straw looked over his shoulder at the glass shelf where the china menagerie stood, spotless amid a faint aroma of furniture polish. (A reliable cleaning lady came in to dust and clean and polish every day.) Of course there was no-one there.

'You've just imagined it, Mummydarling,' he said sweetly.

'Don't be silly, John. She was standing on that very spot. Oh, look. My donkey's not in his right place! She picked him up to look at him. Put him right for me, please.'

'Certainly. Sharon must have left it like that this morning.'

'Sharon did not. Sharon left it the way she knows I like it. The little girl was looking at it.'

'Mummydarling, there was no little girl here.'

The old woman sighed with exasperation and rustled her hands back and forth over the counterpane.

'John, you may think I am just a senile old woman, but there *was*, and I was talking to her. Now *please* go and put my donkey in his right place!'

An ugly look came across the peaceful countenance of her son as he turned and walked over to the glass shelf. One of the little china ornaments was indeed standing at the wrong angle, about an inch from true. He stretched out his hand—

There was a bright drop of blood on the glass shelf. Straw frowned and touched it gingerly with one finger. There could be no doubt: it was wet and newly spilled. He caught his breath.

'Mummydarling—' he began. *Heart*, whispered a voice within him. 'Have you, ah, hurt yourself?'

'Hurt myself, did you say?'

'Yes. I, do you, can I get you – a plaster?'

'John, make sense. What do I need a plaster for?'

'If you have hurt yourself.'

'I haven't.'

'Oh.'

He pulled out his handkerchief and carefully soaked up the red spot. Then he moistened one corner of it with saliva and, as carefully, wiped the place clean.

'John, what *are* you doing?'

'Nothing, Mummydarling. Nothing.'

'Don't "nothing" me! I want to know, I will know, I *insist* on knowing, John!' – and the old woman made balls of her fists and began to smack them angrily up and down on the counterpane with pathetic soft whumps. Jack Straw knew his mother of old. He glanced at her face and saw that querulous, zealous expression on it which meant 'please me or I will throw a tantrum'.

(Jack Straw did not believe it, but his face often wore the same expression. A girl he had once known, the *only* girl he had *ever* known, and at that not very successfully, had said to him, 'You're so like your precious Mummydarling, Daddydarling doesn't seem to have had much of a hand in you – for God's sake, Jack!' That girl, of course, turned out to be very fascist and reactionary, and Mummydarling, who had not been bedridden in those days, had soon put paid to *her* plans.)

He told the truth because he didn't have the
        Heart
to lie.

'Blood? Oh, my goodness, the poor dear must have cut herself on the glass! She told me she fell off her rocking horse earlier. Children are so careless these days.'

'Rocking horse?'

'Yes, she was riding it. Where did she put it? John, do you see a rocking horse anywhere?'

Jack Straw shook his head slowly.

'What did she, ah, look like?' he asked in a strange casual voice.

His mother described her.

Jack Straw jumped a little. His mouth flapped open and shut. The sound that came out was beyond human hearing.

'. . . toilet?'

'Huh?'

The old woman moaned her exasperation.

'John! *John!* MUST I repeat everything three times? I said she is probably in the toilet putting a dressing on her cut.'

'Yes, yes, oh yes, probably she is,' he gabbled, immobile.

'Well?' she said.

Jack Straw forced himself to move. He pressed his fingertips to the wall and pushed himself away from it.

'Yes – I – I'll go and see,' he said.

'What a clever little boy I have to be sure,' said his mother, and she clapped her withered hands together sarcastically. 'Don't be long. I have to go soon too.'

With an idiotic grin on his face, Straw tottered out of the bedroom and on to the landing. It was carpeted. A few feet away stood the closed door of his mother's upstairs toilet.

A rocking horse was standing right in front of the toilet door.

'No,' said Jack Straw hoarsely. 'No, no, no.'

He leaned his head against the wall and closed his eyes.

Heart, I need to take heart pill, it's overdue, there's nothing there, nothing there at all, just tired, that's all, worn out, if I hear it move I will go mad, heart, heart, oh my heart.

He opened his eyes. There was nothing there. The toilet door was still closed. What was on the other side of it? He turned back into the bedroom.

'Ready for the toilet, Mummydarling?' he cried heartily.

'Was she there?'

'Yes, yes, oh yes! All right. Everything in order. Everything fine. Excellent in fact. Got an Elastoplast on her finger. Yes. Nothing to worry about. Tiny little cut, that's all. – Here, let me help you. – Gone now. Downstairs – home, I mean. Gone home. Yes. Thanked you very much. Yes. – Careful . . . '

And he helped the old woman out of bed, slowly, so slowly, and up behind her walking-frame. She shuffled forward, pushing the frame. She was small, stooped; her spindly legs and arms were bent and shaking so the frame rattled slightly. Jack Straw had one hand under her elbow and he could feel the sharp bones trembling. The net she wore over her dirty white hair was six inches below his chin, and she smelled of must and mildew. Mummydarling, go out there and tell your frightened little boy that the bogeyman isn't waiting to, to –

He pushed the door open, his eyes thrusting out like bayonets.

Nothing.

He did not look into the toilet. He let his mother go first. Then he backed out and waited for her, with the crown of his head resting on the door.

It took fifteen minutes to get the old woman back and into bed. Jack Straw performed this service, or a variant on it, every night. If there were ghosts about, the old woman saw none. Nor did Straw. His duties finished at last, he kissed her:

'Goodnight, Mummydarling.'

'Goodnight, John.'

'Sweet dreams.'

'Humpf.'

Then he put out her light. There was nothing on the landing, no girl, no rocking horse, no blood.

Slowly he went down the stairs, his left hand running on the smooth solid banister. One step from the bottom he paused. There was an ominous fluttering under his left ribs . . .

Bump

And a feeling—

His ears prickled.

Bump, bump

A feeling as though the lobes of his ears were being stroked with fine steel wool.

Bump!

He took the final step and turned slowly, oh so slowly—

The little girl was sitting on her rocking horse on the landing above him.

Rosemary.

She stared at him solemnly and did not move.

Jack Straw stared back at her, conscious of, but not comprehending, the fiery sledgehammer blows in his heart. His mouth jerked convulsively and filled up with hot saliva *(I'm going to be sick)*. His glasses began to slide. He raised one leaden hand and managed to catch them as they fell off his nose. *(I need my pill!)* His face was cold and greasy with fear *(I'm not well, can't you see I'm not well?)*, and he turned and staggered, eyes half closed and unseeing, to his own bedroom where his pills were kept.

He vomited painfully into the floral-patterned china basin beside his bed and rinsed his mouth. He took one of the pink pills for his heart and sat breathing slowly and deeply for a while.

'Overwork,' he said. 'Stress – and overwork.' He nodded to himself, and his eyelids fluttered.

When the thumping in his heart had subsided, and his breathing was no longer painful, he got up and barricaded the door with the back of a chair under the knob. He had an en-suite toilet of his own, and made use of it, rummaging in the medical cabinet for certain other little things that would not just help but positively make him sleep. Then he took down a book and pretended to himself that he was reading, until he felt his eyes grow heavy.

There was no sound in the house. He put on his pyjamas and turned down his bed. Then he switched off the main light and – a habit of his since childhood – opened the curtains a crack to look out at the night. A slight sickle moon shone in the dim starlight above the great glow of the distant metropolis. Then he looked at the lawn, faintly illumined by silver.

He sobbed at what he saw crossing it, and stumbled back into his bathroom.

What he took there this time was highly illegal, but other men ridden to madness have done the same. When he fell on his bed he lost consciousness within seconds and dreamed phantasmagorically. In the world of his dreams he committed horrible sins, and got away with them.

36

The Train

That night Janis was sitting up in bed reading when she heard the noise. She put down her book and listened.

The night was loud and wild. The wind lashed the aerials on the rooftops until they rattled and cracked like whips. It tore through the trees on nearby Hampstead Heath and made the skeletal branches dance and throw up their arms and whistle with a dry, harsh voice. Janis felt as if an endless procession of people was sweeping round her house, shaking at the windows, trying to get in. Her husband lay by her side under their electric blanket, a great substantial bulge, gently snoring.

Janis went to the window and pulled one half of the curtain back. With nothing but the dim light of her bedside lamp behind her, she could see out into the night quite clearly. She could see clouds like black rags being torn across the face of the moon. The pale streetlights below her stepped up the hill to the Heath, and strange animal cries sounded from the darkness of it. What were they? she wondered – Owls? Foxes? And weren't they getting nearer? Now they seemed to be among the streetlights and the hedges.

Janis shuddered.

She was about to turn away when she suddenly saw a young girl walk out of the shadows and stand in the middle of the road looking up at her window. She was wearing a yellow frock with a red pattern, and she looked just like the old caretaker's girl who had died on that terrible night. But of course it wasn't. It *wasn't*. Janis tried, and failed, to remember the girl's name. After all, she was dead. But this little girl looked so like her, so like her that—

Janis felt her heart falter for an instant. The little girl's frock hung lankly down to her knees despite the wind that was weeping and sobbing about her. Not one strand of hair did it disturb. Her eyes stared up at Janis with terrible glazed intensity.

   `Mummy, I need you`

And the little girl rose like a demon through the air, her eyes locked with those of the woman at the window. Janis backed away into the room, making an incoherent sound deep in her throat, her fists clenched in the material of the curtains. The curtains stretched out taut, and the threads that held them to the plastic rail hooks began to break – snap, snap, snap.

Janis didn't notice.

The girl's face came closer and closer, until she seemed to be hovering just outside the window like some gigantic insect. And on her pinched face was an expression worse than hate.

'No,' murmured Janis, 'no, please, no.'

The little girl nodded relentlessly and pointed at her, one tiny fingernail scratching the windowpane, such a slight sound. Beside her a second face materialized; white and long with red-rimmed eyes and thin bloodless lips, and on the broad-crowned hat the badge that she could now see was a five-pointed red star.

Both halves of the curtain broke away and the rail came crashing down.

Janis began to scream.

Outside, the wind shrieked.

* * *

It says a lot for Janis's courage and determination that the events of the days and nights which followed did not destroy her entirely.

She rejected her concerned husband's plea that she should see the doctor, who was a friend of theirs, or the psychiatrist, who was also a friend of theirs, or a strange woman whom they knew only slightly who made ornamental wax candles in the Cotswolds and was deeply into meditation and nature remedies. Her husband looked through their library of glossy paperbacks full of cruelty and intolerance and picked out a volume which said that mental stress was caused by capitalism and Americans.

She had told him about the vanishing man in the alley and the two ghostly faces at the window where no faces could possibly be. Her husband said he believed her, and, oddly enough, she felt that he did. He supposed, he said, that she might have picked up bad psychic vibrations from the activities of the anti-communist renegades in Moscow. Something like picking up the telephone receiver and hearing somebody else's conversation, he said.

Janis supposed it might be so.

After her third brandy they went back to bed, and in her sleep Janis heard whispering voices and woke cold and shaking, but her husband had heard nothing, and was once more snoring gently by her side.

On 22 April every year the Friends of *The Red Flag* held their Annual General Meeting. The date marked the birth of the Great Leader and Teacher, Vladimir llych Lenin, in 1870. Communists throughout the world celebrated the event: soldiers did the goosestep; concentration camp guards got a special spirit issue; and guerrillas killed people. The Red House exchanged greetings with the Kremlin; someone in Moscow would hold the receiver in the air and the editors in London would hear the sound of clinking glass and Russian laughter. A heartwarming spiritual communion – or so it had been every year hitherto. But in 1990 . . .

Let Janis Ulman's diary for the third week in April tell the tale:

APRIL 16.

For the first time there is to be no anniversary celebration in Moscow. I feel very saddened. Still don't know whether Gorbachev, Yeltsin, et al., are simply dupes or really traitors in the pay of the CIA. I think history will show that the events of last year were a gigantic and successful plot by the Americans. Everyone in the office feels the same way. Joe in a bad temper. Finlay drunk (again!). Jack missing. My own nerves are badly shot. I hear whispering. But see nothing.

APRIL 17.

Nothing in Moscow.

Interviewed by Capital Radio. I gave the agreed line, approved of the 'Reforms' (!) etc, used the words 'fascist' and 'right wing' quite a lot to describe Stalin, Pol Pot, et al. Avoided 'communist' and 'socialist'. Good. It's what John Pilger does. Went smoothly. After that I went into the rest-room and cried. Couldn't stop. Everything is so terrible. As I was crying I heard a child's voice say, 'Please take this.' I held out my hand and took the tissue. Then when I looked up – *It was her!* She was standing there smiling at me in her yellow frock. She turned and walked into the corridor. I was too shocked to follow her. I – Please—

APRIL 18.

I can't go on like this. Yesterday I decided not to go back to the office, just to drive home. My car was in the underground park, so I went down in the lift. The whispering started again. *Her* voice. I'm not a criminal. What does she want with me?

Man in car – *Him.* Red Star badge. Uniform. What sort of

joke – He looked at me, and got out of the car still looking at me. *Nobody else seemed to see him!*

These last six words are so heavily underlined that the pen has torn into the page. The diary continues:

APRIL 19.
Last night – I had that dream again – the one about—
I saw – I saw – *Them*. Wanted to talk to Jack, but he's avoiding me. (Why?) Maybe I should go away, but I have the feeling that *They* won't go away, no matter where I am. Stress, it's all stress.
It's the Tories.

APRIL 20.
I must make—
I must see—
I'm going mad.

Then the last entry, in handwriting which is nearly illegible:

APRIL 21.
I can't. I can't. God. Please. Help me.
Never meant any harm.

APRIL 22 . . .

That day.
Janis ran.
To get away from *Him*: a bus – a taxi – anything!
A bus pulled up at a stop on the other side of the road, and she ran over to it, dodging a car and a van that swerved in opposite directions, horns screaming. The man followed her, remorselessly, slowly closing the distance between them. No matter how she ran, or how slowly he seemed to move, he

came nearer and nearer, passing through the traffic like a fine mist – and Janis heard, impossibly, above the noise of cars, the monotonous pounding of his heavy boots.

She jumped on the bus, fumbled in her pocket for change, and slapped it down in the coin trough beside the ticket machine – and screamed when she saw the driver's face.

His skin was grave pale, darkening to deep shadows under eyes that were hungry and reddish. He grinned.

'Comrade,' he said.

There was a pneumatic hiss as he touched the chrome lever that worked the folding doors. In a single flash of utter lucidity, Janis realized that if the doors closed behind her she was lost. Without pause for thought she twisted around and flung herself against the doors, her shoulder hitting the rubber fingers just as they came together. The doors shuddered and parted enough for her to force her arm through, then, hissing, they began to slide open again. Janis pushed through them, her coat tearing open and losing its buttons. She staggered and fell forward on to the pavement, picked herself up and fought her way into the rush-hour crowd that was flowing towards the doors of a nearby Underground station. She barged towards the doors, glancing over her shoulder to see if she was being pursued.

Janis seldom travelled on the Underground.

She didn't like the sooty democracy of the place, or the stolid nine-to-five humanity who used it, and she hated the racists and religious cranks and macho-thug types who rode with it like fleas in a cat's coat. But now she welcomed it – oh God, yes! – the noise, the light, the bustle. She needed to hide herself in crowds – they were the People, after all, the working class. However stupid, however treacherous and unworthy, they were what it was all about, and Janis believed in them with all her heart and soul.

She passed the doors of the Underground into the entry hall and fumbled for change for the ticket machine. Would you believe it? – five pence short! She went over to the kiosk where a big black woman sat and handed her a ten-pound note. The woman looked at the note as though it was an obscene postcard and was about to say something cutting about the dickheads who used up all her change when she saw the expression on Janis's face. She stared at Janis for a moment and dispensed her ticket and change without comment. Janis grinned and gabbled something incomprehensible at her and made off in the direction of the escalators. The woman stepped out of her kiosk and looked after her.

Down the escalator went Janis in a solid column of the dreaded nine-to-five humanity: women struggling with shopping bags, men reading the lingerie ads on the wall, people of both sexes staring straight ahead in a trance. The moving steps hit bottom and Janis let the crowd take her to the nearest platform. She didn't bother to find out what line the trains were, or where they were going – *He* wasn't in sight, and that was all that mattered now.

In front of her was a horde of school children, dressed like street kids (that was okay), several of them black (doubly okay), none of them looking like private-school bourgeois brats in the sort of stupid uniforms Janis herself had had to wear thirty years ago.

She followed them on to the platform and found to her joy that a train was already in and standing with its doors open. Janis didn't care what direction it was going in, she just followed the kids into the red carriage, and a moment later the doors closed. She leaned her back against the doors and sighed with relief. If *He* was chasing her, *He* was still behind her somewhere. *He* wasn't on the train. Janis began to pray, addressing some unknown force, begging it not to let the doors open again. They didn't. Instead the train juddered briefly and began to trundle forward into the tunnel.

The windows became suddenly black.

Janis remained standing, her body swaying involuntarily to

the rhythmical cheka-cheka, cheka-cheka of the wheels. All around her were children laughing and screaming.

Janis found herself listening to the sound the wheels were making.

Cheka-cheka, cheka-cheka, it got louder and louder.

And all sorts of strange metal thumps and bangs came from underneath the floor where the mechanisms were. There were harsh shrieks and staccato explosions like distant pistol shots.

Cheka-cheka, cheka-cheka, cheka—
CHEKA!

The train suddenly stopped dead in the tunnel and all the lights went out. There was silence, utter and complete. Then the windows and walls of the carriage swam back into Janis's vision suffused in a pale wintry glow from some unknown source. The carriage furnishings were white as moonlit snow, and the children, sitting on the seats, standing in the passageway, were black and immobile as statues. Janis couldn't see any of their faces. Even when she could see the front of their bodies, their necks were twisted away so that it was only the backs of their heads that she saw, and—

she saw—

that the back of each head had a jagged red hole in it. Usually above the hairline: sometimes below. Sometimes there was no blood visible except for the crust round the crater's edge, but usually a dried trickle of blood ran down the neck and disappeared into the clothes. The hair around the hole was sometimes torn up in errant sheafs or burnt down to stubble, and the smell – the nauseating rich smell of raw blood and burnt skin, the sweet sticky smell of children whose flesh has been ripped open by bullets . . .

And then they began to move. Their twisted necks righted themselves and their small bodies shuffled round to face her; they leaned over each other's shoulders, rows upon rows of bitter white eyes; and they smiled, dreadfully.

He walked down the passageway towards her. Janis opened her mouth but no sound came out. She felt a sickening drop in her gut. Her legs buckled and she sank slowly to the ground. The white eyes followed her down, the twisted smiles leered over her. She reached out her hands pleadingly, her lips quivered and her voice made a hoarse crack. The abortions regarded her with a remorseless lack of mercy. Then *He* was there, miles high; her fingertips shivered blindly round the tops of his high boots.

He raised his executioner's gun.

And performed surgery.

It was dark. Janis knew she was alone. And cold. So cold that her body was weightless and numb. None of her nerves were in contact with anything. Only her eyelids moved – and her chest very slightly with the sigh of her breath. She felt a strange encroaching otherworldliness like a climber going to sleep in the snow.

'Please,' she said, but her voice was so faint she hardly heard the sound. 'Please, I'm dying. Don't leave me . . .

'Please don't leave me . . .

'Please . . .

'Someone.'

Her eyes closed.

A gentle light began to flicker. When she opened them again she saw a little girl's face looking down at her. But she wasn't one of the abortions in the nightmare. She was, she was—

'Rose-mary . . . ?'

The little girl nodded and smiled. Her smile was neither sinister nor malicious. Janis's hands lay on the floor, already dead, but she felt as though the little girl were holding her hands and comforting her.

'I'm dying,' Janis whispered. 'Help me – please. I don't want to die.'

Rosemary smiled sadly and shook her head. 'You have to,' she said quietly. 'You don't have any choice.'

'But why?'

'Why did my daddy kill me? He was lonely without my mummy and all the cruelty drove him mad. He threw me out of a window and I was killed on the railway line below. Do you think I wanted to be thrown away? I screamed and cried, but no-one cared. Then I left my body and a train went over it. The engine driver didn't know what had happened until next day. Then he felt ill and went home from work. He told his wife he wished he were dead instead of me. She told him it wasn't his fault, but he cried and cried. I was there because he cared about me, even though he had never seen me, and I loved him for that. He took a sleeping pill and went to bed, and I came to him and told him that it was all right. And he woke up feeling better, and couldn't remember his dream.'

Janis felt even colder, but she didn't shiver. When she spoke again, no-one living could have heard her voice.

'I'm sorry. I didn't know. I never really hated you. You see, I have no children. I've always been alone. In the important things of life. Always alone. Always – hated it. Always . . . The man. Why did he?'

'He can't help it. He's doing what he was trained to do.'

'I – I didn't mean to . . .'

'It doesn't matter. Sleep now.'

Rosemary leaned over Janis and kissed her cold cheek with lips that felt like snowflakes falling. Janis sighed and closed her eyes. She wasn't afraid or alone any more. She felt at peace. It was a relief to leave the world in which such lies were told.

She left it as the train came out of the tunnel into the next station. Rosemary stood and watched over her. When the train doors opened the people waiting on the platform found Janis lying dead. She was quite alone in the carriage, though one old woman thought she saw out of the corner of her eye the ghostly shape of a little girl in a yellow dress float through the carriage window and out into the brightly lit air of the station. But she kept that to herself because of course she knew it was impossible, and she didn't want people to think she was a crank.

37

The Doors

That morning Tam had finally handed in his notice. He had written it in a slow, painstaking hand on a page taken from the writing pad in which he had once hoped to write his account of the great strike of 1968, which would cause the world to break out into cheers. He had folded the page over and over and crammed it into the envelope of a leftover Christmas card with a robin. Then he put it on Finlay McRath's desk.

After the sullen commissionaire arrived, Tam went out as usual to buy his breakfast rolls. Finlay McRath arrived an hour later. Tam gave him another twenty minutes and knocked on his door.

'Did you see my letter?' he asked, diffidently.

Finlay nodded vaguely.

'Janis Ulman's dead,' he said. 'The police have just phoned me.' That was the second phone call Finlay had had that morning, and he was still trying to recover from the first.

'I'm sorry,' said Tam. 'She, er . . . ' He tried to think of something to say about her. 'Well, I'm sorry,' he repeated.

'Charlie Feaver, Harry Haytor, Janis – it's getting like one of Stalin's purges,' said Finlay. 'They were bourgeois, of course,' he added.

'They were?'

'Oh yes. Of course. People who get purged are always bourgeois,' said Finlay, in the most matter-of-fact voice. 'And women are almost always bourgeois anyway.'

'They are?'

'Oh yes. Incapable of genuine vision, prone to all sorts of stupidity. Soft, sentimental, fascist. Look at Pat and Alice! Some nonsense about ghosts. *Ghosts!* My God, how ridiculous! Claptrap! Twaddle! 1990 and they *still* believe in . . . '

And Finlay shook his head, and began to laugh loudly, as though he really had heard everything now. But the laughter was no longer the jovial condescension of the past. It betrayed a shrill, hysterical note.

Tam opened his eyes wide and stared at him.

'You know, don't you?' he said. 'You know.'

Finlay's noisy laughter cracked. He stared back at Tam, his face flushing slightly and his eyes overbright.

Tam gave a short barking laugh of his own. 'Admit it, you bastard. You've heard him too, haven't you? Have you seen Des at the end of his rope? Have you seen *her*, eh?'

'No – !'

'Oh? That pleasure's still to come, is it?'

'No, no—'

'And maybe you'll feel that cold touch on the back of your neck, like I did.'

'No, no, no!' shrieked Finlay.

So shocking was the sound he made that Tam gaped, and in the neighbouring office the secretary's typing halted.

'No,' said Finlay, coughing and looking flustered. 'I apologize. I – I don't know what you're talking about. No I don't. Nor would any sane man. Not even the Tory press would believe you, so there's no point in running off to the *Sun* with your little pack of lies. No. No point at all. Understand that? You're going to have difficulty getting a job at your age, and we can make it impossible. Understand? Im-possible. We're powerful, you know. You may think we're not now, just because those *fascists* have taken over in Berlin and Prague and – other places. But we'll be back. Oh yes. We're right, you see. We're the powerful ones. History is on our side.

Always has been. Yes. You're just dross, you know that? Just refuse. I suppose you were a scab back in '68. Stabbed your comrades in the back, like Mikhail-fucking-Gorbachev, eh? No use for you, boy. The bullet for you when we come back. Eh? Bang-bang, eh? When we come back,' he murmured, and buried his face in his hands. 'We will come back, you know,' he whispered, as Tam left the room. 'We will . . . We will . . .'

Joe Steele and Jack Straw were standing in the foyer. Their eyes were furtive and fearful. Various secretaries stared through the glass walls with shiny, ghost-like faces. Nobody said anything to Tam as he passed.

That was an hour, or maybe two hours ago. Now Tam was walking along the Third Floor. It smelled cold and musty as always. Lenin's photograph was missing from the wall, leaving a pale rectangle on the paintwork underneath. It didn't surprise him. After leaving McRath, Tam had lain down fully clothed on his bed and tried to sleep. It eluded him. Instead he had lain there staring up at his ceiling.

Suddenly it seemed to him that the ceiling of his bedroom was becoming transparent and that he could see through it into the Ground Floor where McRath was fumbling with a whisky bottle and the commissionaire sat reading the sports pages. Then the Ground Floor ceiling became slowly transparent in turn and he was looking into the First Floor offices where Steele and Straw sat in their fear, unable to talk to each other; then into the Second where Peter the printer was doing a bit of moonlight work on his machine, menus for Tony's Takeaway Pizzas, cash in hand and no questions asked.

Tam got out of bed and climbed up the western stair to the Third Floor.

It was deserted, as he knew it would be, and full of grey daylight. From outside he could hear cars on Leveller Street and the rattle of Underground trains.

Then the toilet door opened and Rosemary came out on her red-and-yellow tricycle. She rang the bell on the handlebar, *ching-ching*, and smiled at him. Tam smiled back crazily. After what he had experienced in the Red House, nothing seemed impossible to him. He opened his mouth to ask—

But she held a finger over her lips and motioned him to follow her.

He walked behind her to the bottom of the east stair. Rosemary jumped off her tricycle and began to climb the steps, looking back at him over her shoulder. Tam took a deep breath and followed. When they turned the bend he was one step behind her.

The wall that bricked off the Fourth Floor was open. Where the cement had been crumbling there was now a horseshoe-shaped portal. Beyond it was blackness, and in the far distance shone a single speck of light.

Tam froze.

Rosemary took his hand. Her little hand pressed his big one, and her hand was warm and natural as that of any living child.

'Don't be afraid,' she said. Her voice was soft and sweet.

Together they entered the portal.

The dim grey light from the stair vanished and a bright crimson glow replaced it. Tam stared round unsteadily. They were in a long narrow corridor, but one which seemed to run at right angles to those of the floors beneath, and to be much longer than the dimensions which the Red House he had patrolled night after night for so many months could possibly contain. Yet Tam did not think of turning back. Rosemary's hand was pressing his gently, and far away, at the end of the corridor, that speck of light he had seen now shone like a tiny silver star.

They plunged on down the corridor. The air grew colder and the ground began to crunch under foot. There was a drip-drop sound as though water were falling from a height.

Tam wondered numbly if there was a hole in the ceiling of the Fourth Floor and rainwater was getting in. Now the ground was getting treacherous; Tam had to lift his feet over lumps of crimson rubble and almost lost his balance. He stretched out his free arm to steady himself and touched the wall of the corridor.

A hand darted out of the wall and grabbed Tam's arm. At the same instant a piercing scream stabbed into his head.

Tam staggered.

Scream after scream ricocheted down the corridor, and more hands came snaking out of the wall – hands on the ends of long bare sinewy arms and raw torn shoulders. Faces turned towards him, terrified eyes held him, delirious eyes, eyes too maddened with pain or grief to focus on anything; mouths open, groaning, crying, screaming, slobbering great gouts of scarlet froth.

And Tam saw that the walls were not made of bricks or concrete, but were piles of bodies, heaped up, twitching, with flailing limbs, and the drip-drop was the sound of blood running from them and splashing on to the floor.

'Oh, my God!' cried Tam.

He backed away from the hands that were clutching at him, and those on the other side reached out and clutched at him too. Blood dripped down on him from the tops of these huge human pyramids, and more blood sprayed from mouths and squirted from open wounds. Blood got into his eyes, and he tried to wipe it away with a hand that was already sticky and red.

Rosemary held his other hand firmly in her own. The blood didn't touch her.

'You can't help them,' she said. 'They are all dead. They won't harm you. Come with me.'

She floated in front of him along the corridor that was now so long Tam felt he was looking at it through the wrong end of a telescope, and its entire length was made up of naked bleeding bodies that cried and screamed, and whose hands reached out to claw at him as he passed, trancelike, between them. Hands closed briefly round his ankles, cold clammy fingers crawled over his face, and sometimes a dangling foot kicked him on the shoulder.

'Don't be afraid,' said Rosemary gently, and pulled him onwards.

At last they came to the place where the light was. It was a great gate behind which shone a light so bright it was painful to look at. On either side were towers of barbed wire topped with red flags, and on the arch between them was written in bloody dripping letters:

ONWARD TO THE VICTORY OF SOCIALISM!

Underneath it was a great trough full of excrement from which a legion of creatures with pig bodies and rat snouts was eating.

'Don't touch it,' said Rosemary.

She called across the trough, and two of the pig creatures extended a long plank over to touch the frozen ground at Tam's feet. Still leaning on Rosemary, who floated beside him in the air, Tam walked slowly along the plank that creaked and bent under his weight. All he could see of his body was now a congealed mass of blood: his trunk, his arms and legs, oozed and dripped blood, blood squelched out of his shoes with every step he took and fell into the stinking muck below.

As they reached the other side, the two pig creatures bowed from the waist.

'This way, comrade,' snarled one.

'Very elegantly dressed, comrade,' growled the other.

Tam caught sight of his face in the brightly polished gun barrels which the creatures wore slung across their chests. It was a single huge blood clot. Even his eyes were blood-filmed sockets. He tried to open his mouth, but the gluey salty taste of blood kept his lips closed.

'Don't be afraid. It's not far now,' said Rosemary.

She led him through the gate and out into the open. They were on a hillside covered with snow and strewn with bodies. These bodies were cold and hard. For the most part they were dressed in ragged coats and caps with earflaps, in clumsy mittens and torn boots. There was very little blood on the snow because it was too cold for the flow to last long, but there was some. A little girl lay at Tam's feet. She had been shot through the head. Both her eyes were open. The clot of frozen blood hanging from her temple looked like raspberry sherbet.

They went on.

Bodies sprawled under foot, hard as boards. Tam tried not to step on them, but it was impossible to avoid doing so. Sometimes when he stepped on them they creaked like planks and their frozen clothes crunched. One moment they were walking through ruins, the blackened ends of houses coated with ice whose people were mounds under the snow; the next through the streets of an empty city, where not even dogs remained. Sometimes their way took them beside an interminable fence on which raw men and women hung upside down. Sometimes over a battlefield littered with broken weapons.

At last they came to a field crossed by tank tracks. They looked like the marks of a prehistoric hunting beast. The corpses heaped in this field were mere skeletons, broken and smashed with bullets, torn by hungry animals.

There were five moving bodies in the field. Four of them were dancing to a thin high-pitched whistle.

As Rosemary guided Tam up the tank tracks they passed a grim kilted Scottish poet with the face of a terrier who was hopping with first the left foot raised, then the right, and swinging a great two-handed sword over his head. 'The

Cheka's horrors were nothing to this,' he shouted. 'Have at the English imperialists!' And he slashed the defenceless air.

The next one they passed was a German playwright with a round greasy face topped with porcupine bristles. In one hand he had a criminal's flick-knife, and in the other a policeman's truncheon, and he stabbed and hit himself with them alternately. Whenever the blade or truncheon made contact with his body, the swollen skin burst like a soft fruit and a spray of pus erupted from it. He seemed to enjoy his suffering, and paid no attention to the bones that lay all around his feet.

Next there was a French philosopher who was really an ugly old hoptoad in glasses. The toad carried a laser gun in his paws. 'It is all absolutely meaningless,' he croaked at Tam and Rosemary as they passed. 'Nothingness, that's all there is. None of this is here.' He looked at a skeleton pockmarked with bullet holes, pointed his laser gun at it, and fired. The skeleton crumbled to dust and disappeared. The toad rolled his eyes to the sky and croaked, 'Nothingness. Alas and alack. Woe is me . . .

A naked woman was leaping up and down on top of a pyramid of bones. She was heavy and pot-bellied, and had long seaweed black hair that tossed and billowed about her shoulders. 'Liberation!' she cried, ecstatically. 'I feel free! I am at one with the universe!' Her feet and lower legs were bleeding from the sharpness of the bones, but she didn't seem to notice.

Rosemary led Tam by the hand past these four to the place where the tank tracks ended, beside a vast pile of skulls.

The last man was leaning against the side of the tank with his arms crossed. Round his feet lay the tank crew, their uniforms recognizable, their torn bodies rotting into next year's manure. The man was also in uniform with a broad-crowned hat that had a red star on it.

The face Haytor and Janis had seen before they died.

Vladilen.

He was whistling the tune to which the four ghouls were dancing. It was *The Red Flag* ('The workers' flag is brightest red, / It covered oft our martyred dead . . . '). He stopped whistling as Rosemary approached, and the five instantly collapsed and lay quivering among the bones and corpses.

Vladilen looked at Tam. 'So, you've come,' he said.

Tam shuddered when he heard the voice, that harsh cruel voice. It was the one he had heard in the Red House, the one that had driven him mad. He tried to talk, but blood poured into his mouth and made him splutter and retch.

'You people don't like blood, do you?' said Vladilen. 'Blood makes you shiver. Your hearts may be hard, but your nerves are weak. You want the butchery to happen somewhere else. You want your meat nice and clean. You don't want to hear the animals scream, do you? You don't want to smell the offal. Well, what do you think of the slaughter-house, *comrade*, the one your friends created?'

Rosemary stood on her tiptoes and whispered into his ear.

'She says you're different from the rest,' said Vladilen. 'Well, we will see. I do the work of historical necessity here. That's what I was told. I'm the liquidator. I need people to liquidate – that's what I was turned into. That's the job I was trained to do. I do it very well. I spent my life as a slaughter-house assistant. Year after year people got fat with the meat I provided, and they weren't troubled by blood because I had it washed all away.

'Now it appears that the meat-eaters don't want to know me any more. Ashamed of me, they are. Since I came here I've been ashamed of myself. I pulled the trigger, you see. But *they* provided the gun! She says that you are not one of them. She wants you to be given a chance. Very well. She even wanted *them* to be given a chance, the ones who did nothing when she was murdered. Very well, they have had their chances. None of them have passed. Let us see if you are any different.'

The scene changed.

Darkness surrounded them. Out of the dark came the Night People, spectral grey in grey convict clothes, numbers painted on their heads. Some of them were children. These were Rosemary's friends, the ones she played with. They sat and listened.

As Vladilen began.

38

Any Mother's Son

My proud parents christened me Vladilen in honour of the great Vladimir Ilych Lenin, but I didn't grow up great. I grew up just like any other mother's son. I was lanky and had tousled hair, played football and liked girls. In 1948, when I was eighteen years old, I was told to leave my parents' home in a village on the Kirghiz Steppe and go to report for military service at the office of the Military Commissariat in the provincial capital.

There a man, whom we called in Russian 'the military buyer', came and selected boys for the Ministry of the Interior Troops. He selected maybe one out of ten – the other nine boys went to the army. The ones he chose were the tall strong ones. He chose me, although I wasn't all that tall or strong. After I had been selected I was allowed to go home for a few days. I told my mother and sister and girlfriend that I was going to join the famous Bluecaps, the élite Ministry of the Interior Troops. My sister and girlfriend looked at the table and said nothing. My mother said that 'some people' – she didn't name anyone – were afraid of the Bluecaps. I laughed and said that decent law-abiding folk had no need to be worried.

When the day came I joined the other two boys who had been selected, and the buyer drove us on the back of a lorry to another town where another couple of boys were added, then on to yet another town where the same thing happened, until eventually there were about twenty boys. We sat in the back of the lorry and laughed and talked about football and girls. Then we took a train trip, and then another lorry took us to a big building sitting in the middle of nowhere, on top of a dusty hill surrounded by trees. There the tarpaulin on the back of the lorry was yanked open and we got pulled out.

The guys who pulled us out were Bluecaps, and they flung us on to the ground like rubbish bags. They kicked us when we didn't get up fast enough, and whacked us across the back with leather belts when we did. An officer stood by looking at us.

The officer was a young man, but he was wearing a whole paintbox of medal ribbons on his chest, including the famous Order of the Red Flag, the Order of the Red Star, and the Order of Honour, because he had fought in the Great Patriotic War against Fascism.

The officer let his Bluecaps smack us around for a while, then he shouted, 'Okay! Hands behind your backs! Line up in pairs! No talking!' – and we rubbish bags were marched into a compound. We fell into a military step, left-right, left-right, and then we were made to stand in a line. The officer walked up and down the line. He was a brutal young man with the build of an athelete. He called us 'fascist trash' and 'the scum of the earth'. He called us 'cocksuckers', 'wankers' and 'gutless yellow-bellies'. He called us 'fascists' again. He called us 'fascists' several times. Then he stopped in front of me and punched me in the face.

I rocked crazily like something a dog was shaking, and righted myself. I thought the whole world had gone mad. The officer asked me if I was going to hit back, and when I didn't, he asked me what sort of yellow wanker I was. Then he ordered me to do fifty press-ups in front of the others while he walked about making sneering comments and the rest of the Bluecaps laughed.

This was only the beginning of my miseries in that place. They went on and on for weeks. All the boys suffered the same. We were continually abused by shrieking guards, called 'fascists', and punished by being made to do the exercises we had learned in the school gymnasium – knee-bends, press-ups, sit-ups, straddle-jumps, and others, over and over again. And all this time not one of us rebelled.

I reckon the military buyer had had a good instinct for the ones who would not rebel.

In this time we learned two lessons.

The first was:

If we can put up with all this shit and not bellyache about it, then other people can put up with a lot of shit and not bellyache about it either.

And the second lesson was:

Anyone who does bellyache about it is a fascist and an enemy, and they are people you can do any fucking thing to that you like.

Or, as an old Russian proverb puts it:

'If God had not wanted them to be fleeced, He would not have made them sheep.'

I remember one thing that happened during those miserable weeks. It was the hour before lights-out. We had all done fourteen hours drill on three bowls of thin cabbage soup and a fist-sized hunk of black bread. This, although we didn't know it, was concentration-camp diet, and it hurt our bowels. Now we had an hour's free time before lights-out.

We were numb with disgust and humiliation and sheer weariness. A Bluecap stood at either end of the dormitory and yelled at any boy who slumped over on to his bed. On the wall at one end, a couple of feet above the Bluecap, was a huge portrait of Comrade Lenin in a three-piece suit and a cloth cap. On the wall at the other end, a couple of feet above the other Bluecap, was an equally vast portrait of Comrade Stalin in a military overcoat with red tabs. The boys would have loved to murder someone, just to get their own back – the two Bluecaps, or someone – Lenin and Stalin, or someone – but there was no-one we could reach. The only thing we could do was go to the toilet. We could only go one at a time, and we had to put our hands up and ask permission.

My turn came. I went along the dismal corridor and into the wet, smelly toilet. I went into one of the white cubicles and pissed my cabbage soup down the bowl. Then I sat down on the lid and took out my girlfriend's photograph, because this was the first time that I had been alone all day. The cubicle door didn't have a snib on it. I didn't hear the two sergeants tiptoeing up. They kicked the door open and dragged me out.

The sergeants were both tough, windburned men with faces like sides of ham and biceps like cannonballs. They were laughing. They told me that wanking wasn't allowed. They took my girlfriend's photograph. They told me that my girlfriend was a whore. One of the sergeants told me to repeat the word. I felt my face go red, but they represented authority. What could I do?

'Whore,' I muttered.

The other sergeant made out he couldn't hear anything. He put his hand behind his ear and cocked his head. The first sergeant ordered me to repeat the word.

'Whore,' I said.

The sergeants told me that my girlfriend had sucked off the whole of Hitler's army during the war, and gone on to suck off police dogs, ponies, and rams. They were still laughing. They ordered me to say yes each time.

'Yes,' I said.

And of course the deaf one couldn't hear me so I had to say it again.

'Yes!'

Yes yes yes.

Then they ripped up her photograph and dropped the pieces on the ground. Her pretty face lay there in several pieces on the floor of the wet, smelly barracks toilet. They ordered me to run on the spot, at the double. My boots stamped up and down on her face.

It went on, day after day, and week after week. One of the boys went mad, tried to slit his wrists, and was taken away. Three others disappeared. No-one knew where they had gone, and no-one dared to ask. The Bluecaps jeered, and the portraits of Lenin and Stalin stared down. Stalin looked like somebody's uncle. Lenin looked like an undertaker. They both looked like guys who thought that death improved people. You wouldn't believe what we went through.

Then one day the miracle happened.

At breakfast the tables in the mess hall had on them cartons of cereal and pitchers of milk, toast and marmalade, white bread and butter and jam, hot coffee and sugar. We stopped smack in our tracks and stared at it. Some boys thought they had finally gone mad; others thought they had died and gone to heaven, and some thought that it was a trick to poison us.

You know what I thought? I thought that we would be ordered to stand to attention there for hours, and look at all that food with our tongues hanging out, and not be allowed to touch a single bit of it. *At least,* I thought, *that's what I would do if I were a Bluecap.*

Then the young officer came in. He was wearing all his ribbons and a great big smile.

'Eat, boys, eat! Don't just stand there – enjoy!' he cried.

We looked at each other, and jumped in, poison or not. We gorged ourselves.

After we had finished eating we saw that bundles with crisp paper coverings were being laid out on one of the long tables. The young officer, smiling, said that here were our uniforms. *Uniforms!* Each of us got two khaki tunics, two pairs of khaki trousers, four fawn-coloured shirts, and four sets of underwear, two for summer and two for winter. Each of us also got a heavy fur-lined greatcoat, a less heavy overcoat, and a light shiny raincape. And two pairs of jackboots with leather shafts that stood up by themselves and came to just below the knee.

The last thing we got was the blue cap itself. This was the famous badge of the Interior Troops. It was blue, with a broad crown and shiny black peak, and in between the broad crown and the peak was a red star. The officer handed each man his cap with reverence. He actually raised it above the man's head in both hands and lowered it on his hair like a crown, saying:

'You're one of us now, lad! You're one of the Cheka!'

And he beamed, and the two sergeants beamed, and nobody sneered at us any more. Instead, everybody said what *real men* we were, and how tough we were. They said that all the torture and misery had been to test us, to 'separate the wheat from the chaff', to 'temper the steel', and so on, and we had come out of it with flying colours.

I was so glad that all the torment was finished. I was like a schoolboy when the term is over and the holidays are about to begin. And it's true, I *did* feel like a real man now that I was treated with respect and fed properly.

A real man.

A great lad.

A true socialist.

One of the Cheka.

My first posting was to a camp in the Urals. I had a uniform and a gun and the right to shoot without warning, but I was still an apprentice at the job, still a green kid. All the other guards were hard-nosed veterans. They had all done it. I hadn't done *it* yet. I was still a virgin. The other guards were polite but chilly with me. I wasn't really in on their horseplay, their wild nights in town, any of that. I wanted to be – God, yes! So I wanted to do *it* as soon as possible, whatever *it* was, since *it* was the ticket of admission. And I did.

The way it happened was like this:

I was off-duty and polishing my boots when the lorryload of prisoners arrived. There were several other off-duty Bluecaps in the barracks, a radio was playing, somebody was plucking a guitar, somebody else was writing a letter to his mother, and the rest were mainly cleaning their boots because it was spring and the ground was muddy with thaw.

We heard a sound from outside. It sounded like dogs yapping. It was actually the trusties shouting, 'They've brought the fascists!' The trusties were men who were in for petty things like murder, rape, robbery and so forth. They were called 'the socially friendly', got short terms, good treatment, and came out alive. The fascists were people who were supposed to have disagreed with the government about something or other. They got long terms, bad treatment, and unmarked graves. We Bluecaps crowded over to the window to have a look at the fascists. We began to snicker. We were bored and we felt like a bit of good cruelty to liven things up. A junior sergeant pointed at one of the prisoners, turned to the corporal standing beside him, and said:

'Let's have a tea-party.'

Everybody agreed that that was a great idea. The corporal went off to arrange it. The other Bluecaps talked about the tea-parties they had had in the past. The junior sergeant put his hand on my shoulder and said, 'You never had a tea-party, son?'

'Tea-party?' I said.

The sergeant laughed and winked. All the other guards laughed and winked too. The corporal stuck his head back round the door. 'Tea-party!' he yelled. The boys whooped and rushed out after him. There were about a dozen of them. The sergeant pulled me up by the arm. 'Come on, son,' he said, 'this'll be fun!'

We went along the corridor to a little room that we used for hanging up damp coats and piling wet galoshes and things. There were some coats and galoshes there now. There was a picture of Lenin on the wall. There was also a middle-aged fat man with glasses who was going bug-eyed with terror looking at all the husky young Bluecaps crowding round him.

'Looks like a fucking professor! – Fucking Yid! – Real Hitler lover! – Cunt fascist! – etc,' jeered the Bluecaps.

Actually, the middle-aged fat man had been a schoolteacher. What he had done was this. During the class geography lesson he had taken down the map of the World which hung on the wall above his desk, and put up a map of Europe instead. He spent the lesson talking about how the rivers flowed and where the mountains were. The map of Europe was bigger than the map of the World and consequently part of it covered the picture of Comrade Stalin which always hung there on the wall. One of the pupils was a good Young Communist. He denounced his teacher to the Cheka after school. The teacher was arrested in the early hours of the next morning, charged under Article 58, Section 10 of the Criminal Code – defining counter-revolutionary propaganda – and given ten years hard labour.

Well, the boys suggested various things that the middle-aged fat man looked like. None of them was a compliment. Then they began to push him round in a circle, faster and faster, jeering at him, catcalling, calling him a homo and a wanker, a cocksucker, a four-eyed nosewipe, and things like that. Then one really tough boy swiped him on the side of the head and sent his glasses flying. Another really tough boy stamped on them and smashed them into a thousand bits. They all had a great laugh about that.

'Take your stuff, fascist!' they said.

The only Bluecap not taking part in this disgrace was me, Vladilen. I stood silent and apart, looking at it all. Occasionally I glanced up at the Great Teacher, Comrade Lenin. I clenched and unclenched my fists by my side. The middle-aged fat man came hurtling towards me like a football.

'Let him have it, Vladi!' I heard someone say.

I caught the human ball in my hands, held it at arms' length, and steadied it. It was the critical moment of my life. My head was fizzing with hate. Suddenly all the sergeants and the officers, and the military buyer, and Lenin and Stalin, and, oh, *everybody*, were right there in my hands, in that one middle-aged fat man who was all soft and smelly and sweaty and blinking like an idiot because he'd lost his glasses. I heard myself give a crazy whimper of pure pleasure, and I slammed my fist right into his flabby gut.

The boys gave a great cheer. They kept on cheering as I beat the living shit out of the fascist. Then I kicked his bloody, unconscious face and ground the heel of my boot down into his torn mouth until the teeth cracked.

Everybody applauded.

The other Bluecaps milled round me like I was a hero, hugging my shoulders, pumping my hands, telling me what a great guy I was, saying, 'Great to have you along, lad. You're one of the team!' They walked all over the blood and urine and vomit of the middle-aged fat man lying on the floor, the one who had insulted our Great Leader, and they ignored him: they were all telling me what a great man I was, and I – I was way up over the moon in the place where dreams come true.

After that I went places.

Though still a private in the camp guards, I soon had the reputation of being a torturer superstar. It was easy in the camps out there in the middle of nowhere for guards to become lax and lazy. I was proud to be one of an élite group of Bluecaps that was sent here and there around the camps to ginger up our more slothful comrades.

And, boy, did I!

I broke ribs in Kolyma, tore out fingernails in Magadan, stamped on testicles in Angren.

Trouble in Karaganda camp? Send for Vladilen! And the train wheels said:

Che-ka, Che-ka.

You've never heard of these places, I suppose. Yet they were bigger than Auschwitz. Many times bigger!

They knew me in Svobodny and beside the ocean at Sovetskaya Gavan. Promotion followed me. I shouted orders:

'Hands behind your backs! Line up in pairs! No talking!'

I was a bastard, and I was proud as hell of the fact!

I killed, and the click of my gun said, *Cheka!*

I got a medal with a picture of Lenin on it.

I became a disciplinary officer, and my tea-parties were the best ever.

They knew me on the road of death in Yakutsk Province where they used skeletons to give better grips on the muddy surface when the spring thaws came. I was famous in Nyroblag and on Yenesei River. In Temir-tau I entered legend. And wherever I went, barefooted corpses marked my path, laid out by the roadside awaiting the garbage truck, turning blue and ivory in the winter cold, swelling black and red and rotten in the summer heat.

All this was the land of the Cheka, the dark legion that walked with their guns and their howling dogs under the midnight moon.

And in Britain the Friends of *The Red Flag* looked on it and thought it was great. They got erections like gun barrels.

39

War Criminals

'So you see,' said Vladilen, 'there is a great deal to be put right. We fought a war against our own people for seventy years – and lost. I am a criminal of that war, you see. I pulled a trigger. This trigger.'

He took a large pistol from the leather holster on his belt and examined it casually.

'I've forgotten how many people I've shot personally. I never even counted how many were shot on my orders. And as for all those I sent to the camps who died of hunger and cold – well . . . ' He shrugged his shoulders and gestured to the circle of pinched grey faces that surrounded them. 'Who cares about such things? No-one but the sentimental bourgeois. And was I a sentimental bourgeois? No, no. The sentimental bourgeois was one of the targets I shot at. So I've come back to find out. I was *wished* back by a war criminal one night when he was drunk. Britain, it seems, is full of war criminals – people who crept after our prison convoys, sucking up the snot and calling it caviar. So I'm going to ask each one of them, how many did I kill, eh, with this little machine?'

And Vladilen raised his pistol.

All this time Tam had been crying for the murdered millions, and for the lonely boy, named after the father of murderers, who had done his share of it. The tears had washed the blood away from his eyes, so he could see without having to look through a red film, and they had run down his cheeks to loosen the clots that had kept his lips gummed shut. Now he opened his mouth, coughed, and threw up a sticky black lump of blood into the snow.

'I . . . I didn't know,' he croaked.

Vladilen snorted.

'You didn't know!' he repeated contemptuously, then spat. 'You know now!'

And he pointed his pistol at Tam's face.

The grey clad convicts stared at Tam with eyes that had seen too much and consequently didn't seem to see him at all.

(But hang on I'm having a nightmare vision bad dream something I'm just imagining just imagining it tell myself it's not there not real not and it will go away and if it doesn't Oh my God I've gone mad!)

A real gun was pointing at Tam's face.

(He's going to shoot me!)

He closed his eyes.

'Let him go,' said Rosemary in the darkness. 'He's innocent.'

Tam passed out.

40

The Day of the AGM

Downstairs this special day, which would mark the 120th anniversary of Great Comrade Lenin's birth, was getting under way.

The offices were full of phoney work.

Finlay McRath, after having ordered Tam out *out* OUT! (he thought), sat and looked at the phone like it was a tarantula waiting to scuttle over and—

It rang.

'Yes!' he yelled into it. And fearing—

But it wasn't.

The choked voice belonged to Janis Ulman's husband, who had just discovered that he was a widower.

Finlay commiserated briefly and fell silent.

The man babbled.

Joe Steele was genuinely affected by Janis Ulman's death. She had been a fine comrade. But he mourned her in socialist fashion, acknowledging the debt and looking to the future. He went over to his fax machine and glared at the flow of weakness and treason in the *Tass* report from Moscow.

Jack Straw busied himself with the preparations for the evening's great event. He talked on the phone with the caterers, and took receipt of the drink brought by delivery van from the off-licence. He fussed in and out of the Lecture

Theatre, where the meeting was to be held, and the Library, where the subsequent reception was to take place, and admired the red crepe which two secretaries were looping around the portrait of Lenin and over the books of cruel dead people which adorned the shelves.

The nerves of all three men were shot to pieces, yet none would show it – for fear of what the other two might say.

Jack Straw was the first to hear it.
Comrade, said the voice behind him.
'What?' he snapped, turning round.
The two secretaries looked at each other, then at him. Neither had said a word. Nor heard one.
But Joe Steele did.
So did Finlay McRath.
Comrade, cried a thin voice issuing faintly from some crack in the wall.
Finlay began to shake . . .

> The year slipped away through that crack in the wall, the terrible year which had brought unimaginable defeat, the collapse and betrayal of all he had believed in. It was still 22 April, Great Comrade Lenin's birthday, but no longer 1990: no, it was 22 April 1989, the Anti-Fascist Wall stood in Berlin, the German Democratic Republic safeguarded socialism in central Europe, and a successful Annual General Meeting, was remarking with dignified restraint upon certain alarming signs of weakness in the Union of Soviet Socialist Republics and the Peoples' Democracies . . .

Joe Steele stared at his fax machine. Blank. Zick. It didn't matter anyway. It was all lies and dirt. For the past year the world had stopped turning, and great silt-like masses of lies and dirt *in which filthy little fascists swarmed and bred like baccilli!* began to ooze up out of the sewers and cess pits and cracks in the earth's surface and reactionaries, religious maniacs, cranks, nationalists, creatures of darkness all of them, whom he had thought had been safely shot or imprisoned years ago, were coming back from the dead dark ages, monsters from the primeval swamp, with their swastikas and blood myths . . .

> And Des the caretaker they had had here a year ago had wandered round and round looking so bewildered it could have been funny if it hadn't been so awful. He was Class-Conscious but not properly Educated, you see. He was one of the Working Class who follow, and don't have the brains to do anything but follow, the lead of the Vanguard, the Party members and intellectuals who do all the thinking for the Working Class and make all the decisions, because the Working Class (God love it) is thick as pig shit . . .

Jack Straw walked unsteadily back to his office and closed the door. He tottered to his desk and sat down heavily behind a mound of peace pamphlets *(war is caused by the internal contradictions of capitalism)* that no-one wanted to buy any more since it didn't look like the hated US of A was going to unleash Armageddon after all, and it was so unfair, he wanted peace, he really did, but not if it meant – but not if – but . . .

Jack Straw put his head in his hands . . .

> None of the Friends of *The Red Flag* had paid too much attention to their for-Chrissakes *caretaker* as he wandered round – uninvited, please note – listening to them lambasting the fucking so-called Working Class for its lack of discipline, for its flabby uninformed democracy – it had actually elected Reagan and Thatcher, for fuck's sake, and if that didn't condemn democracy, what

did? – And hearing Finlay McRath and Joe Steele in particular grimly prophesy a time when American-paid fascists/racists/sexists toured Britain in death-squads standing the children of workers up against the wall (Jack Straw, Janis Ulman and Henry Haytor adding their shrill chorus), Des went

> due entirely to the internal contradictions of capitalism mad
>
> and committed *a certain unfortunate act*.

Bump

Time passed. Backward. One year. To the day.

Des lurching crazily up the stairs, his pretty little crying daughter in his arms.

US marine fascist sex-and-drug-fiends gang-raped girls that age and younger in Vietnam, Joe Steele had told him.

Des shouting hysterically,

'THEY'RE NOT GOING TO DO IT TO MY BABY!'

Janis Ulman backed against the wall, her eyes bugging.

Haytor, face downcast suddenly, sneering at the ground.

'I WON'T LET THEM!'

And Jack Straw tented a large peace poster over his head—

Joe Steele froze on the steps and fiddled his hearing-aid down to nil as the screams came—

And Finlay McRath turned his blind left eye.

Bump
`   bump bump of the rocking horse`
BUMP

The three men stalked their office floors with haunted ghoul eyes.

And so the day passed.

41

The Annual General Meeting Itself

Evening of that day, 22 April.

The AGM was set for seven o'clock.

By 6.30 they had begun arriving, the Friends of *The Red Flag*. They came from Victorian bits of Hampstead and Chelsea, from suburban homes in Slough and council flats in Tower Hamlets; one butt of many jokes came from darkest Neasden, one from a Tudor farmhouse in the wilds of Hertfordshire. They parked all along the grubby length of Leveller Street, and amongst the grid of fragmentary side-streets that sprayed off on either side of it; and in ones and twos, in threes and fours they entered the portals of the Red House like bees returning to the hive.

Most of the staff had gone home. Tam, with two weeks notice to work out, was not expected to emerge from his lair until eleven. (Tam wasn't in his lair, but no-one knew that.) Peter the printer and a couple of secretaries had stayed behind to play spot-the-celebrity. The commissionaire was there on overtime.

In they came.

By seven o'clock there were forty-five of them. Finlay delayed the grand opening for half an hour in the hope that more would turn up.

More did.

By seven-thirty there were fifty-four.

The previous year there had been more than three hundred.

The Anglican bishop, who had always turned up in his purple robes with Anti-Apartheid and Campaign for Nuclear Disarmament badges glinting, was in his palace composing a letter to the press saying that he had always opposed 'Stalinism'.

The peer of the realm, whose ghost-written memoirs were in the final proof stage, was making it clear to his publishers that he had rejected 'Stalinism' right from the start.

All the Labour MPs were telling their constituency parties that they were good democrats really.

All the television persons were making documentaries about the collapse of Communism in Eastern Europe.

Some of the actresses who had been famous in the sixties were raising charity money for Romanian orphans.

Jimmy Glasgow was at his wordprocessor rattling out the next chapter of his next grant-awarded prize-winning wonderwork *A Tough Time In The Tenement* – 'an unanswerable exposé of the evils of monetarism at work in our so-called free society' (blurb).

None of them were in the Red House that night.

Across the foyer, where Tam had heard that cold harsh voice, and across which Des had rushed with his little daughter in his arms, marched the hard core of bitter, lonely, disappointed, compromised and uncompromising zealots of whom the great Finlay McRath had once written:

> In time of stress
> we learn who is best.
> The red workers' brigade
> has got it made:
> as Lenin said –
> and the remark was incredibly profound.

The last of the fifty-four guests strode into the Lecture Theatre; and Finlay McRath, and Joe Steele, and Jack Straw followed them. Deprived of celebrities to spot, Peter the printer and the two secretaries went home and lived to see the morning. The commissionaire removed the fire-extinguisher which had been propping open the Lecture Theatre doors, let the doors swing shut, and settled down at his desk to read the sports pages.

The Lecture Theatre in the Red House was a large, windowless, rectangular room carpeted in tough light green, painted in durable pale yellow, and ceilinged with grey chipboard tiles in which a dozen fluorescent lights were recessed in two rows of six gleaming panels each. In between the rows of lights were two large grilles above which the ventilation machinery hummed monotonously.

At the back of the room, beside the main entry door, was a control room little bigger than a cupboard – with a projector, sound equipment, a video screen, and six light switches beside which Jack Straw sat sucking the remnants of his dinner out of his teeth. Twelve rows of fixed seats with red velvet upholstery, twenty-four seats to a row with a passage down the middle, stepped down gradually towards the dais at the other end, where there was a table, lectern, water flask, tape recorder, and several plastic chairs.

Jack Straw took off his glasses and busied himself in polishing the lenses. Janis Ulman's death had deeply upset him. He would miss her, with her endless petitions and her sweet, desperate smile. He had always felt that, because she was a woman and he knew nothing about women, he could always confide in her if things went wrong.

(Things are wrong.)

Of course, he hadn't actually confided in Janis because he didn't want – it just wouldn't do – to get the reputation of being a

(mummy's boy)
sentimental bourgeois or anything. But the fact that she was a *woman*, and the feeling he had (based on all the feminist books he had read) that women are inherently more peaceful and loving and socialist than men, meant that her approval was important to him when he had to advocate murder in the cause of peace. When, for example, he said, as he was going to say again tonight, that peace needed a huge Soviet Army, nuclear missiles and all, he would glance at her pleadingly, and she would nod emphatic approval

(yes, yes of course)

and he would feel vindicated because this left-wing woman agreed with him. It was like being in touch with the life force.

And Jack Straw gulped and blinked and polished his lenses feverishly.

Finlay McRath and Joe Steele entered together from a small side door to the left of the dais. Finlay's glass eye was flashing. Joe adjusted the whine of his hearing aid. They sat down at the table. Finlay looked at his notes. Joe stared at Jack Straw at the other end of the room.

'Ready, Jack?' he boomed in the tone of bomber pilot to rear gunner.

Jack Straw's head jerked up. He dropped his glasses, fumbled for them on the floor, and emerged with a face as red as the crepe round Lenin's picture.

'The lights, Jack,' said Steele, stonily.

With a mumbled apology, Jack Straw went into the control room and dimmed the lights over the audience slightly. Here and there cigarettes began to smoulder.

Finlay McRath stepped to the lectern.

'Comrades,' he said jovially, 'and I use that word not in any Stalinist sense, but as a good, non-discriminatory, non-sexist term of greeting – comrades . . . ' And he launched himself into a warm-hearted peroration in which *he*, good old Finlay, working-class born and bred, for seventy years a fighter in the cause of Socialism who had seen and done it all, told *them*, the workers, how it was.

Steele scanned the audience with a basilisk stare. Salt of the earth! he thought, without irony. They weren't lovely to look at, but they were *true*. All the middle-class sympathizers had fallen away and left the fifty-four members of the audience, not one of whom had a reason for being here other than genuine unadulterated commitment.

The men might be beer-bellied louts with sadistic kinks and raucous voices, the women might either look like female impersonators, paratroopers, or Alice Cooper, but it was to such as they that young Lenin had talked, and John Maclean, and Keir Hardie, the Tolpuddle Martyrs, the leaders of the General Strike, and the Peasants' Revolt, and Jesus Christ and Spartacus. They were the bedrock, those who, in the beginning, were chosen to receive the Word.

' . . . remember our beloved comrades, Henry Haytor and Janis Ulman. They will be sadly missed, but not just missed. The reactionaries may have won a battle in the present, but the past – and the future – belong to us! Their example, the example of these two dear comrades, is a torch which shall be passed on . . . '

Jack Straw felt the shakes coming on again, just as he had that afternoon when he heard, *thought* he heard: that voice, that terrible terrible voice which no one else seemed to hear.

It suddenly came to him with a bright blinding certainty that he was having a nervous breakdown: that the dreadful news, the catalogue of defeats and disasters he had had to listen to over the past months, had launched this creeping carnival of craziness that was slowly engulfing him.

(My heart.)

He thought that he could even smell it in the room now, a lavatory stench of hatred and intolerance laced with a thin acrid stink of fear.

(My heart, my heart, my heart.)

'. . . the Romanian children who are being systematically exploited by the West,' Finlay McRath yelled, with a flourish of his arm . . .

'Got to take my pill,' said Jack Straw to no-one in particular. He slipped out of the door.

Steele saw the door open and close as Jack Straw crept away. Probably going for a piss, he thought. Even if he had known that Straw was after a glass of water to wash down his heart pill, he would have said the same. *Straw* and *piss* sat together in his mind. The man was full of piss. Fucking hypochondriac. Bloody bleeding-heart liberal. Whiny bourgeois bag of shit.

McRath was saying something very witty about 'people who make a King Charles's head out of anti-communism,' and the audience made a snottering sound that indicated mirth and merry agreement.

Joe Steele laughed with and at them. He sounded contemptuous and ugly.

One of the audience caught his eye. He was a terribly thin man in shabby grey clothes that seemed to have some number on the chest. It could just have been the fashion – you could never tell with 'fashion' these days – except that he didn't have the look of your average follower of fashion. He looked like a drug addict on his last legs. His face was pale, no, *white*, his cadaverous jaws were covered with grey stubble, and his hair was cut brutally short. He was staring unwaveringly straight at Joe Steele.

Steele winced. The poor bugger's got AIDS or something, he thought. He averted his eyes. The room seemed to darken and grow cold, while McRath's voice gurgled on, and on, and

(put a sock in it, you bastard)

on.

Steele gazed at the ceiling. *(I'm not going to look at that white-faced creep.)* It had previously had plaster cornices and dim light bulbs in bowl-shaped shades full of dead flies. Gloomy photographs of dead revolutionaries had stared down from the walls, frowning.

Steele remembered it well.

He had stood in this very room in 1956 – when news of the Hungarian revolution was coming through, behind a table just about at the spot where he was now sitting, and condemned the Hungarian *fascists* who had dared to raise their ungrateful clammy paws against socialist power. He had roared against them, he had called for the tanks to go in, he had demanded blood and heads and mass arrests. He had got them. He felt proud. In those days progressive people walked tall, heads back, a frank clear-eyed expression on their features. (He looked for the white-faced man again. Where was he?) Yes, in those days – those good old days—

And Joe Steele gave a short harsh laugh which seemed to relieve him mightily. Everybody looked at him, and he coughed and fiddled with his hearing aid.

It was his turn to speak.

He stood up.

42

Peace

Jack Straw pushed open the door of the Lecture Theatre and went out into the corridor with Finlay's voice booming in his ears. He took a deep breath. Through the glass panels of the foyer door he could see the commissionaire at his desk. Reading the eternal sports pages, he supposed. Worlds come and go, but the sports pages last for ever. He took a step towards the toilet to get water for his pill, then stopped.

Toilet? The little girl on her rocking horse? Her father gone mad? No, no way, not here, not tonight.

He turned and walked to the door of the Library, feet away. He opened it, switched on the light, and closed it behind him. Finlay's voice vanished. Peace, perfect peace. He was alone with Lenin, shelves of hate books, and a table laden with buffet food and drink. Lifting the small plastic box from his pocket, he took out his pink heart pill, popped it into his mouth, and unscrewed the top of a bottle of Perrier Water. He looked up at Lenin as he took a swig to down his pill.

You don't have the answer to everything, do you, matey? Scientific atheism can't explain what I've seen and heard these past few days.

(Strain, heart, I'm having a nervous breakdown.)
Can it?
Hmmm?
Lenin stared back glumly, frilled with red crepe.
Gone all silent? Nothing to say?

You're about as much good as God, you know that? Fuck all.

'*Comrade*,' said a voice behind him.

He spun round, his heart—

She was standing there between the table and the bookshelves, smiling at him, and her voice was sweet and innocent as morning dew. Jack Straw's mouth fell slack. He tried to back away from her, but his feet refused to move and he swayed crazily from the ankles like a tiring clockwork toy.

Rosemary approached him and held out her arms.

'Please kiss me,' she said. 'Kiss me good night, the way Daddy used to.'

Her eyes burned with a phosphorescent glitter. Jack Straw felt a warm gush as his bladder let go. He tried to say something but only an insane choking sob came out. Slowly the little girl rose in the air until her gleaming eyes were next to his. She twined her arms around his neck.

'Peace,' she said.

The Perrier bottle hit the floor. Seconds later Jack Straw's body followed it.

43

Fascists

Joe Steele coughed again and began to speak.

Straight to the point.

Unlike Finlay McRath, he told no jokes, made no pretence of urbanity. His voice was cold and loud and deliberate, his words a mixture of rage, hate and pain:

'Comrades! A spectre is haunting the world, the spectre of post-Communism. The reactionaries are hugging themselves happily. So are American spies, millionaire capitalists, Zionists, pornographers, and the corrupt racist police of this rotten fascist government! . . . '

With none of the hated bourgeois press present and neither television lights nor camera bulbs flashing, Joe Steele was unrestrained. He knew his audience. They wanted to hate and be strong. Joe Steele let them hate. His voice shook with malice. Britain today was like Russia in the 1880s, he said, when Lenin was but a lad and the socialist movement in its infancy. He prophesied the second coming of the revolution when the enemy, the treacherous resilient power of capital, would finally and for ever be exterminated with many firing-squads, much imprisonment, and a great cleansing bout of blood and torment. Only then would the workers inherit the earth. Either that or the planet would spin through space, a lump of cold rock devoid of human life as it had been in the beginning, before the dawn of man.

Finlay McRath winced, judged the audience, gave a desperate grin, and began to nod his head vigorously, saying, 'Yes – of course – quite correct – absolutely!' and things like that.

'Supporter of the underdog!' shouted Joe Steele, his hearing aid whining. 'Friend of the dispossessed! – Fascists to the wall! Shoot the buggers! Kill them! Go for it! Bang, bang, bang!' – And he fired his finger into the audience – who loved it, laughing and cheering. Joe loved it too. He looked round, grinned happily—

(blood! executions!)

blinked—

The white-faced man was there again.

Another one sat by his side.

Stiff. Staring. Faces blank, and yet somehow familiar. Clothes of some harsh grey material. Numbers painted on their chests. Heads shaved to the skull.

Steele looked at them for an instant, and for an instant only his mouth hung open and no sound came out. Then he gave a rough spluttering cough, smacked one hand down on the lectern, making his notes ruffle and jump, and continued belligerently:

'The right-wing and philistine destruction of the peaceful anti-fascist Wall in Berlin can only serve one end. We all know the CIA is plotting with the Pope and the Zionists to oppress the Arab workers. The creation of a unified neo-Nazi state in Germany in alliance with Israel will be the greatest blow to the international working-class since . . . '

And he sneaked a glance.

They were still there.

And there were others. All in the same grey, torn prison clothes – he recognized the uniform now – some bareheaded, some wearing battered greasy caps whose flaps hung down over their ears. Some were women with grey shawls over their heads and skirts like canvas sacks. They sat among the audience, they stood around the wall, and they stared at him, stared with sad, suffering, unblinking eyes. Then one raised an arm and pointed at him with a rotting claw-like hand, blue under the nails. Then another – and another – and another . . .

Steele's thoughts were no longer on his notes. His mouth, working automatically, trundled on awhile along the well-worn route: American aggressors, bourgeois plotters, fascist tyrants – these decrepit phantasms crept out of his mind and danced around him while he stared at the dead in their rows. Then it croaked and was silent.

The audience began to murmur. McRath leaned over and touched him on the sleeve. 'What's wrong?' he whispered.

No answer.

'Buck up!' cried McRath with his usual affected good humour. 'What's wrong, man?'

Joe Steele stood sideways on to him, hugging his shoulders with his hands and shuddering slightly.

'I don't feel well,' he said quietly, without raising his frowning eyes from the ground. 'Excuse me – take over – you have to take over . . . *It's the fascists!*' he barked suddenly. *'They're getting in everywhere!'*

And with that he looked up, and for a moment Finlay McRath saw an altogether different being in his comrade's eyes – someone who was terrified, agonized, and lost. Then the accustomed sneer of cold power returned and Joe Steele shook himself, turned away from the audience with a snarl, and strode out of the room – keeping his eyes all the time away from *them*.

He rushed past the astonished commissionaire and out of the Red House. The night beyond the door was cold and forbidding, the wind wet and shrill. There were few cars on the road, and fewer pedestrians. Some lorries and buses rumbled along Leveller Street; the buildings on either side, which seemed so dirty and dismal during the day, now shone like polished ebony; and the graceful lampposts formed a long perspective of gothic arches topped with globes of golden light. But Joe Steele saw none of it, he who had seen it all ten thousand times.

He ran – at first he ran – then stopped, leaned against some anonymous grimy brick wall, laughed, and said, 'Whew! Too much of the jungle juice, my son!' gave another attempted laugh that was more like the dry caw of an old crow – and looked round fearfully.

A noisy car hissed past him on the road, spray splattered round his legs, and a white face with rimless glasses flashed past, grinning malevolently, and was gone. Joe Steele stood flattened against the wall, nailed there by some hammer that was pounding at his chest. No, he dared not look back: *they* were there, he was sure of it. And because he dared not look, he *made* himself look and to hell with it. The crown of his head was pressed against the brick, he stared up at the streetlights on the other side of the road and didn't see them; slowly his head turned as though an invisible hand had cupped it and a will other than his own was making him move, and he looked back the way he had come.

They were there. They were shuffling slowly towards him. Their feet were bare, their skin grey as their clothes, withered as the season, shrivelled as the dead. They shuffled forward slowly, so slowly. One had a rope about his neck, another – a woman, he noticed – was puckered with bullet-holes, dark red rips that zig-zagged across her chest in a ragged stitching line. Many appeared to walk on their toes, leaning so far forward, their arms stretched out so far in front, their long gnarled fingers quivering and clawing so precipitously at the air that they seemed about to stumble and fall down on him.

With a stammering cry Joe Steele backed away.

A knot of cheerful people came along the street under umbrellas, talking in some foreign language that he didn't understand, and they seemed to laugh at him, and one turned and looked in his face, and passed on. He ran after them and called to them. 'Yes?' they said turning, still laughing. Their eyes were untroubled. *They couldn't see!* Behind his back he heard the shuffling feet draw closer, and closer. His mouth croaked open, and shut. He wanted to hide among people so much, and yet, perversely, he turned from them with an angry grimace and a violent gesture – at which they just laughed even more – and darted across the street.

He walked swiftly now, without looking back. At length he came to an area of bright signs and glowing shop windows. He stood and looked in the window of a newsagent's that was full of embossed paperbacks and glossy magazines. Of course, there were no such things as ghosts, although . . . he was sure he had seen them . . . Besides, all the rivers flow – for ever, and ever, and . . . Besides, the world was purely material; had Lenin seen ghosts for all the thousands he had had killed, had Stalin for all the millions? – although Stalin *had* killed a few million too many – but what was a few million when you were talking about a species? – and the old sod hadn't given a damn anyway. I must be careful, said Joe Steele to himself, when Marxists stop believing in Communism, they take up astrology, religion, or start studying tea leaves.

He leaned against the window. 'That's better,' he said. He straightened his jacket. For the first time he noticed that he wasn't wearing a coat. He was soaking. 'I'll be angry with myself later,' he said – 'I'll laugh about this later. Ghosts indeed!' He was careful not to look round, and derived a dim sort of pleasure from the conviction that they were still there.

He went into a pub, one that he knew well. It was noisy and garish and packed with people shouting to each other over the jukebox, and whole veils of thick cigarette smoke hung in the cold stagnant air and made his eyes sting.

He ordered a pint, shouting happily at the barman. He

bought some peanuts. He spotted someone he knew and exchanged half-heard shouts about something or other. He ate a little, drank a little, turned round – and there they were.

He spun back to face the bar. He was trembling. His glass clattered down. He pushed it to one side, disowning it, and ordered another for the pleasure of speaking. He laughed out loud, and again. The barman looked at him strangely. Everything was real and hard and solid – the gossip, snatches of which he could hear, about football scores and offices, the names on the beer pumps, the bright colours, the glowing bottles that hung upside down beside the mirror behind the bar. He examined that mirror. It was the pub he knew: real people, shouting, smoking, drinking . . .

'Ah-ha,' he said, looking suddenly very cunning; 'but I know you're there!'

He turned. They were standing, more and more of them, staring in his direction with blank sightless eyes.

With a sound somewhere between a laugh and a sob, Joe Steele pushed himself away from the bar and waded towards the door.

He had to pass through them, because they stood before the door, and as he did so the first one said soundlessly:

Magadan

and Joe nodded without turning. And the second said:

Dzhezkazgan

And the third:

Vorkuta

Kolyma

said the fourth.

Karaganda

the fifth.

Temir-tau

Tonshayevo

Angren . . .

Other names followed.

And Joe Steele nodded, recognizing the names of the concentration camps he had denied and lied about so coolly, so brazenly, so many times.

He passed through them out into the night, and they followed.

He fled, and still they followed.

Whether he walked, ran, stood still, turned right or left, there they were with their slow shuffling gait and outstretched arms, half a dozen steps behind him – and their continual whining noise, muttering names of massacres best left forgotten. Eventually, coming to a crossroads where the traffic lights shone green, he spun round, his face twisted and jerking with frenzy, and shook his clenched fists at them.

'Fascists!' he screamed. 'What right have you to persecute me? Lenin was right! Scum! Insects! You should be killed! All of you!'

And with a muffled shout in which fear, hatred and rage were horribly mixed, he dashed out into the street.

There was a scream of brakes. Joe Steele spun round. The tank was coming down on top of him.

'*Them!*' he shrieked. 'Not *me*! Kill the fascists! Kill *them!*'

There was a heavy thud, the wheels of the huge lorry ground over him, and along the line of the kerb the grey ones stood and stared at the mangled thing that once had been a man.

44

Blood

Back inside the Red House all was confusion. Steele's flight had stunned everyone – except one. Some attributed it to a stomach upset, some (unsmilingly) to a sudden onrush of diarrhoea or vomiting caused by the nauseous fascist triumphs of the last few months. The more imaginative saw the hand of Zionism at work and suspected poison. Soon all suspected it. A clamour of conspiracy theories arose in the Lecture Theatre. The faces of the faithful, the fifty-four who made public their belief in ideologically motivated murder, were shuddering with leers and grimaces.

Only Finlay McRath knew.

He knew because he had seen, as Joe Steele barged out of the Lecture Theatre's doors, shapes indefinite as grey vapour swirl and crowd around him.

```
It's coming!
```

For ten minutes Finlay McRath the Great, who had won so many prizes and so much praise, sat with the thud of his heart beating at the floor of his palate.

When he felt strong enough he crept to the door and out into the foyer. The commissionaire, standing at the street door, glanced incuriously at Finlay over his shoulder.

Finlay went to join him.

Together they looked out into the street. The rain was falling. What monsters were cavorting there in the dark land of democracy? What fascist horrors?

'Where did he go?'

The commissionaire shrugged his shoulders. 'Dunno.'

'Didn't he say where he was going?'

'Nope.'

'Was he – alone?'

'Dunno.'

Finlay sighed. 'Did you see anyone with him?' he asked.

The commissionaire pondered this. 'Nope,' he said.

Finlay leaned his back on the glass door and looked up at Lenin.

The commissionaire took out a packet of cigarette papers, a pouch of tobacco, and began rolling up with slow, sweet, nicotined fingers.

Creeeeak-bang—

Finlay jerked. 'What's that?'

'Huh?'

'That noise.'

The commissionaire hadn't heard anything.

It came again, a few seconds later: *creeeeak-bang.*

'That?' said Finlay.

The commissionaire shrugged, his mind on the smoke he was building himself with such loving care.

'Must be a window open somewhere, or something,' he said.

'Look and see, will you?'

'Okay,' said the commissionaire, putting the perfected roll-up in his mouth.

McRath didn't want to be alone. He hurried back to the lunacy in the Lecture Theatre.

The commissionaire's name was Lenny.

He was a grey-skinned little man approaching retiring age and the only things that really interested him were on the sports pages. He liked his little flutter, did Lenny. His grudge against capitalism was that he never won anything more than peanuts, not on the races, not on football, not on nothing. Under socialism every 2.30 hot tip would romp home a winner, every English team would score, and bookies would sing 'The Red Flag' in chorus while they shoved wads of crisp ones into his hands.

That's what socialism meant to Lenny.

Meanwhile – stuff it. 'Find me bursting my guts over a—'
He heard it
creeeeak—
for himself this time
bang.

'What the – ?' Lenny frowned, forgot to inhale, and some of the smoke stung his eyes. He walked to the foot of the east stair and stared up.

Then he began to climb.

Finlay McRath changed his mind, walked past the noisy door of the Lecture Theatre, and past the door of the Library, inside which Jack Straw's body was lying, and went into the toilet. He felt hot and sweaty. He began to run water into a sink.

Lenny, frowning deeper, passed the First Floor and began to climb up to Second, the sound now turning into a muted rumble above his head, for all the world like somebody was driving a train along the Third. Sounds like the pipes having a fit. Maybe the heating's gone wonky. Next thing to do is check the boiler room.

In the Lecture Theatre the comrades were passing a resolution calling for executions in China and other places. Many executions. The proposer of the resolution was standing out on the dais, screaming. His arms and legs were bent and his hands were clawing the air. The other fifty-three raved along with him. They did not hear the rattling in the air vents above their heads; they did not notice the fluffy grey dust that began to fall out of the grilles in the ceiling.

Finlay stood in front of the sink in his shirt sleeves and washed his hands furiously. Then he took a paper towel, soaked it, and began to wipe his face. His jacket was hanging over the back of a cubicle door and his tie was loose. Be calm, he said to himself. Be calm.

The face of a geriatric war criminal stared back from the mirror.

The noise was getting louder and louder and Lenny didn't like it at all. He was in the Third Floor corridor, which was enough to scare the shit out of him anyway, standing at the bottom of the dead-end stair that led to Fourth, and what he wanted was to do a runner back down to Ground and phone the police, or the fire brigade, or somebody. Only he didn't quite know what to say. He was putting it together in his head, leaning one foot on the bottom step, when the sound changed abruptly. The hammer blows (or whatever) were replaced by the crumbling roar of falling masonry. Chips of flying concrete hit the wall where the stair did its elbow bend and came tumbling down on him in a cloud of stinging grey dust.

Lenny hastily withdrew his foot and leapt out the way just as a sizeable lump of concrete came bouncing down the steps and thudded on to the linoleum just where his own sweet self had been. He turned and ran, taking the steps two at a time. He was halfway down to Second when the gurgling started. His ears told his brain and his brain said it was impossible, but he heard it, a long wet slithering on the stair behind him, the slurp and suck of some glutinous liquid.

A heavy drop of it flew past him and struck the wall. It left a long red smear of – that looked just like – that was—

Blood?

On Second he left the east stair and began to run along the

corridor to the lift – no, forget the lift, the whole building's falling apart – to the west stair. He had got a few feet along it when the ventilator grille in the ceiling blew off and struck the floor inches away. He jerked his arms up to shield himself from the red mess that followed it and

BLOOD, MY GOD, IT'S BLOOD!

swerved, banging his shoulder on the printing-room wall, hurting himself but stumbling onward, flinching again as the remaining grilles blew out of the ceiling like a row of corks popping and the red stuff came pouring down, soaking him in thick warm glue.

He slipped on the wet linoleum and heard himself, for the only time in his adult life, scream. Then the roar came at him. He raised himself long enough to see the door at the west end blow inward off its hinges and disappear under the rushing red wave that reached halfway to the ceiling. In its echo a second explosion came from the east end.

But this is impossible!

The two waves collided in the middle of the Second Floor corridor. Seconds later the weight of blood on the floor above brought the ceiling down.

The noise was coming from above his head. Finlay looked up. The ceiling tiles were vibrating. Then out of the ventilator grille came the first red drop. He stared at it numbly for a moment as it hung on the grille growing, growing, and then fell – splat! – on the linoleum. Bright scarlet, bright, too bright. Then another drop, and another. Finlay closed his one good eye, raised his right hand and cupped the palm over the socket. His glass left eye goggled out at the dripping blood.

Drip-drip-drip—

He shuddered and shook his head. 'No,' he said.

His hand fell away. He opened his eye and looked cautiously at the vent. Nothing – nothing.

Then it came in a huge red splash that struck the floor a

263

couple of feet away and leaped up, soaking his trousers to the groin. Finlay staggered back with a sob of fear and disgust, and the edge of the sink jabbed itself into his spine. He reached the door and pulled it open. It jumped out of his hand, and he just managed to get through before it slammed behind him, grazing his elbow and ripping his sleeve on the way.

The corridor ceiling was bulging.

The light-weight tiles were soaking up the blood until they turned into dripping red cardboard, bulging and dripping, bulging and – . The first one fell, then another; a third hit Finlay on the head and there was no weight to it, just a dull wet slap across the skull, but suddenly that awful wet coppery smell invaded his nostrils that was hot BLOOD which he had never smelled before in the whole of his long life.

(So that's what firing-squads do.)

And he ran, or tried to, but his traitor body slowed him down to a monster's lurch.

He clawed his way past the Library and tried to yank open the Lecture Theatre doors, but they were jammed shut. People were screaming inside and the doors were trembling as fists pounded upon them. Finlay abandoned them and made for the foyer, his feet wading now through a muddy mess of blood and saturated chipboard that slowed him down pitilessly until he was moving in slow motion.

He reached the foyer doors . . .

The screaming in the Lecture Theatre came swelling up like surf waves. The whole ceiling had fallen in – and with less space to fill, the blood level was rising faster in there than out in the corridor. The blood had no outlet. The paper-thin crack under the door was soon clotted solid, and the wall-to-wall carpeting and old linoleum beneath prevented any from draining off between the floorboards. A man wrapped his jacket round his fist and punched out part of the thin glass panel in the middle of the door, but it was too narrow for him to get through.

The blood storm rose.

In the Library Jack Straw was covered. It wasn't yet deep enough for his corpse to float. He lay under a table like an alligator in a swamp. The bookshelves began to give way. *The Collected Works Of Lenin* in innumerable volumes – SPLASH! – *Collected Poems Of Finlay McRath* – SPLASH! – MacDiarmid, Shaw, Sartre, Brecht— SPLASH!—

Shelfloads of socialist realism from Progress Publishers, Moscow – SPLASH! – whole cases of unread dogma from American campuses—

SPLASH! it all went, SPLAAAASH!

Some paperbacks were already floating.

The lifeless thing that was Jack Straw began to move.

Finlay burst into the foyer looking like the maniac butcher in a slasher film; from his crown to his toes he was dripping and clotted with blood, and his one eye bulged in his head like a golf ball.

But it wasn't the foyer. He stared uncomprehendingly. His weary feet lumbered forward a couple of steps and crunched on the hard-packed snow. Before him, where the door should have been, was a barbed-wire fence, and in front of it stood frozen grey spectres in rags guarded by other spectres in uniform.

The uniformed spectres were beefy in long coats and carried submachine guns across their chests. Red stars were on their hats, and round their feet lay spectre dogs, the white steam of their breath rising up in clouds on the harsh air.

The only thing from the familiar foyer was Lenin's portrait. It was there – or rather Lenin was there, the Lenin of the portrait, the familiar suit, the beard, the merciless staring eyes; but he was real – there was no paint, no portrait frame.

He stood on the other side of the wire, a vast colossus a hundred feet high, towering over the insignificant human insects shivering there in their rags; and he did not deign to notice them; his indifferent, God-like countenance was fixed on some far far horizon.

Deep inside Finlay McRath a little voice screamed: *It's here! It's true! You've known it all along!*

Suddenly the spectres became aware of Finlay. One of the uniformed ones advanced towards him shouting wordlessly and making threatening gestures with his left hand while his right swung up the barrel of his gun. The spectre's head was a skull.

Finlay backed away, sobbing. Stopped. Where to? God, where to? The blood?

Above the ruins of his mind, a single thread of decency remained, fluttering like a shot-up battleflag. *Tam. He can save me. They won't touch him.*

Why they wouldn't touch Tam, Finlay didn't know. He just knew they wouldn't.

Somewhere, he thought, are the stairs down to the caretaker's flat and the boiler room. Tam will still be there, asleep. I'll promise him his job back. I'll promise him anything—

Anything—

And Finlay fumbled his way towards where the stairhead would be if this were the Red House in London instead of Marx's nightmare in Siberia. He tripped, nearly fell to his knees, but righted himself in time (just) and found it. Yes! He gave a little cry of triumph as his feet found first one step, then a second. And he looked down as he ran, expecting to see the well-known reality of concrete steps materializing through the haze of hallucination, and saw the shelves of corpses encased in ice over whose broken remains he was rushing. He yelped, but he was at the bottom, there was a door, there was, the door of the boiler room, exactly as he remembered it. He pulled it open—

I've come, said the Statue, bending its granite head. Behind it, where the boilers might have been, was the curl of smoke and the crackle of fire.

With his last moments of life Finlay stared up into the hard face of the truth.

Dear Comrade, said the Statue, opening out its arms and pulling Finlay unresistingly into its cold crushing embrace.

45

Fire

Tam opened his eyes. He was lying under cover on a pile of polythene rubbish bags. A drizzle was falling, splashing on the slabs at his feet, and there was a strange hee-hawing noise in the distance. He pulled himself up warily and looked around. He was in a basement area beside a pizza house whose name he could see overhead. He knew the place, he had passed it often, it was only a couple of blocks away from the Red House. A streetlamp shone down from the wall, and the rain hung in its glow like fine mist. A car went sizzling by above his head, its tyres hissing like frying pans on a stove.

And he remembered; everything, the cold, the corpses, the blood.

He ran his hands over his face and through his hair, but there was no blood. He got to his feet and stood in the rain under the glow of the yellow lamp, stared at his hands, his legs, what he could see of his body. No blood. But—

But

Then the sound came again, that hee-hawing, and he recognized it this time: sirens, passing close and fast. *And he knew.*

He scrambled up a short flight of steps and climbed over the small metal gate at the top, on to the pavement. A few yards brought him to Leveller Street. There were more lights on than usual. He saw people at windows looking up the street. He followed their eyes. There, where the street bent, the night sky was shot with crimson.

He began to move towards it. Other people were moving too; they had come out of doorways, some in dressing-gowns, some with coats thrown over their pyjamas. A swarm of blue lights flashed and flashed under the crimson glow, and a salvage truck passed at high speed, its siren whooping. Tam followed it until he came to a place where a policeman stopped him and directed him to stand with the small crowd of people that had formed on the pavement opposite.

The Red House was on fire.

The windows had shattered and sheets of flames were leaping inside. Part of the roof had already fallen in and a roaring spiral of flame and sparks was lashing the black riven beams and sending a great column of smoke up and over the roofs of the city. Rain fell on the inferno but did not lessen it. Four fire engines had their ladders extended, and firemen were hosing thousands of gallons of water down through the windows and the break in the roof, but the fire had taken invincible hold.

It burned.

The whole Ground Floor was an oven. In what had been the Library the remains of Jack Straw were barbecuing in a pyre of books and celluloid. The doors of the Lecture Theatre had collapsed, but no-one came out. The drowned comrades lay in piles. Some had their nails dug into others' cheeks and eyes; one had his teeth embedded in the scalp of another who lay beneath him. As the flames lapped them the blood that had poured into their lungs and stomachs in great gouts boiled until their guts exploded. Where Tam had walked night after night among the offices and the printing room, the desks and filing cabinets, typewriters, wordprocessors, fax machines, computers, VDU screens, all the accoutrements of deceit, were one vast unstoppable bonfire.

In the basement the mirror in Tam's flat split from side to side. Part of the back wall had blown out over the railway lines when the boilers had exploded, and the cadaver in the boiler room would never be recognized by anyone as having been human. In the foyer Lenin's huge portrait was burned to less than ashes. Fire purged the toilet on the Third Floor, and on the Fourth –

All that was on the Fourth was opened to heaven as more and more of the roof gave way, and it burned and could not be extinguished until it was no more. Then, as the crowd gasped and the police waved the onlookers further and yet further back, the iron frame which had held the red luminous lettering of the name THE RED FLAG in its place for nearly seven decades – since the world's first concentration camp was young – broke loose from the crumbling wall and hurled the remnants of that once terrifying and now tawdry sign down to shatter into pieces on the hard stone of Leveller Street.

'Night ends, the evil things depart.'

The voice sounded, not in Tam's ear, but, as it were, inside himself. He looked round.

Standing across the street with a knot of other people he saw a tall gaunt man whose face was overshadowed by a broad-crowned hat, and, holding his hand, a little girl with long hair and a red-and-yellow dress. She smiled at Tam joyfully, and waved.

Dawn was breaking over the roofs of London.